To Polly a̶n̶d̶ 2

Best

Carol M Creasey

2019.

THE POWER OF LOVE

Also by Carol M. Creasey:

Biography:
    My Life is Worth Living!

Fiction:
    Fatal Obsession
    Not Just an Affair
    Evil Woman
    Evil Woman...Takes Revenge

THE POWER OF LOVE

Carol M. Creasey

UNITED WRITERS
Cornwall

UNITED WRITERS PUBLICATIONS LTD
Ailsa, Castle Gate, Penzance, Cornwall.
www.unitedwriters.co.uk

British Library Cataloguing in Publication Data:
A catalogue record for this book is
available from the British Library.

ISBN 9781852001810

Printed and bound in Great Britain by
United Writers Publications Ltd.,
Cornwall.

I dedicate this book
to all mothers of
children with special needs.

Chapter One

1959

Laura stood in front of the mirror, admiring the way her skirt stood out with the hooped petticoat beneath. She loved the black and white check skirt, and the matching black top with tiny buttons down the front. She wore it tucked inside her skirt with the elasticated wide belt, which really accentuated her small waist. She frowned as she turned sideways to inspect herself. Clive, the school swot, had looked disdainfully at her through his disgusting National Health glasses and called her "skinny" yesterday, and she had felt mortally wounded. She spent half of her time disliking some of the boys, and the other half wishing that someone would notice her. She liked the idea of having a boyfriend; someone with dark hair in a quiff, nice and high on the top thanks to Brylcreem, his hair would contrast with her blonde ringlets that she tried so hard to straighten and tame.

She looked approvingly down at the white pumps, which fitted her slim and dainty feet; so when Judy put on her Elvis records, she could jive, and maybe one of the boys might notice her. Mum and Dad thought she was too young for boyfriends, but what did they know? At fifteen, Laura felt really grown-up.

These rock and roll afternoons, which were held monthly on a Saturday, with each girl in the class taking a turn, after persuading her parents to hold it at their house, had been inspired by Elvis Presley and Cliff Richard. It seemed the girls in her class had divided opinions about who was their favourite. Laura was firmly an Elvis fan; she loved his quiff of black hair which frequently

7

fell across his brow. Oh how she would have loved to gently push it back for him. Those eyes to die for, so full of expression, and his beguiling smile which showed his white teeth. He was such a beautiful man, and she felt she would love him forever.

But Judy had different ideas. She was mad about Cliff; he curled his lip and Judy said it made him look sexy, and she boasted that Cliff was attainable, he was British, he performed in this country, whereas Elvis was in Germany, right now doing his National Service, and it was rumoured he didn't like flying, so he would never come to England. But it was maybe that reason that made him even more appealing to Laura; she might never meet him, but that didn't stop him from occupying her dreams at night.

Today it was Judy's turn to hold the get together at her house. There would probably be about a dozen from the class. Some didn't come, mainly the boys, but the ones that did maybe came for the biscuits and cake provided by enthusiastic mums, who were so pleased that their teenage daughters brought their friends home instead of hanging about on street corners.

None of the boys danced, that was too much to expect; they just hovered near the girls watching them jiving, skirts twirling furiously to the beat, unashamedly getting a glimpse of legs, but the whalebone stayed put, swaying like a lampshade, so the view was minimal.

Laura grimaced as she heard her father's voice coming from below. Dad was always moaning these days, he didn't like her make-up, her clothes or her friends; but tough, there was nobody more of a square than him. He didn't like Elvis, he thought when he swivelled his hips it was disgusting. Mum had tried to smooth things over by saying he should live and let live, and just because they were used to crooners like Bing Crosby and Frank Sinatra, it didn't mean that there was anything wrong with the current trend of rock and roll which the teenagers loved. But it had made no difference, her Dad had made up his own mind; he didn't like it.

"Laura, come down and see your Dad and I before you leave, I have a few small cakes I baked that you can take with you." tried her mum, always the family peacemaker.

Laura wondered how her mother had managed to put up with him for so long. When he grumbled she didn't fight back like Laura did, she let him have his way over everything, she was just a doormat. Her mother was typical of most women, they were not considered as important as the male sex, but Laura didn't agree with that. No man was going to treat her like second best, and certainly not her dad.

It wasn't that she didn't love her Dad, it was human nature to love your parents, no matter what. She had memories of having fun with him when she was a little girl, but since she had hit her teens he had changed and nothing she did was ever right, and unlike her mother, she couldn't just accept his wrath, she had to fight back.

Trevor Clark steeled himself as he heard his daughter Laura's springy step on the stairs. What sort of sight would greet him today: black false eye lashes, mascara, painted slits at the corner of her eyes, a skirt that looked like a crinoline? His Laura didn't need any of that, she had her own natural beauty, and as proud as he was of how she looked, it was making him protective of her. He didn't want to lose his little girl, he didn't want her taking up with spotty teenage boys, he just wanted to keep her safe.

Most fathers were distant figures to their children, often going to London on the train early in the morning before the children even woke up, and getting home just before they went to bed. It was only at weekends they saw each other, and mother was the central figure in their lives. But it had been different for Trevor; he had a good job at an engineering company in his home town, so his children had seen him in the morning and the evening, but he still left all the care of them to his wife. He had never changed a nappy in his life, and never intended to; that was women's work.

Emily Clark was busy in the kitchen making pastry, but she washed the flour off her hands and paid attention as Laura stood by the door. She was proud of her beautiful daughter. Laura's deep blue eyes, almost violet in colour, met hers. Her hair curled around her small doll-like face, and the curls bounced with enthusiasm, flowing around her shoulders. She reminded Emily of an older version of the famous child star Shirley Temple, whose eyes and curls had captivated the world and made her very successful.

Not that she wanted that for Laura; the world of show business was very superficial, and there were so many dangers these days for young girls. Laura was quite an intelligent girl; not as clever as her brother Sam maybe, but he could follow his father into engineering, whereas once Laura had left school after taking her

9

GCEs, hopefully she would find a nice young man, the sort her father would approve of, then marry and settle down. If girls wanted to be a lawyer, or doctor, or have some sort of long career, then university would have been another option; but in Laura's case, and with the looks that she had, there would not be a long career. She would become a wife and mother in not too many years, then stay at home to do the cooking and cleaning, just like Emily had done.

Laura presented herself very briefly before anything could be said about her appearance. She had seen that look on her dad's face, and she didn't have time for any sort of conflict right now. She had promised Judy she would come early to help her.

"Lovely cakes mum, thanks," she said encouragingly, as she put them in the plastic tupperware box and fastened the lid. Cupcakes were always popular, and her mother had baked and then decorated them in a variety of colours. They would not last long.

She gave both her parents a quick kiss on the cheek, which made Trevor soften a little. Well at least her skirt was a suitable length, and if she wanted to walk around looking like a lampshade why should he worry? Emily's cakes had caused a diversion long enough for Laura to leave the house and be on her way, and Emily had the sense to keep some back, which would now be given to Trevor with a cup of tea. Even her thirteen year old son Sam had sniffed them out like some eager bloodhound and appeared at the door like magic.

Emily smiled at them both. "Time for a cup of tea, I think," and then dutifully went to fill the kettle. Trevor sat down in the chair to read his newspaper, whilst Sam flopped on the sofa, welcoming the break from his studies, and they both waited for their tea to be brought to them.

Laura would have skipped down the road if it hadn't been for the container of cakes; if she swung it about they would end up damaged, so she carefully made her way to Judy's house. They lived two roads apart, but Judy's parents' house was quite small, with just a scullery kitchen and a tiny garden, so today the French windows of the lounge had been opened and there was access to the patio, which was where the record player was set up. It was warm and sunny today, so most people would be outside. Laura thought Judy's parents were much more free and easy than hers, and frequently wished she were as lucky as Judy. And today they had gone out. They had left the teenagers to their own devices.

Judy answered Laura's knock very quickly, she looked flushed and excited. Her hair was in complete contrast to Laura's, it was jet black and straight, and she wore it long with a full fringe. Her eyes were very dark brown, she was stunning to look at, and she was poised and confident which belied the fact that she had not quite reached her sixteenth birthday.

They hugged briefly and then Judy spotted the cakes.

"Oh great, your mum's been baking again; these will go down well."

As Laura entered the hall, her attention was arrested. Just outside the dining room door stood a boy, who she guessed to be about a year or so older than herself. He was breathtakingly handsome, with the most expressive brown eyes she had ever seen. His hair was dark brown and he had brylcreem on it, except for one piece which he was continually pushing back from his face. His face was tanned, and she noticed how tall he was. He was wearing drain pipe trousers with a long jacket, it was expensively cut with velvet lapels, but even if he had been wearing a black sack he would have made the same impact on her. The feeling she felt inside was completely new to her, but it drew her to him like a magnet.

"Oh, by the way," Judy said casually, "Laura, this is Simon, Kate's brother. He's given her a lift as he's just passed his driving test." She turned to him. "You can stop you know, if you want to."

Simon clasped Laura's hand to shake it, and she felt like an electric shock passed through her body. He smelt of aftershave, and when he smiled it showed off his very white teeth. His nearness was disturbing and exciting at the same time. She made a supreme effort to come back to reality.

"Hi, I didn't even know Kate had a brother," she said lightly, thankful that no one could see the way her heart was thudding.

"Oh yes, I think I might stay," said Simon. He liked what he saw, so why not?

11

Chapter Two

Simon Richards and his sister Kate were not particularly close, mainly because he was the favourite of their parents. But that was because he was a boy. They lived in a big house in a private road on the other side of town. Most of the houses in their road had elegant conservatories, and a swimming pool, so these were taken for granted.

Simon's father Ken was a city banker; he had made so much money he didn't even work now, he just enjoyed the fruits of his endeavours. His mother Elizabeth had never worked, she spent her life shopping and arranging coffee mornings. They had a housekeeper to take care of them all, which was just as well as his mother was very untidy. She tried on just about everything in her wardrobe when she went out, and then left her clothes in an untidy heap on the bed and the chair, until Jane came in to clear up.

Simon and Kate had both passed their 11-plus exams, so were eligible to go to a Grammar School, and Kate had been accepted for St John's Grammar. Her main reason for going there was that several of her friends from primary school, which included Judy and Laura, were also going there. But two years earlier, when Simon had passed, it had been different. His parents had wanted him to go to a private school named Wilson House, and it was supposed to be the best private school in Surrey. Pupils from there had gone onto Oxford and Cambridge Universities, and they wanted nothing less for Simon.

Simon found school work easy. He was naturally bright, and

with this knowledge came a very strong confidence. Nature had been kind to him; he was blessed with good looks and an extrovert personality, and with this came a jauntiness and an attitude that nothing would ever be too hard for him to obtain. He knew in Kate's eyes he was cocky, vain and full of himself, even giving her a lift to Judy's house had been more about showing off the new car his dad had bought him, as a reward for passing his test the first time, rather than helping his sister.

He had not intended to stay with a bunch of nearly sixteen-year-old giggly girls. At seventeen and a half he felt so much more mature than them, until he saw Laura. Simon changed his girlfriends as often as he changed his socks. He knew he could get girls easily, someone had even commented that he looked like Elvis Presley's younger brother, and being charming came easily to him. After all, life was good to him, his family were rich, and anything was within his grasp.

The moment he saw Laura he knew he would stay. It wasn't just that she had a very beautiful face and gorgeous blonde ringlets; those violet eyes did something to him, the look of innocence about her roused his desire to protect her; from what he didn't know, but he felt a magical connection with her, and he was certain she felt the same; he could sense it.

He had such a desire to know her. He watched her circulating with the other girls. She had a ready smile and a bubbly personality, they all seemed to like her, even his sulky sister Kate. Then he watched her jiving with Judy. There were only four other boys there, but like the others he stood watching, not wanting to make an idiot of himself. As she twisted and turned, her petticoat swayed, and he caught a glimpse of her shapely legs. She was a good dancer, her body was lean and lithe, and how he longed to encircle that tiny waist of hers in his arms.

He strode over to the record player. Cliff Richard was singing about his *Living Doll* and the song was just finishing. Maybe he could find something a bit slower to suit his purpose. On top of the pile was an Elvis record, *A Fool Such as I*; surely that would do. He removed the former record and placed the new one on the turntable, gently placing the arm of the record player onto it. As Elvis's velvet voice sang about unrequited love, he made his way over to where Judy and Laura were standing, getting their breath back after an energetic jive.

"Laura, can we take a slow one together?" he said softly. At this moment he didn't care if he was the only bloke dancing, to have this lovely girl in his arms was all he could think about.

Laura looked at him. She had been about to play hard to get, as her mother had told her that this is what women did, and the man had to do all the chasing, but the feelings inside her were so strong, she couldn't wait to be held by him. She could feel such a strong chemistry flowing between them, could she dare to even dream that he felt the same way?

"Yes," she murmured, and as his arms went round her the world stood still. The warmth of her body melted into his, as the voice of Elvis continued to caress their senses. She kept her eyes closed as they stood barely moving, wondering if she was dreaming that she was in the arms of the most handsome boy in the world.

For them the song was over too quickly, for the others it was back to rock and roll again. Tim, another of the boys, had taken advantage of the fact that there were no parents present, and gone down the road to buy some cider. He offered them a glass of it. Laura wasn't sure; she was only fifteen, and her dad would go mad if he found out, but that had not deterred the others, they were all getting very giggly and even louder. Simon took a glass of it; at almost eighteen he felt old enough to make his own decisions.

Laura's curiosity got the better of her; she had never tasted alcohol, so she took a sip. It tasted really good, and because she was thirsty, she drank it down very quickly, and then found she had a very floaty feeling inside her and she kept wanting to laugh at everything.

Simon went to get another glass, suggesting they went up to the end of the garden to get some air.

"Good idea!" said Tim, winking conspiratorily at him. Normally Simon would have used the opportunity of a female companion getting tipsy as a good reason to have fun. But this was Laura, and although he really didn't understand himself any more, he knew there was no way he would take advantage of such a situation. He also knew that although he had slept with every one of his past conquests, he would not do it with Laura, as much as he longed to, until she was absolutely ready for him. No matter how corny it sounded, he had fallen heavily for her, and he was going to make sure he did nothing to spoil anything between them.

They sat in the warmth of the afternoon sun, and Laura was sipping the black coffee that Judy had made. She had only drunk one glassful, but it was the first time she had touched alcohol and it had gone straight to her head. Judy was getting anxious now, she had shipped the other rowdy ones home and she was expecting her parents home at any time. Simon could see they would need to go, and he was looking forward to driving Laura home and arranging another meeting, but there was Kate as well, and right now she was quite a thorn in his flesh.

But Kate had seen what had happened and there was no way she wanted to be a gooseberry.

"Don't worry about me, I'm going into Croydon to meet some friends in the coffee bar."

Simon heaved a sigh of relief, and after thanking Judy for her hospitality, he offered his arm to Laura. She had sobered up now but had a slight headache. Apparently it would take five minutes in the car, it was just a couple of streets away.

Kate watched as he drove off with a cynical look on her face.

"What's wrong?" asked Judy, curiously. She had always secretly thought Simon was quite a catch and she envied Laura, she had done very well for herself.

"She is so blinded by love, she has no idea what my brother is like," said Kate ominously, then she changed the subject so Judy had no chance of discovering exactly what she meant. Judy decided it was just brother and sister differences; after all, he couldn't be a mass murderer, he was far too nice.

Simon arrived at Laura's house all too quickly. He didn't want her to go, but it was now six o'clock and she was expected home. He jumped out of his side of the car, and went round the other side to hold open her door. She looked composed now, so he walked her up the path towards the house. Suddenly the door was flung open, and the figure of a man with grey hair, who he assumed was Laura's father, appeared threateningly on the doorstep.

"Who are you, and why are you bringing my daughter home in a car?"

Trevor had been watching out of the window. Laura was usually back by five, but today was different, and then he saw the

15

car draw up. He didn't like the look of this young man at all. No doubt she was besotted by his film star looks; but oh, didn't he know it, his whole bearing, the jaunty stride, and the confidence that oozed out of him. Trevor felt jealous, and usurped, he didn't want this young toff with the expensive looking car hanging round his daughter. He obviously came from an affluent home, and Trevor didn't need reminding that he had only managed to provide his family with an average way of life. What was even worse, he was so arrogant he didn't even show any fear of Trevor's displeasure.

Simon looked at the miserable old git in front of him. It wasn't as if it was the middle of the night; but he was very adept at masking his reactions. He used every bit of charm he possessed, simply because it was Laura's father, and he so wanted to see her again.

"You must be Mr Clark. I am Simon Richards, very pleased to meet you."

Trevor ignored his outstretched hand, only intent on getting his daughter inside. He pulled roughly at her arm, but Laura was having none of it. She bristled with indignation; she had done nothing wrong, and Dad was so rude!

She could see the figure of her mother hovering anxiously inside the door, wringing her hands in agitation, so her next words were meant for her, and all women who were under a bullying man's thumb.

"Dad, don't hurt me, I have done nothing wrong. I have been at Judy's house and Simon very kindly gave me a lift home. You could at least shake his hand and thank him."

Trevor gulped, Laura wasn't like her mother, or any other woman come to that, she stood up to him and he wasn't used to it. He believed women should be kept in their place, but she was as arrogant as the young man she was standing next to.

Emily was in a quandary now. Part of her admired her daughter for her courage, but a voice inside was reminding her that they had brought her up to be God fearing and to respect her parents. Now her loyalty was to Trevor, he was the breadwinner and had every right to be concerned about the company their daughter kept. The young man standing beside Laura looked absolutely charming, but he had a car and was older than her, and Laura was still only fifteen.

16

"Thank you so much for bringing Laura home, Simon. Her dad has been worried because we expected her at five, but we can see that all is well now."

She shook his hand and Simon brightened. Laura's mother had a kind face, she had the same curly blonde hair, but her eyes were not as big as Laura's, nor as blue, he guessed her age as about forty-three.

The intervention of Emily seemed to have calmed Trevor. He too shook hands with Simon; but as Laura passed him to enter the hall, he got a whiff of her breath. She had been drinking alcohol, it was illegal, she was only fifteen, and he felt the red mist descending on him!

Suddenly he became master in his own home again, and this time he felt justified. There was no way he would allow Laura to go to any more of these get togethers, and this young upstart could go on his way, out of their sight before he corrupted her.

"Get upstairs, my girl, you reek of alcohol, and don't expect to be allowed out. And as for you, allowing my daughter to drink when she's only fifteen is disgraceful!"

This time Trevor did assert himself, he had good reason to be angry. Laura disappeared from view and the door was very firmly closed on Simon. He wished he had given her some chewing gum to mask the fumes; he hadn't even thought about that. Oh well, it was too late now. But none of this made any difference, with or without the backing of her parents, he wanted to go out with Laura. In fact, he wanted her as his girl, to go steady, because after meeting her the rest of the female sex just paled into insignificance.

Chapter Three

Laura lay on her bed wishing she could see Simon again. Her father had strictly forbidden her to have anything to do with him. He said he was "after no good", whatever that meant, by trying to get her drunk when she was under age.

She had tried to explain that it wasn't like that. She had tried the drink out of simple curiosity. Simon couldn't have known she would do that, and she wasn't that bothered anyway, it didn't taste any better to her than a glass of orange squash.

But the trouble with Dad was he just didn't listen. He had his own ideas, and he seemed to think all men were going to harm her, which was so ridiculous. Simon had treated her with kindness and respect, and she knew no matter what her father said or did, somehow she would find a way to see Simon again. There was a feeling inside her which drew her to him, and it was just too strong to ignore.

She had been grounded for today and she was not allowed out of her room as a punishment, but tomorrow was school, and Kate would be there, so hopefully she could contact Simon through her. But, of course, she would have to warn him not to come near the house; whilst dad was in this mood who knows what he might do to Simon if he saw him.

Simon had been thinking about her all night; such a beautiful girl, and what a miserable bad tempered father she had. If only he'd stopped her drinking a whole glass of cider, or then after, given her some chewing gum. Her parents would never have known. But it was done now, and he wasn't sure he could risk Trevor's wrath by going round to see Laura. It was a shame he wasn't welcome at that house, as he had every intention of seeing her again.

He put Rover on the lead and went for a walk whilst he tried to think of a plan. There was a wooded area not far from where she lived. It was quite a long walk from his house, but he didn't care, he would have crossed the Sahara Desert to see Laura if he had to. It was just a vague hope that he might see her, because it was a place where teenagers did meet up on a Sunday. To his great disappointment Laura was not there, but Judy was, and she explained the situation.

"Laura's been grounded. She can't leave her bedroom today. I phoned her and her mum told me."

Simon frowned with annoyance. "They can't keep her locked up all the time. She has to go to school tomorrow."

"True, it's her dad you see. He doesn't want her to have a boyfriend, he is very strict, and her mum always agrees with him."

"Well, I am the cause of it all. I should have stopped her from drinking that cider!"

Judy laughed. It was all a bit ridiculous in her opinion, just a storm in a teacup.

"Would your parents have reacted like that?"

"No, but they aren't strict at all."

She could have added that they were always so busy with their own lives, they scarcely had time to notice her. But to Simon she wanted to sound cool and grown up, not as though she was lacking in confidence or had any hang-ups. If Laura wasn't allowed to go out with him, tough; Judy was, and would, if he showed the slightest bit of interest in her.

But to her huge disappointment, Simon's heart and mind were set on Laura, and only Laura, and already he was working out how he could arrange for their paths to cross on the way home tomorrow.

He called Rover to him. He had found another German Shepherd dog to romp around with whilst his master was chatting, but he was very obedient, he came back and stood patiently whilst his lead was put on. After checking with Judy

19

which bus Laura got home, and at what time, he spent the next hour, whilst he was walking home, making plans. He came out of school fifteen minutes later than Laura. If only he had the car, but his parents had bought it on the understanding that he only used it socially outside school. Well, one way or another, he would find her tomorrow.

At school on Monday, Laura found it really hard to concentrate on her work. Thoughts of Simon invaded her mind: his ingratiating smile, the tenderness in his limpid brown eyes, and the way he had held her when they danced. But despair swept over her at the thought she might never see him again.

Kate had been at school, of course, but she had said nothing about Saturday, so clearly Simon had now forgotten her. If he had wanted to see her again, Kate would have been the messenger. She felt angry with herself for imagining that the magic he had created inside her had affected him too. All the lessons that day went straight over her head. She had given her heart away, and the futility of the situation hit her.

She left school after all the other girls had gone; somehow she didn't want to hear any of their cheerful banter. She wanted to be alone, she had just had her first taste of unrequited love and it really did hurt.

She glanced out of the window idly as the bus took her home. It stopped outside Wilton House, and suddenly her heart stood still. He mounted the step, and the conductor rang the bell. His gaze held hers; she could feel crazy waves of emotion inside her, so strong, and then he sat down beside her, politely saying:

"Do you mind if I join you?"

Did she mind? She was ecstatic with happiness. He was here and suddenly her life seemed wonderful again. But her reply gave nothing away.

"It's fine."

Then he launched into conversation, apologising for upsetting her father, and saying how much he had enjoyed his time with her on Saturday. He knew she had been grounded and he was out of favour with her family, and he hoped she could forgive him.

Laura smiled, he had hardly taken a breath; it seemed as if he had wanted to get those words out as quickly as possible. But she knew the blame didn't just lay with him. She had acted impulsively,

20

and in this instance her parents were justified in being angry with her.

"It was my fault, Simon. At my age I should not be drinking cider at a friend's house and then going home and expecting my parents not to be angry. You only got the blame because you were with me."

She had got up now for her stop, and Simon got up too. There was no way he was going to let her go now, even if he ended up walking home. They both got off the bus and walked towards the alley that opened out to the wooded area near her house. Simon gently took her hand; it was as soft as he had imagined. He was really smitten with this girl and he had to let her know.

"Laura, since meeting you I realise I have met someone really special. I am sorry I've managed to fall foul of your parents, and if you turned me down I wouldn't blame you. . . Please will you be my girl? I want to go steady with you."

Laura gazed at him in wonderment. So she had not imagined it; he cared about her too, and they hadn't even kissed yet.

"Yes, I will go steady with you," she said quietly, scarcely able to believe her own words; and when he bent his head and kissed her, his lips were so soft and gentle, her first kiss was everything she had dreamed it would be.

This was the beginning of a powerful teenage romance. For the next year they spent whatever spare time they had together. Simon met her every night from school and walked her home, Saturday afternoons were spent at the cinema, or the local coffee bar, and because her parents had no idea what was going on, they didn't meet on Sundays; instead Laura dutifully attended church with her parents.

As time went on, Laura fell even more deeply in love with Simon. His kisses aroused her passion, and sometimes in the privacy of his car, he put his hands up her jumper and touched her breasts. When she felt her nipples hardening she knew that no matter what her parents had told her about sex being sinful, it was a sin she really enjoyed, and so did Simon. So their petting continued and it became the most enjoyable experience she had ever had. Her shyness was now forgotten when he took her top off and bared her breasts. Spurred on by her response, Simon became bolder, his hands now progressed up her thighs and inside her panties, where he touched the most intimate parts of her body.

It was inevitable that one Saturday evening their passion would spur him even more. Laura felt after a year spent with him, that she knew Simon inside out. She felt no shame, only wonderment, when they lay naked in the back of the car and he made love to her for the first time. All thoughts of "sin" as she had been led to believe sex was by her parents, were banished from her mind. How could something so enjoyable, that bound you both in body and spirit to the person you loved, be so wrong?

At seventeen she now felt she knew her own mind. She was about to leave school and become an insurance clerk. She had passed the O-levels necessary to do the job until such time that she wanted to marry and become a housewife, so going into sixth form for more studying and then on to University wasn't really necessary. There were not that many jobs around, but Laura was one of the lucky ones, the careers officer had been able to point her in the right direction, the rest was up to her, and she had passed her interview and got the job which she would start in September.

But it was different for Simon; so much more was expected of him. He would marry one day and be the breadwinner. Maybe his parents did have money, but Ken didn't want his son to be a rich layabout, he wanted him to make his own way in the world and prove his worth, so there was going to be no string pulling to get him into merchant banking. His A-level results had been outstanding, and his father and mother puffed their chests out with pride when they told everyone he had been offered a place at Oxford University. Their son was about to achieve his true potential, but then everything changed. It was now 1960, and Simon was among one of the last young men at that time to be called up for National Service.

Chapter Four

"He's very serious about her, Daddy, they have been together for over a year now, I think he may want to get engaged to her." Kate looked directly at her father without flinching. She was sick to death of hearing about how her wonderful brother had got to Oxford, and what a genius he was. Couldn't her parents see just how arrogant and superior he thought he was?

"Well, how can he?" said Ken Richards impatiently. He scratched the top of his bald head and looked thoughtful. "He's going off to Oxford."

Kate shook her head; her tawny brown hair tumbled around her shoulders, and her green eyes gleamed with spite. When she smiled Kate was very beautiful, but more often than not her expression looked angry, she really felt second best to her brother. Now she was trying to do something about it.

"That won't stop them, Daddy, and Simon can always drop out of his studies."

She wondered if she had gone too far when she saw her father's face darken. These were desperate measures to get attention back to herself, but she was telling him words he didn't want to hear. She felt no conscience for betraying her brother's trust. She didn't feel she owed him a thing.

Ken had visions of his bright son wasting his life by not getting a University degree. Damn the girl for being such a distraction at this crucial time in Simon's life! What would the neighbours say about him dropping out of Oxford? They would never live it down.

"Where does this Laura live?" he barked at Kate.

"Oh, it's in those small semis down by the woods."

Ken bristled. That settled it. His son going out with a girl who lived at the poorer end of town. This would never do, they were in a completely different class from them. There was one way out of this that would keep their reputation and dignity intact. His son could be excused National Service because he had got to Oxford, but Simon didn't know that. He would tick the box and return the letter that they had left in the drawer pending his exam results. The next letter that came would be the one stating when he would be called, and that would be the one Simon would need to sign. Three years away would get that floozy out of his mind, and it would also make a man of him. His son had always had it so easy, now it was time for him to grow up.

He smiled kindly at his daughter, who smiled back. She was growing to be a stunner; a bit sultry, but her smile was captivating.

"Thank you for telling me that. It's our secret. If you work hard your mother and I will think seriously about sending you to stage school."

Kate exulted inwardly. She could read her father's mind exactly. Her parents were snobs, they wouldn't want anyone to look down on them, so to save their faces, her darling brother would be shipped off to the army, and that was just what Kate craved. Three years without him. She would be the centre of attention, and if they sent her to drama school, who knows? She might end up a successful actress. She might not be as clever as Simon, but she was far more devious, and Daddy would do this without even consulting Mummy, but Mummy would agree to it anyway, she would be just as horrified at Simon's choice of girlfriend.

"You are welcome, Daddy," she said, trying not to look elated, and then her acting skills came into play.

"I had to tell you because Laura is a gold digger. Poor Simon has no idea," and then she allowed her face to show an expression of concern, and her father was impressed by her loyalty.

"You did have to tell me, so now we can do what is best for everyone."

*   *   *   *

24

Simon still couldn't quite believe that he was going to do his National Service. He had wanted to go to Oxford University, and his only reservation about it had been leaving Laura behind. He was deeply in love with her, and had hoped that now she was seventeen she might tell her parents that they were together. He was tired of having to hide their relationship; only a few close friends knew, and he was so proud of his beautiful girlfriend, and hoped to get engaged to her before the year was out.

He was being posted abroad, somewhere in Europe. A feeling of hopelessness swept over him; at least Oxford was not that far from Surrey, they could have still seen each other, but wherever he was going would be too far for Laura to visit. Oh, how tough life was. His heart ached, and he wondered how he would get by without her. Her sunny smile and bubbly nature was everything he needed. His girl was really special, but it was now August, and he was unlikely to see her for a while now, even if they allowed him a few days of leave at Christmas.

He hadn't even told her yet. He just couldn't believe it was happening. He had been in denial, even hoping his father, with all his wealth and contacts, would be able to sort it for him. Dad and Mother had both been disappointed that he wouldn't be going to Oxford, but going in the army was his duty and he could not avoid it. He was in good health, and his father felt it would be character building, so that was that, he had to go.

When he found out the date had been moved forward a week, he panicked. Laura was away on holiday with her parents right now. She had gone under sufferance. She felt she was much too old to be taken on holiday, but soon she was due to start her first job, and her mother had apparently talked her into taking a family holiday for the last time. Her father had packed them all into his Ford Cortina and they were touring the Scottish Highlands. They were away for another two weeks, and he realised to his horror, that he would have been gone for a week when they got back. He couldn't even say goodbye to her.

His bags were packed with the little amount he was able to take with him. Life was going to be a lot harder for Simon than he was used to. He had no way of contacting Laura, so he did the only thing left to him. He sat down and poured out his heart in a letter to her, and declared his undying love if she would only wait for him.

When he had finished writing it, he carefully sealed it down.

b

He wouldn't put it past her dominating father to intercept her post, so putting it through her letterbox might not be an option. But there was Kate, she was friendly with Laura. She hadn't exactly been thrilled about their relationship, but he reminded himself, she hadn't leaked it out either, she just looked the other way and pretended she knew nothing. Kate could deliver the letter right into Laura's hands.

Laura was missing Simon so much it hurt. This was the longest time they had spent apart. The beauty of the scenery in Scotland was wasted on her, and her kid brother Sam was being particularly childish and annoying. Her parents could see she was not being a ray of sunshine. Their normally happy and bubbly daughter seemed troubled, and Emily secretly wished they hadn't put pressure on her to spend this holiday with them. It hadn't worked, and the atmosphere was tense and awkward.

During the second week she didn't feel very well. Her mother had told her to wear a headscarf to protect her head from the sun like she did, but Laura didn't listen. She liked to feel the breeze ruffling her hair, and anyway, Mummy was being such a fusspot, as if she would get burned by the summer breeze! But after a day spent walking quite a distance, later that evening, she discovered to her horror, that not only was the top of her head red and sore, even through her thick mane of curls, but her face was red. No wonder she felt nauseous. Maybe Mum had been right.

Emily didn't reprimand her, what was the point? Maybe Laura had learned her lesson, and it was bad enough listening to Trevor berating her for not taking heed of her mother. She gave her some aspirin, and insisted she drink lots of cold water, and packed her off to bed.

Laura went willingly. She felt totally exhausted, and although her head felt better the next day, she had to rush to the toilet when she got up and she vomited, and then didn't feel like much breakfast. Her mother made her spend that day very quietly and she kept out of the sunlight. Emily stayed with her at the hotel, and Trevor and Sam went out on their own.

When she got up the next morning, Laura felt the nausea sweep over her again and she had to rush to the toilet, and then fear swept through her. She remembered that sickness in the morning was often a sign of pregnancy. Maybe it wasn't too much sun, maybe she was pregnant. Her passion for Simon had completely dominated her, and in her naïvety it hadn't occurred to her she might conceive.

She couldn't believe this was happening to her. She could never tell her parents. They would disown her! Her father had frequently warned her about "Getting into trouble with boys". But in her mind this wasn't trouble, this was her love for Simon and the child they had created. She had no intention of having a back street abortion, she was going to tell Simon; they would work it out somehow.

Maybe she was too young to marry without her parents' consent, but if necessary she would move to Oxford to be near to him, and maybe when he had his degree, then they could get married. She would find a room and get a job; anything, she thought wildly, their love would get them through, but in the meantime, she had to hide this pregnancy from her mother.

She couldn't wait for her holiday to end. For her it became such an ordeal; first trying to hide just how ill she felt, and secondly the realisation at just how miserable she felt being away from Simon. Every morning when she got up, she had to go to the bathroom and hide her nausea, trying to stifle any vomiting. Then there was a distinct aversion to tea and coffee; she didn't fancy either, she just drank water, but she had to pretend to drink a cup of tea at breakfast, just so her mother would not notice anything different. It was all such a strain.

When she finally arrived home, there was only one thought on her mind. She had to see Simon and tell him they were having a baby. She didn't need a doctor to confirm it, she marvelled that inside her body was a tiny little life growing, a human being created by their love. Although she feared the wrath of her parents, with Simon by her side she felt she could weather the storm because they were in love.

Her dad was at work and her mother had gone shopping when she came to her decision. She was going round to Simon's house to tell him the news. After all, with a baby coming, his parents would soon find out about their relationship. Although she did not like the term "shotgun marriage", she knew many would call it that. She was sure Simon would marry her, and in years to come people would see he hadn't just married her because she was pregnant; they really were in love.

27

She had felt particularly nauseous that morning; was it nerves at the news she had to break? Her mother had given her a sideways look when she said she couldn't eat breakfast. Laura wasn't ready to tell her before she had his ring on her finger. It wasn't long before she was due to start her new job, and she was apprehensive about that, especially as it wouldn't be long before her pregnancy showed. Would it cause her to lose her job before she really got going?

When she arrived at Simon's house the affluence of it all made her feel at a disadvantage. All the houses in the area were detached and it had a beautiful garden. As she entered the gates, she noted a couple of gardeners tending to it. Her Dad could never have afforded that. The swimming pool was glistening in the morning sun and another man could be seen sweeping the bottom of it. There was no sign of any of the family, and as it had taken all of her courage to come here, she fervently hoped her mission was not in vain.

She directed her steps towards the front door with the gleaming polished step. Everything here looked so perfect, she almost felt she shouldn't step on it in case she left footprints. The brass door knocker shone, and she lifted it up in her hand and knocked.

She should have realised that Simon wouldn't open the door. A middle aged lady, wearing a nylon overall, stood there with a polite smile on her face. It wouldn't be his mother, of course, but the housekeeper. Rich people like this had housekeepers.

Laura summoned every bit of confidence she had, but still her voice faltered.

"Good morning, please can I speak to Simon?"

"I'm afraid not, the young master's not here."

Kate had seen Laura come into the grounds, so she was ready for the knock at the door, and not far behind Jane, their housekeeper, and she cut into the conversation quickly. It was clear that Laura didn't know her brother had enlisted, and Kate wanted to be the one to tell her. With Simon out of the way, she could afford to be kind. She had the power now and life was going just the way she wanted it to.

"Hello Laura, I haven't seen you for a while. Did you have a good holiday?"

Then she turned to Jane and asked her to make them some

coffee, whilst she took Laura into the study to talk. Now she could drop the bombshell.

"I am afraid you missed Simon. He enlisted last week, he asked me to tell you."

"Enlisted!" echoed Laura, totally unable to comprehend this news. "But he was going to Oxford."

"Not now," said Kate, scarcely able to contain her delight. She had always pretended to like Laura at school, because everyone else did; she didn't want to be the one left out, but secretly she had always envied her. It wasn't just her beauty and her lovely hair, it was her personality, it drew people to her like a magnet, whereas Kate knew she couldn't quite match that. There was a certain naïvety and niceness about Laura that shone out of her, and a bearing too. She may have lived at the poorer end of the town, but she still had class. There was no way Kate wanted her to stay with her brother and threaten Kate's position in this family as their father's darling.

"Daddy decided the army would make a man of him; teach him lots of things. He's already very clever, so he will get a job when he needs one. Going to Oxford isn't everything."

It was just as well that Laura was seated when she heard that news. She couldn't believe Simon had gone just like that. He wouldn't have wanted to leave her. Misery swept through her, and the nausea became worse. She gritted her teeth, she must not vomit, but suddenly she felt an overriding fear engulfing her too. Fear of having to tell her parents she was pregnant. Fear of being on her own, an unmarried mother, and fear for the future of her and her baby. But then she told herself sternly; he hadn't gone forever, even in the army they got leave. No doubt Simon would have left her a note, he wouldn't have gone away without leaving his address either.

"That is a shock, but no doubt he's left me a note and you know his address so I can write."

Absolute horror swept through her when Kate shook her head.

"He hasn't given anything to me, sorry, and we don't have the address, as they are not allowed to write. However, he may get leave at Christmas."

Kate smiled encouragingly at her. She could see how upset Laura was, and it gave her a certain satisfaction; she wasn't so sure of herself now. Kate had destroyed the letter. Probably by

Christmas they would have both forgotten each other, but if Simon remembered he had left the note with her, she would just say she had lost it. They were always fighting anyway, so it was just another thing to fight about. She really didn't care.

Laura had only one hope left, that Simon had written to her home address. During their wonderful year or more together he had written her many passionate love notes. Maybe this time he didn't care about her parents, and he had posted it. She would go home and look through everything. She clung to this thought, because right now her future was looking very uncertain and she had never felt more alone.

Meanwhile Kate rubbed her hands together with glee, and did not allow her conscience to trouble her. She had been presented with an opportunity to achieve her own aims and she had taken it. Jane entered the room with a tray and two coffee cups.

Laura took her leave, politely declining the coffee and choking down her nausea.

"Have one with me Jane, there are two cups," pointed out Kate, smiling. Jane was surprised to see her face wreathed in smiles, because that in itself was unusual, but responding to Kate's temporary good mood, she poured herself a coffee and sat down gratefully for a short break.

Chapter Five

During her journey home Laura was unable to stop the tears from flowing down her cheeks. She walked quickly, with her head down, not wanting anyone to see her distress but totally unable to suppress it any more. The nausea was welling up again; it seemed every time she got stressed it became worse, and when she reached home she had to run up the stairs quickly, and just made it into the bathroom before she vomited.

Afterwards she washed her face with cold water and rinsed her mouth out. Now she had herself under control and she knew what she had to do. There was no other choice, she had to tell her mother. Telling her dad was out of the question, but surely her mother would help her?

But she didn't need to tell Emily. As each day passed, her mother had been watching her, noting her pallor, and remembering she had felt the same when she had been pregnant. She was amazed at her daughter's behaviour. Hadn't they always brought her up to be God-fearing and know right from wrong? Sex before marriage was a sin, and who was the man in all this? She didn't even realise Laura had a boyfriend.

Most of her animosity towards her daughter was because of Trevor. He must never know. He had a quick temper, but in the past had never struck his daughter. However, in this instance she could not be sure that wouldn't happen. Laura had brought disgrace on the family. Unmarried mothers were outcasts from society, and in an effort to protect her daughter, she had very carefully thought out a plan. She heard her come through the door. Trevor was out with Sam, so she seized her opportunity.

"I know you are pregnant Laura, how could you do this to us, and who got you into this mess?"

Laura felt relief that her mother had guessed, and guilt that she had let her down so badly. If she could only explain just how her passion for Simon had got out of control and they had both wanted to make love so much, but she didn't dare. She had only found out about sex and babies at school, her mother had never discussed it with her, the subject was taboo, and she felt embarrassment sweeping over her at the very thought of discussing it with her mother.

"I am so sorry, Mum, but we do love each other, and it's all gone wrong. He's been conscripted for three years, and has gone to Europe."

And once again her tears of anguish flowed, and because Emily wasn't made of stone, she gathered her daughter into her arms and promised to help her, and in return she must never tell her father. But there was still one question for Laura to answer.

"Who is it, and does he know about the baby?"

"It's Simon. I went round to tell him, but he's joined the army."

Then it all made sense to Emily. Of course it was Simon, the boy who had brought her home that day when her father had been so angry. So they had continued to see each other, and she had no idea, nor had Trevor. It wouldn't have been so bad if Simon could have married her to stop all the tongues from wagging, but if he was in the army they had to face this alone, and keep it from Trevor.

Well it was no good berating Laura now; it was too late, but that would not stop Trevor if he knew. She shuddered inwardly at the thought. If Emily felt let down by Laura's behaviour, she tried not to show it. Her mind was already in action, working out how best to salvage some sort of normality from this mess.

"We can't go to the doctor yet, we won't know for sure until you are three months."

Laura was so grateful for her mother's calmness, and now the initial shock had worn off, it felt like her mother was supporting her. This eased her feelings of nausea a little. She had absolutely no doubt in her mind that she was pregnant, and she realised just how much she needed her mother's support. Simon was not here to stand beside her and protect her; it looked like he had not given

32

her a second thought when he went away. The pain in her heart this caused her was like a sharp dagger continually thrusting into her, and once again her tears flowed, whilst her mother administered to her and packed her off to bed, insisting she would feel better if she laid still for a while. Laura wearily agreed; she had no other choice, so she pulled up the blankets and tried to block out all the misery of her first love.

Agnes Frost went out into the hall to answer the telephone which was ringing imperiously. She had been listening to a play on the radio, but the strident sound could not be ignored, so she was slightly irritated with whoever it was invading her privacy.

Agnes was tall and thin, she always wore tweed suits and lace up shoes with a small heel, and no stockings. Her grey hair was drawn tightly back into a bun and she never wore make-up. Because of her severe appearance, she looked much older than her fifty-five years. She was the complete opposite of her glamorous younger sister Emily.

She had worked hard at school because right from the age of fourteen, she knew she didn't like men, never wanted to marry, and had a desire to be a schoolteacher. She felt that children really needed to be educated and she would be the one to do it. So over the years she had seen many children mature and leave school equipped with the knowledge that they would need in life. Agnes was stern and forbidding, it was hard for her to be any other way, but she got good results. Her pupils were in awe of her, and she insisted that they all exhibit good manners at all times. She felt that her life had been more successful than her younger sister's, who, in the eyes of Agnes, was totally under the dominance of a very assertive husband who always thought he was right.

She picked up the phone and repeated her number. It was Emily. After the preliminary enquiries about how she was, Emily rushed on, anxious to share this problem with an older and wiser person.

"There is no easy way to say this, Agnes: Laura is pregnant, the father has gone away, and I don't want her to have an abortion, it's too risky. And Trevor must never find out!" she finished, almost pleadingly.

Agnes slowly digested her words. What a scandal this would be.

Unmarried mother, no father around. How would unstable Trevor, whom she heartily disliked, deal with this? She didn't really do pity, and she hadn't really experienced love herself, apart from when she was a child; a time almost forgotten now. But Laura was her niece, she had been brought up with manners and a sense of right and wrong, so Agnes was surprised to hear she had got herself pregnant. Maybe the man had forced her? She didn't really even want to think about it. All men in her eyes were selfish greedy takers. At work she had been regarded as an oddity by the men because she had chosen to have a career and stand on her own feet and be independent. Maybe one day other women might follow her example. After all, the Land Girl's had worked hard during the war whilst the men were away, and they had proved they could do jobs that normally only men did, and drive tanks. Agnes had done a bit of that herself and thoroughly enjoyed it.

"Well, that is a shock Emily, Laura should have known better."

Emily swept all her elder sister's moral principles aside with her next words. The pregnancy had now been confirmed and already there was a slight roundness to Laura's normally flat stomach.

"Agnes, I know what you are saying, but Laura needs help, she needs somewhere to stay until the baby is born, then it can be adopted and she can come back home. I can't let her father find out!"

"So you want her to come and stay here. Won't Trevor wonder why that is?"

"Well he knows you are recovering from an operation. I had to write to the company she was due to start work for and say she had changed her mind, and then say to Trevor she hadn't got the job, it had been a mistake. You have no idea how deceitful I feel, but Laura is not a bad girl, only a foolish one, and she needs our help to allow her to pick up her life again without fear of any scandal."

As independent as Agnes was normally, the idea of having someone around who could share chores was pleasing. She had never been that close to her niece as a child, but Laura was seventeen now, and to Agnes, having just got back on her feet after a stomach operation, the idea of having Laura there to help her for a few months was a good one. Agnes had retired from work now, but she had been given a cash sum when she retired, so when she was back to full health and strength, Laura could return to the bosom of her family, and Agnes would be free to take a cruise.

"OK Emily, she can come here. I will arrange a midwife for her confinement and I will also make enquiries for you about having the baby adopted."

"Oh Agnes, I am so lucky to have you for a sister," said Emily, relief flooding through her. She knew how much her sister loved to be in charge of everything, and in this instance it was so important to have a sensible plan so it could all go through without a hitch.

"Just put her on the train and I will meet her at Victoria," said Agnes a little gruffly, not allowing any emotion to penetrate her very thick armour.

When Emily put the telephone down she went up to Laura's room. She was laying on her bed listening to Elvis Presley records, her face looked pale and her eyes had dark rings. She knew just how uncertain her future was, and Emily could not help feeling a wave of pity engulf her. Laura was scarcely more than a child herself, far too young to be a mother.

The sickness that had dogged her relentlessly seemed to be lifting, and her father had noticed nothing, but the fear that he might had kept them both in a state of nerves. Of course, if he was here right now, he would blame Elvis, with his gyrating hips, as the reason for his daughter's pregnancy, which in itself was ridiculous, but Trevor had wanted to keep Laura away from boys for as long as he could. Emily had wanted to trust her, and she had, so probably Trevor would blame her too.

"Aunt Agnes has agreed to let you stay at her flat in London with her whilst she is recuperating from her operation. She is going to make arrangements for your confinement, then after the baby is born, it can be adopted and you can come back home and get back to normal." She tried to keep any emotion out of her voice, nor dwell on the fact that this baby would be her grandchild. It was a sacrifice they both had to make to ensure Laura's future had no stigma. One day, hopefully, she would marry and bear her husband children, but no one would want her if they knew she had already borne an illegitimate child.

Laura gazed back at her mother. She had known it would come to this. She was being sent away so her father wouldn't find out, or anyone else come to that. Laura had spent the last month getting her head round the fact that Simon had gone away without a backward glance, so he certainly would not have wanted the responsibility of fatherhood. She had told herself repeatedly that she no longer loved such a person, although her heart argued back.

She wanted to be independent, not like her mother, so maybe marriage was not for her. Her aunt Agnes had managed without a man, so maybe going there was a good idea. Someone else could give her baby the right life that Laura could not manage. All she could offer that tiny life, that was growing inside her, was love; but that wasn't enough, that was not the answer to everything, although it was what all the films and love stories would have her believe.

A feeling of relief swept through her, it was all going to be OK. She had made a mistake, and it had cost her dearly, but she was to have a second chance. Her father would have no recriminations to hurl at her when he was in a bad mood, she would not be the reason for her parents' marriage breaking up. Everything would carry on as normal.

Just one feeling of pain persisted deep inside her. The baby that had been conceived in love, still safely inside her womb, would be separated from her. But then, she reminded herself, the love had all been on her side; if she kept that child, she could never forget him, and she really needed to. No matter how painful, she would allow no man to destroy her sanity.

Laura suddenly felt very vulnerable, and sensing that, Emily hugged her gently, saying simply, "It's all going to work out, don't worry."

"Yes, I know Mum, thank you. I need to get my clothes together and pack."

Later that evening, with her bag packed ready for the next day, Laura went to bed and slept fitfully for the first time that month. Emily came to say goodnight and was relieved to see how well Laura had reacted to the plan. It looked like the crisis was over and they could all relax again. Next time Laura saw her father it would all be over, as he was in Germany with his company, helping to provide car parts, and would return after she had gone to Agnes's. Their secret was safe.

Chapter Six

Agnes lived in a flat at Battersea. It was one of the old Victorian houses with large rooms situated over three floors, and her flat was on the ground floor. The houses, although large, were situated in a terrace not far from Battersea Park, they had just a yard out the back overlooking similar houses and no front garden to speak of either. People who owned cars had to park them in the road, but many of them who worked in London just used the facilities that trains and buses offered. Cars were a luxury, mostly used for holidays and family outings, and usually driven by men.

Agnes had never seen the need for a car. The school she had taught at was a bus ride away, and any part of London was reachable by tube, so all her life she had used public transport. She had met Laura at Victoria, and they had taken the tube to Battersea and then walked to her flat. She had inherited some of her parents' furniture when they died, including a big dark wood bookcase, which was crammed full, as Agnes loved to read. It had been nailed into position and took up the whole of her lounge wall on one side. It was a big room with high ceilings, it contained a table and two chairs, a sideboard and a radio.

She didn't have, nor did she want, a television, they may have been getting popular with the public, but Agnes could not see the point of soaps such as Coronation Street, which showed actresses like Violet Carson sitting in their local public house drinking stout. In her opinion it sent out a bad message to young people of today. She preferred to listen to The Archers, and some of the very good dramatic plays that were on the wireless.

The kitchen was situated at the back, with a door out onto a small yard, just big enough to hang out her washing. It was a narrow galley-like kitchen, but it had an old gas cooker that she lit with matches, a sink and a very deep food cupboard with a meat safe inside. The kitchen wasn't big enough to house a boiler, there was a coal cupboard outside the back door, and opposite a toilet. She no longer used the outside toilet which was a haven for spiders. The one luxury she had allowed herself was a bathroom, which had been created from what would have been the third bedroom. It had a modern toilet and a hand basin, as well as a deep bathtub; no more tin baths by the fire for Agnes, her childhood was now over.

The kitchen floor was covered in linoleum, as was the hall, lounge and two large bedrooms situated on the other side, although both bedrooms and the lounge did have a rug in the middle of the room. The lounge had an open fire when it was cold, and hot water was obtained by a water heater situated on the bathroom wall, which was very noisy when the tap was turned on.

Agnes owned her flat and had lived there for many years. It was worth quite a bit of money because of its proximity to London, but sometimes she had dreamed of having a small bungalow by the sea and walking on the beach with a dog. It wasn't fair to have a dog in these surroundings, she knew that, but as each year passed, her inclination to move was getting less, it was too much of an upheaval so she would stay put.

Although the house was divided into three flats, Agnes rarely saw her neighbours, they all came and went at different times, so as far as keeping Laura hidden away from the world, this would be ideal. As she put her key in the lock and gestured Laura to come in with her suitcase, Tiddles, her black cat, slid gracefully along the hall to greet them and then he rubbed himself against her legs, just to remind her that it was his meal time.

Laura was struck at how old fashioned the flat was. In recent years her dad had prided himself on being able to afford fitted carpets for their rooms at home; lino was gradually disappearing and going out of fashion. But then Aunt Agnes had been living here for years without changing much. However, she was glad to see the outside toilet was no longer in use, and Agnes did have a nice bathroom which was modern with a bath tub, even the walls were painted a delicate shade of pink, which was quite in contrast to the drab and dark wallpaper in all the other rooms, including the kitchen, which although it was very small, had bold pictures of knives, forks and plates against a black background, which in her opinion looked just awful.

But, she reminded herself, she was not here for the décor, she was here to live quietly for a few months, have her baby, then after it was adopted, return home and pick up her life again. Even at this early stage of her pregnancy, a wave of pain shot through her heart at the thought of it. She didn't feel like this baby was her shame, it was the result of her love for Simon, and even though she had to constantly remind herself that he hadn't cared the way that she had, and it was useless spending her time pining for him, it did not lessen her love towards the little one that right now lay protected from the world inside her womb.

Agnes strode down the hall and opened the door of the room which was opposite the new bathroom. "This is your room," she said, allowing the ghost of a smile to cross her face in an effort to be hospitable.

Laura followed her. It was a large room with a big bed, covered by a brown candlewick bedspread, the wallpaper was floral with yellow flowers and brown leaves, the lino on the floor was brown, and an old dark oak chair stood at the side of the bed. She squashed down her dislike of the drab surroundings, she must not be ungrateful, Aunt Agnes was allowing her to stay here and her parents had always taught her to have manners. She put down her suitcase on the brown rug beside the bed, and murmured, "Thank you very much, Aunt Agnes."

"I just need to heat up the stew I made and then we can have dinner, so if you want to unpack your things, and organise yourself, it should be ready in about half an hour."

"Yes, I will." Then remembering her mother's words, Laura added, "If you need any help, just ask me."

"You can come and lay the table in a while and fill the glasses with water."

Agnes went out into the kitchen, she had already cooked the lamb stew, but now she lit the gas ready to heat it up. Seeing Laura in the first stages of her pregnancy had brought back a very unpleasant memory, that she had shared with no one and had spent the whole of her life trying to forget. But maybe this was why she had agreed to have her niece here and support her, maybe it would help her to move on. Something inside her had urged her to do it when Emily had asked her, and she was utterly determined to see it through. Helping Laura might well help herself to come to terms with what had happened on that day in 1920, because try as she might, even though it was now over forty years, she had never been able to erase it from her mind.

For the next six months, Agnes found the presence of Laura in her flat agreeable. They usually went out for a walk each day, as Agnes firmly believed in fresh air and exercise. They ate their meals together, but each afternoon they both rested in their bedrooms, and then again in the evening, Agnes retired to her room to listen to her wireless, and Laura, who was used to watching television at home, made use of the local library by borrowing Agnes's ticket. She could have died of boredom without a book to read. She was missing her family and friends, as well as Simon, so reading kept her mind off her misery.

Agnes had arranged a midwife for the confinement. Daisy lived the other side of the River Thames, but she cycled over regularly to see her, dressed in her blue and white uniform. She was a very down to earth girl, probably not much older than Laura herself, and to Laura's relief, not at all fazed by the fact she was attending an unmarried teenage mother, who was having her baby adopted shortly after its birth.

Three days before she was due, Laura felt her first pains. They were not that severe and for most of the day she carried on normally, although Agnes took the precaution of telephoning Daisy and letting her know. At six o'clock in the evening, her waters broke and the pains became unbearable. She screamed with terror, and Agnes telephoned Daisy again, and this time she pedalled over as fast as she could.

Doctor Porter arrived at the same time. Daisy was there to assist him, and between them they managed to calm Laura. She was given some pain relief and then urged to push. As she pushed and panted with pain, Agnes found she had to leave the room. It was unbearable for her to watch Laura like this, those memories surfaced to torment her once more, and her fear that this baby might not survive the trauma of its birth was too much to bear. Agnes may have appeared to have a tough exterior, but life had allowed an armour to protect her from further pain.

Just as Laura felt she could take no more pain, it happened, the head of her baby appeared, and Daisy and the doctor urged her to push just a bit harder. She was panting and moaning at the same time as it emerged, they then told her to rest for a few seconds before one final push, which brought her baby into the world, safely received by Daisy and wrapped gently into a cotton blanket.

"It's a boy!" exclaimed Daisy, whilst the doctor helped Laura to deliver the afterbirth.

Every birth was so special to Daisy; the miracle of life, seeing a newborn baby enter the world was quite unlike any other experience, babies were a gift from God in her opinion and she felt sad for Laura that she couldn't keep her baby.

As soon as Laura held her son in her arms a wave of fierce maternal love coursed through her heart. His very vulnerability aroused a feeling of protectiveness deep inside her. His eyes were open briefly, and she saw his shock of dark brown hair peeping out of the blanket in wisps, Simon's hair. And after he had been washed, they put a white cotton nightie on him and she asked to hold him again. She felt the warmth of his tiny body beside her, she marvelled at his tiny fingers and toes; he was so perfect, and when she touched his hand, his little finger grasped at hers, and it was at that moment Laura knew there was no way she could give this little boy up. He was hers, a miniature Simon, and if she had to she would lay down her life for him.

Daisy opened the door and spoke to Agnes.

"Laura has a little boy, he's really bonny," she said encouragingly. As she looked at Agnes, who always had a severe expression, she was relieved to see her face relax into a smile.

"Can I see him, and is Laura all right?"

"She's fine, of course you can see him."

Agnes held her breath as she entered the room. Her expression might have looked impassive, but her heart was thudding, as her memory took her back to that moment her little boy had been born. He had been as perfect as the little mite that lay in the carry cot before her. He was asleep, and she gently touched his downy head. This baby was alive, but her little boy had been born dead, and even now she could feel the pain deep inside her that had remained hidden for all these years.

"You have a perfect little boy," she said to Laura, with as much cheerfulness as she could muster.

"I know, he's so beautiful," said Laura, and already a plan was forming in her mind, she was trying to work out how she could keep him.

"Get some rest then," said Agnes rather awkwardly, and then left the room very abruptly. It was all a bit much for her, unlike Laura she had no one to turn to when she had been raped on the way home one evening. She had been too scared to tell her parents and had carried on day after day in sheer desperation, getting bigger and wearing looser clothes, and unbelievably nobody had noticed anything.

Then one day at seven months, she had been out walking to the shop when she felt the pains, so strong, and she knew what was happening to her. She had spent all those months despising what she felt was the parasite growing and feeding inside her, and when he was born, out there on the waste ground, on a cold and windy day that no one would choose to be out in, she had held him in her arms, so tiny and defenceless, and she felt such a love for him, her poor little baby who had never really lived, except when he was growing inside her. She had realised at that moment, that the fact she had been raped by a stranger just didn't matter, it was not the fault of this tiny being, and if God had allowed him to live she would have loved and cherished him.

But it wasn't to be, so she had buried him beneath a bush. He had never been found and she had never returned to that spot, it was just too painful; and when she got home her mother had scolded her because she had walked across the common to get some potatoes from the shop and come back without them. Agnes had said nothing, she just walked back again and got the potatoes, well aware that she had to keep everything normal. But in her bed that night she sobbed quietly beneath the sheets, and for many more nights afterwards. She made up her mind that she would never marry or have children, she would be an independent woman with a career, and hopefully one day the pain would diminish. Having Laura to stay had been her way of putting her own past behind her. She was so glad the baby had gone full term and lived, but now it seemed so cruel after going through the pain of childbirth, that Laura had to have her baby adopted, but it was her mother's wishes and it was not up to Agnes to interfere.

The next day she telephoned Emily to tell her Laura had been safely delivered. She could see the way Laura was holding him she had bonded already, and her heart ached for Laura.

"Laura has had a son." She tried to keep her voice completely emotionless.

Emily gripped the telephone cable in an effort to remain composed. She had a mental picture of Laura holding her grandson, the grandson she must never meet, and it didn't sit well with her. If only she had the courage to stand up to Trevor, but if she did, both her and Laura would be cast out in the street.

"Right, and Laura is all right?"

Agnes assured her she was.

"Once her son has been adopted she can come home to us. Thank you so much, Agnes, for taking care of her."

Agnes muttered a curt reply to say she had not minded helping out. Emily was silently grieving for the child she would never see and the coldness of Agnes was not lost on her. But how could she expect her severe older sister, who hated men, to understand any of this?

It had been right to send Laura there, where someone in the family would look after her without fear of her getting emotionally involved. This is why she had asked Agnes, and she had done them a good service. If only she could stop feeling as if she had let her daughter down. Laura was scarcely more than a child herself, and as Emily knew only too well, life as an unmarried mother would be a very unhappy one, with such prejudice towards "fallen women". Her only comfort was she had done her best to help her daughter, in spite of what her conscience was telling her.

Chapter Seven

The day after his birth, Laura took charge of her own baby. She was determined she would not be parted from him, so she started to breastfeed him. It was clear to Daisy and Aunt Agnes that she had made her own decision. In the case of Agnes, although she knew that her sister would not be happy about it, she was pleased to see Laura showing a strength of character, because Agnes knew that if her own little boy had lived, she would have done the same.

During the afternoon, whilst the baby was sleeping, Laura got up for a couple of hours. Daisy had encouraged this, as long as she didn't over do it. She joined Agnes in the lounge.

"Aunt Agnes, I know I agreed to have Matthew adopted, but it's not going to happen. I don't care what people think, I am going to keep him and make a life for us both. I may be poor, but he will never want for love!"

Agnes lost her severe expression, her face showed her compassion for her very determined niece, who stood before her, arms folded, as if to ward off any negative comments.

"I am proud of your courage, Laura."

Laura gaped at her. Was she hearing correctly? Wasn't Aunt Agnes hand in glove with her mother, wanting her to have her baby adopted?

"Forty years ago I was in the same predicament as you Laura, but I didn't have a choice, my son died."

Then Agnes went on and told her the whole story. It came tumbling out, and the relief at finally being able to share it with someone after all this time was tremendous. When she had finished, she took out a white handkerchief, blew her nose loudly, and dabbed at the tears in her eyes.

Laura was so moved by this story. Maybe Aunt Agnes was old fashioned, but how she had misjudged her, because clearly she was not hard and severe. Her outward appearance hid a very troubled person who had never recovered from losing her baby. She moved spontaneously to hug her, and although it was unusual for Agnes to display emotion, the feel of Laura's arms around her was comforting. All these years of bottling up her pain, totally unable to share it with her mother or anyone else, but now she had, and maybe the healing could begin.

Laura released her, still trying to comprehend what Agnes had told her. This revelation would bind them together forever, this was the most forthcoming that Agnes had been during their whole time spent together.

"Does my mother know? Is that why she sent me here?

"Nobody knows except you. I don't want them to know, and when I see you with beautiful little Matthew, I praise the Lord he is well and strong. We only get one life Laura, live it with your son, don't worry about what people say. It's your life, stay together, the Lord will keep you safe."

"I will Aunt Agnes, nobody is going to part us. But when I leave, my mother will blame you, and my father may get to find out, and after all the lengths Mother went to keep it from him, you could suffer, and that is not fair after what you have done for me."

Agnes patted her arm gently.

"Don't fret, we will give it some thought. You need a few more days to regain your strength, and then it can appear you left suddenly without my knowledge. I don't usually get involved in deception, but Laura, you have an independent spirit that even your own father could not quell. You are a survivor, and I have every faith you will make it in life."

They embraced again. Matthew could be heard waking up for his feed as his cry came from the bedroom. Laura left the room, her heart was full of compassion for what Agnes had suffered for so long, and she remembered the advice she had given her. She picked up her baby and put him to her breast; she felt complete when she held him against her. As he sucked eagerly, his finger gripped hers and she looked lovingly down at him. The unexpected support from Agnes, and her words of advice, had served to strengthen Laura's resolve even more. She vowed that no matter what lay ahead, she would make a life for herself and Matthew. She would do what her aunt had suggested, take a few more days to recover, and then make plans for herself and Matthew for the future.

Whilst she was feeding Matthew, Daisy made her daily call to check on them. Daisy had seen this before, the bond between mother and child. So many of these young mothers had to give up their babies; most of them had no way of keeping their baby, and families offered no support, either emotional or financial. But she was left in no doubt about Laura's intentions.

"I am not having Matthew adopted. Aunt Agnes knows and she supports me," she said defiantly. Her eyes held Daisy's before she lowered her head to continue feeding him.

"I understand, especially now you are breast-feeding him. Are you going to live here with your aunt?"

Daisy looked around doubtfully. The flat was not that big, not that it was really her business. Would Agnes who was in her late middle age, rue the day she had agreed to offer support. Babies cried and disrupted one's life, would it work out?

"No, she will be in big trouble with my parents, especially my father. I am going to leave and make my own life."

There was no doubt that Laura meant every word of it, and Daisy sighed inwardly. Laura looked younger than eighteen years old, but she knew better than to try and dissuade her from her purpose. So few mothers had her courage and determination; it was rare. Daisy realised that it was now time to become involved and see what she could do to help.

"Leave this with me, and I will see what I can do to help you," she said kindly as she left.

The next day, after she had fed Matthew, Laura decided to go for a short walk. It was her first time out. Agnes had said she would watch Matthew, and had urged her to go and get some fresh air. There was a newsagents at the end of the road and Laura planned to buy the local paper just to see if there were any jobs she could apply for. She realised with a young baby she was limited, but at least she would get an idea of what was on offer. Maybe she could find some sort of child minder to care for him whilst she was at work. She felt such a pang of sadness at the thought of being separated from him at such a young age, but she

46

would have to work to live. She was finding out how tough life was already.

It was nice to be out in the fresh air. Oh, how she wished she had a nice pram to take Matthew out in. Maybe one day she would, she was certainly going to do her best to provide for him. The thought of losing him was more painful to her than being poor, and this spurred her on.

As she reached the shop, the doorbell rang as she entered and an Asian man came out from behind a beaded curtain. Aunt Agnes did not shop here and it was the first time Laura had, she was aware that Aunt Agnes preferred to use another local shop, which was manned by an English family, because she had explained to Laura that she didn't understand the Indian culture, nor did she like the smell of curry that drifted out from the back of the shop.

Laura smiled politely. "Please can I have a copy of the local paper."

"Yes, here," he handed the folded paper, and she opened her purse to pay him.

On her way out, just as she was closing the door, she noticed the adverts in the window. Mostly it was second-hand furniture for sale, no childminders or jobs, and she nearly missed the one on the end; the writing was faded and it looked as though it had been there forever.

"Respectable widower with young daughter needs daily nanny/housekeeper. References required," and there was a telephone number, which she wrote down quickly. Could this be the answer to her predicament?

She didn't stop to think about it. There was a telephone box outside; she found her loose change and dialled the number. When she heard his voice repeat the number, she pressed the button and heard her money go down.

"Good afternoon, I am telephoning about the position. Is it still available?"

"Yes it is, could you come round and see me for an interview?"

"Yes, I can come right now if you are agreeable."

"If you have a pen, my address is The Manor House, Corbyn Close. It's close to Waterloo Bridge.

"I will find it, don't worry, and my name is Laura Clark."

"I am Doctor Ravi Khan, and my daughter is six months old. I will explain more when I meet you."

Laura said goodbye and put the telephone down. Whatever had she done? This was an Indian Doctor. She had no problem with anyone who was not English, she could not understand why people were so against mixed marriages. After all, if you loved someone, what did it matter about the skin colour? Why did children of mixed race get taunted at school? She could never be like that, but what if Doctor Khan did not want an English person as a housekeeper, and also what would Aunt Agnes say?

She picked up the telephone again and rang Agnes's number. She explained to Agnes that she was going after a job, and Agnes reassured her that Matthew was still sleeping soundly. She omitted many details, there would be time enough for that later. Right now she needed to hop on a bus and get to Waterloo, then find his house, which actually sounded very grand. Then she had to ask if she could bring Matthew to work. There were so many obstacles to overcome to get this job, including finding somewhere to live.

She had to run to catch the bus, and when she sat down to get her breath back, she passed her fingers through her tousled curls. Luckily she had put on a dress this morning, a turquoise crimplene; it was a loose style without a belt, which was more flattering right now, because her stomach was still enlarged after childbirth. She had low heels on and a minimum amount of make-up, and her dress had replaced the bouffant styles of the 1950s. The new fashions were now knee-length and straight. It had been in her wardrobe for several months whilst she wore smock styles to minimise her enlarging waistline. But that was all now behind her, and as Daisy had suggested, she was going to do some exercises to help her stomach become flat again.

When she got off the bus, she spotted the private road immediately. Corbyn Close curved round, and when she arrived at The Manor House, the small front garden led to an impressive building, which she guessed probably dated back to the mid eighteen fifties. She took a deep breath before knocking on the door.

Chapter Eight

Dr Ravi Khan felt nervous whilst he waited for Laura to arrive. He had interviewed several women of varying ages since his wife Jenny had tragically died whilst giving birth to their daughter Tasmin. None of them had been Indian, and it seemed that women of other cultures were reluctant to work with someone who was different from them. Some had not even turned up for the interview once they heard his accent, and knew his name.

His big mistake had been not returning to India to practise his skills, but he now had a very well paid job as a consultant at Harley Street, and with a daughter who was Anglo Indian, London seemed the right place to bring her up.

Ravi had come to London after he finished his degree. He had not been looking for a relationship, but a short torrid affair with Jenny had resulted in Tasmin. He had hurriedly married her when her pregnancy was confirmed, even pretending to his parents in his communications with them that Tasmin had arrived two months early.

He had grown up in Delhi, son of wealthy parents, and had a very strict upbringing. Having sex before marriage was considered a sin, and marriage in his country was not as a result of meeting someone and being attracted to them. Arranged marriages were normal in India, love did not really come into it, but a dutiful wife would work hard to please her husband, respect his wishes, and provide him with heirs; and it was important to have sons.

Ravi had not really known Jenny long enough to decide

c

whether he loved her; the hasty marriage and then her pregnancy had complications, and it had all been very stressful. Then, when she was in labour, the baby was in a breach position. She was at a private hospital and a decision was made to give her a caesarian section to deliver her baby safely, but unknown to anyone, including herself, Jenny had a rare heart condition and she never woke up from the anaesthetic. Suddenly Ravi found himself a widower with a newborn baby daughter.

He had employed a nurse for the first few months of her life, but he really needed a nanny and a housekeeper so he could concentrate fully on his job as a consultant child psychiatrist. He had tried everything to get some help, and the advertisement in the newsagents had been a last resort. Even today he did not hold out much hope that it would be any different. Although he really didn't want to, he had decided that he might have to return to India, because he would then get help from his extended family.

If Tasmin was brought up in India she would have to adopt all the Indian customs, including covering her head, but would she even be happily received out there, as she was half English? Right now she was a happy chubby six month old baby; she had her mother's blue eyes, but her father's thick and very dark hair, which was an unusual contrast to her eyes. She was becoming interesting now, attempting to sit up on her own and every toy went into her mouth. He guessed her first tooth would appear soon, and he thanked Allah that she had never known her mother so could not miss her, and he spared no expense to give her everything she needed.

Night time was the hardest, as there was no nurse to pacify her and it rested on him to soothe her if she woke up, and he then had to present himself at work the next day and do his job properly. Being a single father in England was hard with no relatives around. It seemed unfair to him, that at the age of only twenty-six years old, he had been widowed and left with a newborn child. It was no good regretting his affair with Jenny; after such a strict upbringing, her free and open attitude had enthralled him, and although he had taken precautions, still she had become pregnant. He never wanted to regret that, because that meant he regretted his little daughter, and to him Tasmin was so perfect in every way.

When he heard the knock at the door, he moved swiftly. Tasmin was sleeping, her nurse was close at hand if needed, and he wanted to meet this would-be employee first, before he even allowed her to see his daughter. When he opened the door, he saw a blonde haired young girl, dressed smartly in a turquoise dress. He noticed when she smiled her whole face lit up, it was a happy face, and her very deep blue eyes fascinated him. She looked quite young, and he wondered tentatively just how much experience of looking after children she had.

"Good morning, please enter."

"Many thanks."

He noted with pleasure that she took her shoes off before walking on his carpet, that showed good upbringing and manners.

Laura was impressed with the very smart man in the dark suit and white shirt, who gripped her hand firmly in greeting and looked directly into her eyes. He was of slight build and not particularly tall. His eyes were deep brown, and she felt him watching her intently, summing her up she guessed, and his jet black hair was thick but neatly styled. She guessed his age to be about mid twenties.

She followed him into a room which seemed to be a study. There were bookshelves everywhere, and on one stood a photo of him in graduation robes and other photos; clearly family photos.

"Sit here please, and tell me about yourself and why you want this job."

Laura noticed the tone of authority in his voice, but did expect that; it was his house and his child, and he was very young to be a widower. She was probably one of many women who had applied for the job and might not even stand any chance of getting it.

"I am eighteen years old and three days ago my baby son was born. His father could not marry me as he was called up for National Service, and my mother sent me away to live with my aunt because my father would not have been able to accept it."

This was the last thing Ravi expected to hear; in her naïvety she had been completely honest with him. Did she not realise she could have pretended to be widowed? But he liked her honesty, he knew where he was with her.

"So you have only had three days of experience with your son."

"Yes, but I am willing to learn. You said your daughter is six months old. Right now my baby Matthew sleeps and feeds, so I will have plenty of time to devote to caring for your daughter."

"You want to bring your child to work with you?" He wasn't really as surprised as he sounded.

Laura drew a deep breath before she spoke. Her whole future and desire to keep Matthew depended on winning this man over, and convincing him she would be suitable.

"I have no one to look after him, and if you have a spare room, and would allow me to live in, you can adjust my wages to reflect that and, of course, I will be on hand at night when your daughter is teething, or unwell, and needs attention."

Ravi considered her words. Here was a young woman, by her own admission with a child born out of wedlock, but who was he to judge when it had happened to him and Jenny? She was the only one who had stayed long enough to even be considered for the job. She looked respectable, and the happy air about her made him feel less melancholy about his own predicament. She would help to lighten the atmosphere. His next step would be to take her to meet Tasmin.

Normally, outside work, Ravi was a man who kept himself to himself, but Laura reminded him a little of Jenny, and before he knew it, he found himself telling her how his wife had died during the birth of Tasmin and how difficult it had been ever since. She had been shocked to hear that, and her empathy was like balm to his sore spirit. As the conversation continued, a baby could be heard, crying from a distance, and Ravi rose from his chair and went out into the hall. He spoke to the nurse who was on her way to the nursery, and explained that shortly he would be bringing someone up to meet Tasmin.

Within a few minutes, Ravi led the way upstairs. The nursery was a big room, and it had a very pretty wickerwork cot on a side table, which Tasmin had now obviously outgrown. Laura noticed the wooden cot, painted a very delicate shade of pink, and the shimmering pink drapes above it and at the window. There was an assortment of cuddly toys, all shapes and colours, far too many for one little girl, she observed.

"The room is lovely!" exclaimed Laura. She had always loved pink herself and was amazed that after losing his wife so tragically Ravi must have done all this, because until she was born, he would not have known what sex his baby was.

Ravi smiled and explained. "Thank goodness I had nurse Patel here to inspire me about how the room of a little girl should look. Mara, this is Laura Clark, who wants to meet Tasmin today."

"Well I was glad to help," said Mara, her hand extended to Laura, whilst perched in her other arm was a baby with a thick mop of hair that seemed to spike out in all directions, and the most beautiful blue eyes that Laura had ever seen. The little girl was wriggling, clearly wanting to be put on the floor; her determination could be seen. Her skin was paler than her father, and Laura guessed that her mother may not have been Indian.

Mara put a rug on the floor, then propped Tasmin up with several cushions around her, and Laura watched her stretch forward to pick up her toys and then each one went straight into her mouth. She fixed her eyes on Laura, realising this was a newcomer, and gave her a dazzling smile.

"What a beautiful little girl!"

"She is a happy child, but she has a strong will." Ravi said proudly.

Mara nodded her agreement, she seemed to be a woman of few words, but clearly she adored her young charge.

After watching her for a few minutes, Laura held out her arms to Tasmin, who responded by raising hers, so Laura picked her up and was treated to a long solemn stare from the chubby little baby.

Ravi was happy to see the interaction, he felt an ache in his heart when he saw Laura hold her. That should have been Jenny. His baby should have had a mother like all other babies, life had been so cruel to them. Laura was English, and he was anxious for his daughter to be equally comfortable with English and Indian women.

Who knows whether Jenny would have been an ideal wife for him; most of their time together had been during her pregnancy. She had not been that well, although her heart condition had not shown itself. She had been stubborn to some of his ideas, difficult at times, and he was not sure she would have let him mould her into the person he wanted her to be. Indian women were very dutiful to their husbands, but Jenny had not appeared to be.

He took his daughter in his arms, and after responding to her smile, he handed her back to Mara. Laura knew it would not be long before he made his decision. Even though this house and this man were unfamiliar to her, she knew that if he offered her the job, for the sake of keeping Matthew, she would happily accept.

Ravi led her back to the study and indicated her to sit down again. There was a power about this man that made her respect him. In spite of the tragic circumstances, he was still very much in control of his life. She sat there waiting expectantly for him to speak, so glad he could not see how hard her heart was pounding with uncertainty.

He fixed his brown eyes intently on her. "Can you provide me with character references?"

Laura's voice faltered. Was this going to lose her the job? "Only my aunt, if family counts. This would be my first job."

He had guessed what her answer would be, and he had made up his mind anyway. He didn't really have a choice, he had to trust his instincts.

"Miss Clark, I find it very surprising that you are out and about only three days after giving birth."

"I need to find a job so I can keep my baby."

Ravi studied her again; she had despair in her eyes. If she loved her son so much to try and get herself a job already, surely his beloved Tasmin would be safe in her hands.

"For the next two weeks you need to recover from the birth of your baby, but you can come here for two hours every afternoon and get to know Tasmin. Mara will show you the routine. You can also bring your son, and we will see how it all goes."

Hope lit her face up again. "Thank you so much. I am looking forward to getting to know Tasmin."

After she had gone he reflected on his decision. Unless she didn't prove herself, Laura would be working for him shortly. He had been impressed by her courage and tenacity, as well as her naïvety and complete honesty. But as a doctor he knew she must recover her strength first.

Chapter Nine

During the next six months Laura more than proved her worth. She got up every morning early, and after feeding Matthew, she put him back in his cot to sleep whilst she fed and dressed Tasmin. As the months passed, Tasmin sat up, then crawled, and then stood up, and at the age of one year, she was just tentatively taking her first steps. Her nurse was no longer there, so Laura had full responsibility. Not only were both babies really well cared for, but she also kept the house clean and tidy and the washing done too. She was totally exhausted every night when she fell into bed, but she was comforted by the fact that she was bringing her own son up and they were not homeless.

Ravi was quite a stern master; a very private man, who expected a lot from her, and she was determined to cope with all the duties. She only had a very small amount of money as wages as there was no rent to pay or food to buy. It was up to her to manage the food budget out of money she was given for that purpose. However, she opened a building society account, and saved whatever she had left after buying baby necessities, because she never knew what might happen in the future.

She was allowed a few hours off every other Sunday, and she got on the bus and took Matthew to visit her Aunt Agnes, who was always delighted to see them. Aunt Agnes had told her that she thought Ravi was exploiting her; caring for two babies and running a home without any help was a bit much for an eighteen year old girl. Laura didn't know whether she was right or not, all she knew was no matter how tired and drained she felt, she did have a roof over her head.

Matthew was her whole life; her son meant everything to her, and he couldn't have been more different than Tasmin had been at the same age. Tasmin was a demanding little girl and maybe a little spoiled by her doting father. She did not like to be left out in her pram. The moment she woke up, her cries of protest could be heard, and as soon as she was picked up she was all smiles. She was into everything and a very enquiring child, who was, at the age of one year, trying very hard to speak. She knew a few words, and she practised "Daddad" and "bubba" all day long. Laura had grown fond of the little girl, who always held her arms up to be lifted from her cot as soon as Laura entered her room.

Laura felt she had been very lucky that Matthew was a much quieter baby. He was quite happy to lay in his pram kicking, and even when he wasn't asleep he used to watch the branches on the trees in the garden moving, cooing in delight. Sometimes when she picked him up to breastfeed him she had been very surprised that he became angry, as if he had not wanted to be disturbed. She had felt low at that point, having only just given birth and knowing very little about babies, she almost felt that her baby didn't love her.

She had confided in Aunt Agnes; after all, she was the only person she had now. She felt depressed, and she missed her parents, even her brother Sam; she would give anything to have him teasing her and being irritating, but she knew she had made her choice, and Matthew had been that choice. She would never regret having him, but the loss of her family hurt her deeply.

Agnes had worried herself so much about Laura's decision to go and live with Dr Khan. She had never met the man, but in her opinion he was treating Laura like Cinderella. She was running that house full time, and caring for two babies; she looked thin and tired. In fact, she had not wanted her to go there in the first place. But Laura wouldn't be budged; it was a shelter from the world, she had food to eat, a bed to sleep in and a bit of pocket money, because that was all it was, and Agnes partly admired her for her determination, but another part of her felt exasperated by Laura's stubbornness and refusal to realise he was exploiting her for a very lowly wage.

"You need to get yourself to a doctor girl, and not the one you work for!" said Agnes very pointedly. "You are more than likely suffering from post natal depression. Of course your baby loves you, he can't survive without you. You need medication to help you, but don't let the good doctor know, it might affect your job."

"Oh, silly me, I have heard of that, I will go when he is at work, but it's hard with two babies."

"I will come with you. I can sit in the surgery waiting room and watch them whilst you see the doctor," said Agnes gruffly, but she soon softened when Laura hugged her with gratitude. Her heart went out to Laura, she saw so much of her own character in her, and she still felt anger towards her sister Emily, who now knew that Laura had kept her son, but still kept it from Trevor, even though she knew her daughter was on her own. Agnes had told her everything, in the hopes her parents might relent After all, it wasn't as if she had murdered someone, and he was such a beautiful little boy, but still her weak willed sister did nothing.

So Laura visited the doctor and got some medication, and it did seem to help her. She started to understand her little boy more as he grew. He was obviously going to be a reserved child she decided. She left him in the pram, as he wanted her to; she was glad he was not demanding because Tasmin kept her very busy. Matthew fed well and he grew strong. His likeness to Simon, even at such a young age, was uncanny, and she knew that she found this both disquieting and comforting, because no matter how much she told herself she was over Simon, she never would be; that man was the love of her life.

Matthew was a solemn little boy. He didn't smile at everyone, but the first time he smiled at her it gave her heart such a lift; so he did love her, she had not been rejected. He was fascinated by bright lights, especially at Christmas; a decorated Christmas tree gave him such pleasure, he would sit in his baby seat and gaze wonderingly at it for hours. At six months he was now almost sitting up and moving about the floor. But he didn't move towards people; it seemed almost as if he wanted to keep himself to himself. The only person allowed into his world was Laura, and only when he wanted her to enter. Laura knew that all babies were different, just as people are, and she accepted her son's unusual character without question.

Not so Ravi; he said very little, but he noticed a lot. Being a child psychiatrist he could recognise all the signs. Matthew was reluctant to make eye contact or smile, he was a loner, he avoided Tasmin, even when put next to her on the floor. This child was clearly not normal; and as time went on, he felt reluctant to let him grow up with his daughter; she needed normality.

Ravi had read about Leo Kanner of the John Hopkins Hospital, he had discovered that some babies have behavioural characteristics in early infancy that marked them out as being different, and this had been labelled as infantile schizphrenia. The theory was the mother was to blame, and they were referred to as "refrigeration mothers".

Matthew's motor development didn't seem to be affected, but his unusual behaviour, and apparent lack of warmth, and also lack of eye contact were all the symptoms that had been described, and Ravi now decided he wanted Laura and her son out of his life. He had been pleased with the way that Tasmin had accepted her, but there was obviously something wrong with her if she had affected her son in this way; schizophrenia was a very serious mental condition.

Ravi had always intended to marry again. He wasn't looking for love, just a personable young woman who could help to bring his daughter up, and maybe later provide him with a son and heir. He had met Sofia at work, she was also a consultant, an Anglo Indian girl, with long slim legs and dark brown hair, and the biggest brown eyes he had ever seen. Ravi was very sexually attracted towards her and he was sure it would develop into love later.

He was planning to get to know her better before he asked her to marry him. It was scarcely three months, but he felt such unease when he saw Matthew, and the way Laura left him in his pram and rarely cuddled him. He needed to marry Sofia and get her moved in. He confided all Matthew's symptoms to her, and they pored over text books together, and then he invited Sofia to pay a visit and observe Matthew for herself.

Sofia had set her sights on Ravi the moment she saw him. She was twenty-four, just a couple of years younger than him, but he had been a practising child psychiatrist for longer; he was senior to her, and earned quite a bit more money. She felt the handsome doctor was quite a catch, so when he asked her to marry him, she did not hesitate. She was not going to move in with him until they were married, but he assured her, cold hearted Laura and her son would be gone. They had both agreed it was for the best, and Sofia believed a man as comfortably off as Ravi would find a new housekeeper to help her when she took up her position as mistress of the house.

When Ravi arrived home from work, having made his plans with Sofia, he called Laura into the study. He felt no guilt or compassion towards her, she had served her purpose for the last six months, but now it was time for her to go, before her son's mental problems affected his beautiful Tasmin. He spoke to her very shortly.

"I am getting married and there will be a new mistress of this house, so I will no longer require your services."

Laura's face registered her amazement. She had no idea this would happen. But then she chided herself, it wasn't that surprising, Dr Khan was young and probably would want to remarry. But she couldn't help wondering what would happen to herself and Matthew now. Desperation made her bold as she asked.

"Are you giving me a month's notice then?"

Ravi's eyes glittered with annoyance, and then his facial expression closed down like a shutter. "I am giving you until the weekend."

Laura felt fear and anger course through her. Perhaps Aunt Agnes had been right. This man had used her for his convenience, worked her hard, paid her very little, and now couldn't wait to get rid of her. He was allowing her only one day, as it was now Thursday evening, to pack and move herself and Matthew out. She had been loyal to him and never complained, even though she had found the work hard and had been secretly battling against post natal depression.

"Have I done something wrong? Surely you can give me longer than a day."

Ravi studied her, seeing the confusion in her eyes. As a consultant, and if this child was to have any sort of life, he needed to tell her what he knew. Laura may have just been a servant in his eyes, but her son was the future, and she needed to show him more love. He tried to make his tone as polite as he could.

"Miss Clark, your son is suffering from a mental condition known as infantile schizophrenia. It's caused by not being picked up and cuddled, or shown love. I am telling you this so you can put it right before he gets much older. It is a field in which I have studied and I have recognised all the symptoms."

Laura stared at him completely speechless, and at that moment she felt like he had taken the sharpest of knives and plunged it straight into her heart. She loved Matthew more than life itself, and she would love to cuddle him more, but the distress and anger it caused him had made her hold back. The closest she could get was to clutch at his fingers when she fed him, he didn't seem to mind that, but the contact she had with him whilst breast-feeding meant everything to her. Leaving him in his pram was not about neglect, it was accepting that he was happier with his own company, and she would have done anything to make her child feel safe and loved.

But in the midst of her anguish she felt anger. Anger that this man clearly thought she was neglecting her child, and he wanted her to go. Her reply came straight from her heart.

"My son means the world to me. I would love to cuddle him more, but he is not comfortable with it. Sometimes I have to respect that he only wants his own company. He is not sociable and outgoing like Tasmin. I have learned from him, to treat him the way he wants to be treated. I don't care what your text books say. I am his mother and I am doing my best for him."

Ravi secretly admired her fortitude. Her life with this child was going to be a hard one he knew, but he had tried to warn her, and if she wouldn't listen, then there was no more he could do, except make sure his own daughter was safe. He shrugged his shoulders.

"I am getting married on Saturday, so you have to leave tomorrow by the end of the day. I will pay you for this week."

Laura felt such emotion welling up inside her; fear of the unknown, and pain at the thought of her son being mentally ill. She would give her life for him, and she so wanted him to be all right. Her beautiful boy needed more love, and her heart was bursting with love for him, but she knew instinctively he could not cope with her displays of affection. She felt totally alone; no one could possibly understand, and that night she sobbed herself to sleep.

Chapter Ten

Mara the nurse had been brought back to stand in on Friday. It didn't take Laura long to pack her own clothes, but Matthew's took a little longer. She would have to carry him in her arms, as the pram she had used belonged to Tasmin, who never wanted to be left in the garden, she always wanted to be around people.

Laura was painfully aware of the difference between Tasmin and Matthew, but she had accepted her son's character as being quieter and more solitary without question. She spoke to him just before she fed him, told him she loved him every day, and she had been rewarded with a smile which lifted her heart. Matthew only reserved his smiles for those he knew well.

Even though he was not responsive to cuddles, breast-feeding him made her feel very close to Matthew; her body was keeping him alive and he had a good strong suck. She vowed that whatever problems he had, she would face. At this short notice the only place she could go to was Aunt Agnes, she would tell her all about it, and they would take Matthew to the doctor and get some help for him.

She had telephoned her last night and been told they could stay as long as she wanted. Aunt Agnes had proved herself to be a very reliable person. She had stood by her, but she wasn't her mother, and Laura's heart ached because her mother had washed her hands of her, and didn't want to meet her grandson. But then she knew she had to rise above this feeling of depression, for Matthew's sake, and she reminded herself what a good person Aunt Agnes had proved to be. Matthew was heavy and there was too much luggage for her to carry, let alone attempt to get on a bus, so she was getting a taxi which Agnes had insisted on paying for.

When she arrived at the flat, her aunt came out to help her with everything.

"Matthew is getting chubby," she said. He was sitting in his baby chair in the taxi. Ravi had allowed her to bring that with her.

Agnes didn't know much about young babies, so the far away look in his eyes, and lack of eye contact, did not cause her any concern until later, when Laura sobbed out what Ravi had told her and explained that he believed Matthew's mental condition had been caused by her neglect.

"You are an amazing mother. Don't listen to him, I know!" said Agnes angrily. "We will take him to the doctor and get some advice."

Her heart went out to Laura. She had always been such a bubbly happy girl, but right now, coping with motherhood was hard, she was fighting depression too, and only just nineteen years old. For her to be told something like this about her baby was devastating, but together they would get through it.

The doctor did not know much about Matthew's condition. He suggested Laura should take him to a Harley Street specialist, but that would involve Ravi, so Laura declined the offer. She felt she actually knew more about caring for her son than the experts. Agnes insisted they stay for a while until Laura could shake off her depression. She blamed herself for allowing Laura to move out so soon after Matthew's birth, but understood she had wanted to prove she could be independent.

Matthew's motor development was fast. He was a sturdy boy, and he didn't crawl for long, he stood up and was walking before he was a year old. He was easy to amuse. He loved Matchbox cars, and spent his time lining them up; he would spend hours meticulously making sure the line was straight, and instead of cuddly toys, the cars would have all been taken into his cot with him. Laura had only allowed him to take one, and after initially protesting by making screaming noises, which she ignored, Matthew accepted that.

Laura was learning to deal with his unusual behaviour; he

reserved his smiles for her, she felt as if he did know she was his mother, and they did have that special bond. He tolerated her dressing him and changing his nappy, but couldn't wait to get back to his cars when it was done. Baby toys like rattles and keys held no interest for him, but he did love music, and could be seen jigging around to the radio, especially when rock music came on.

Laura and Agnes shared the chores together, and Laura began to feel better and the draining tiredness she had experienced whilst working for Ravi lifted. Then one day Matthew showed her just how close they were; he suddenly made up his mind that hugging was not so bad, and he came over to his mother, his face wreathed in smiles, and gave her the biggest bear hug she had ever had.

Laura's depression vanished overnight; she felt fulfilled as a mother, and in time Matthew would come to treat his great aunt Agnes in the same way. Laura had thrown off Ravi's harsh words and diagnosis, she didn't believe her son was mad; being different did not make you mad. What she learned along the way, was that Matthew liked to initiate the hugging, and she respected that and always left him to make the first move.

At the end of 1963, Matthew was now walking well; it was a harsh winter, and the world was in shock following the assassination of John F. Kennedy. He had been greeting the crowds in an open car and he was shot dead, whilst his wife, Jackie Kennedy, had survived. Agnes wondered what the world was coming to; the president of the United States shot dead. There were so many mad people at large.

Laura watched the progress of her son avidly. He might be unlike other children, but as his mother she was learning to cope. He showed no signs of speaking yet, just the odd baby babbling, and then one day he looked at her, and simply said, "Mummy." This thrilled her for two reasons, firstly he knew who she was, and when he had said that magical word, he had made eye contact with her. Laura had been encouraging him to make eye contact since she had read in a baby book that this was key to a baby's cognitive development, being aware of the world around him.

Although Agnes would have happily let them stay with her, she knew that Laura wanted to be independent and she had thought of a plan which might help her. So when Matthew was tucked up in bed asleep, she shared her idea with Laura.

"I am thinking of selling my flat and moving to Eastbourne. A bungalow near the beach has always been a dream of mine. I should have some money left over, and if you are interested, there is a business opportunity for both of us."

Laura was surprised. With the little bit of money she had managed to save, she couldn't imagine it would stretch far in any business venture. Agnes continued.

"There is a shop with living accommodation in the local paper. It has a reasonable rent, and all they are asking for the goodwill is £1,000. That includes the stock. It's mainly wool and haberdashery, but you know how much I love knitting and crochet, I thought I could knit some baby clothes and cuddly toys, and you could sell them. I will put up the capital and we can share the profits."

"I can't let you do that, Aunt Agnes, I need to put some money in too."

"Listen, my girl, I have everything I need in life, I am comfortably off, but any money you have saved needs to go towards your rent. The only stipulation I make is you visit me at least once a month; you can collect what I have knitted, and also I get to see Matthew."

Laura's mind whirled, here was a chance to make a success of her life. It had been hard living with Doctor Khan. Tasmin had been her focus mainly, and she had got affection back from the little girl, but she had always felt out of place, because it seemed that Indian women had to be seen and not heard; their opinions were not encouraged and, as a servant, she had no status at all. It had not been great for her confidence so soon after giving birth. No wonder her depression had lifted now and her feisty strong nature had resurfaced. Aunt Agnes made her feel loved, and she went over to give her a grateful hug.

The next day they went to view the shop. It was set in a secondary parade of shops, nestling in the middle of a hairdressers and an Italian restaurant. There was also a grocer's shop, and a greengrocer's, and at the end of the parade was a baker's from which the delicious aroma of home made bread was drifting.

Another bonus of its position was that right outside was a bus stop, so Laura was already planning an eye-catching window display to tempt in customers whilst they were waiting for the bus. The living accommodation was set over three floors. At the back of the shop was a small room, where she noted Matthew could safely play in his playpen whilst she was in the shop. There was also a downstairs cloak room, which was useful, as she was toilet training him. The kitchen was up a flight of stairs, it was a fair size, and at the front of the building was the lounge, which was big with a view of the street from its large windows.

Another flight of stairs led to the bathroom and two bedrooms, and they were both of a good size. Out at the back was a parking area, and a small garden with a gate at the end of it which led into a lane which ran behind the terrace of shops.

Laura liked the spaciousness of it. The decor was a bit shabby, it was in need of a coat of paint, but she could sort that out in time, and she really liked the idea of proving herself. This was going to be a home and a work place, and the best part of it all was she could keep Matthew safe and still do her job.

Aunt Agnes's flat sold very quickly, as was expected, and within three months she was settled in a new bungalow with central heating and fitted carpets. It was close to the beach, and she now had a small dog from a rescue centre for company. Larry was what was commonly known as a bitsa, part poodle part terrier, but very friendly, and Matthew took more interest in him than he did with people; they seemed to develop a special bond.

At the same time life changed for Laura and Matthew. They moved into the shop, and Laura vowed to make a success of it and prove herself to Aunt Agnes, who had such faith in her and had been so generous in helping her to remain independent. She taught herself how to make eye-catching window displays, and made use of the stock she already had, giving it a new lease of life by completely revamping the shop.

Agnes had given her an old Singer sewing machine, so in the evenings, after Matthew was in bed, she used it to make girls' dresses and skirts. It wasn't that hard, and it was a good way to finish up old pieces of material. She then put them on a rail marked "Special Offers", and they sold really quickly. Laura used the money to buy new stock, and took pride in seeing her little business growing.

Agnes knitted the soft toys and children's baby clothes as she had promised, and Laura and Matthew visited her as arranged; not monthly, but fortnightly after Laura had closed the shop on a

Saturday, and they stayed until Monday afternoon, as she did not open the shop until Tuesday, then she worked the rest of the week; unlike other shops, most of which closed for a half day on Wednesday, and like her shop, were not open on Sundays.

Laura had quite a few of the local mothers as customers. If they knitted or sewed, they could buy wool and sewing aids from her, if they didn't have the time, she had inexpensive ready made children's clothes. Her ready smile and willingness to help her customers made her shop very popular, and many of them tried to encourage her to join their social circles. Laura politely declined, explaining her job took up so much of her time, but deep inside she knew the reason why she was doing this; it was because she was protecting Matthew from curious stares and comments which might happen when people met him. Just like a lioness, she was protecting her cub.

Matthew was happy to play with his cars in the room behind the shop. He meticulously parked them in lines behind each other, and spent hours scrutinising them carefully. As he grew he learned to speak, but in clipped sentences, saying as little as was needed to make his point. Laura tried not to worry about his lack of communication. Although now only three years old, Matthew had started to read some of the words from the books Laura had borrowed from the children's library to try and widen his world a little, as so far he had never played with any other children.

During one of her visits to Agnes, her aunt, always brutally honest, decided to speak her mind.

"Matthew spends too much time with you. He needs to go to a play centre and meet children of his own age. There is a new one that is opened up the road from the shop."

"I know, Aunt Agnes, and I don't know what to do; he is different from other children. I would have to write down all the things he doesn't like so they will understand him."

"Well, do it then. He's three years old and he needs company other than his mother, he needs to make friends. People have to accept him as he is, and the sooner the better."

If Agnes's words sounded harsh and uncaring, that was far from the truth. It worried her that Matthew, who was not keen on leaving the flat, was happy just to sit in the back room all day with his cars. He had to learn to be away from his mother, and to form friendships. One day he would go to school, so the play school would be an excellent place to start.

Laura knew her aunt was right. Her son needed the stimulation of the world outside and to meet other children, but it didn't stop the fear circulating inside her, wondering how he would cope. Matthew had a lot of intelligence, he could already write his name, read a little, and even do simple sums, but because he had been kept at home with her, he had no social skills. She accepted the fact that he only spoke when he needed to; he was a deep thinker, but maybe she was being over protective, and in a different environment he would become more sociable. She owed it to him to give it a try.

When she told him about it, Matthew was not happy. He threw a tantrum and bit his wrist until he drew blood. It would have been easy just to say he didn't have to go, but his balkiness only increased her determination; this behaviour was both upsetting and bewildering to her. Was she such a bad mother? Ravi's words frequently came back to haunt her, but she turned to the one person who had never failed her; Aunt Agnes, and drew strength from her continuing support.

Aunt Agnes got the train immediately, and stayed with Matthew whilst Laura went to speak to Mary Hunt, who ran the play school. She guessed her age to be about mid-thirties, her manner was professional but kind. Mary's grey eyes showed concern whilst Laura explained falteringly that her son was different, he was not sociable and he had never played with any other children, and was content to spend his time with his cars in the back room of the shop. He always liked to sit in the same chair, he lined his slippers up by the door on the rare occasions when he went out, which was always with her. He was quiet and withdrawn, but he was also very bright; although only three, he could already read a bit, do sums, and write his name.

Mary looked at the young woman who was being so frankly honest with her, and saw fear and desperation in her eyes. She was clearly a young mother, no more than early twenties she guessed, but was she bringing up this child alone?

"I am not trying to pry into your life, but what about Matthew's father? Does he spend time with him, too?"

"We are not together. Matthew just has me and his aunt, who has been such a support to me, and is, in fact, looking after him now."

67

Laura handed a photograph of Matthew to Mary, and sat quietly whilst she studied it. The pain that never went away had burrowed deep into Laura's heart when the word "father" had been mentioned. She was fighting against herself inside, pushing her son away, but fiercely wanting to protect him from himself forever.

"Have you ever explained your worries about Matthew to a doctor?" Mary smiled kindly at her, and then she saw Laura gulp. "He's a very bonny little boy," she remarked, handing the picture back.

"I worked for a Harley Street specialist, and he blamed me for my son's condition, said it was schizophrenia due to lack of love; but I love the bones of him, he is my whole life!" and then the tears came, unwelcome though they were. She had tried so hard to keep her cool and had failed miserably.

Mary handed her a tissue, and then went to switch on the kettle and make some tea. All the while she was thinking as Laura fought to compose herself. Her heart went out to her; she was a mother bringing up her child alone, and instead of helping her, it sounded like this specialist had let her down. But there were good doctors around, and she would encourage Laura to see one. In the meantime Matthew sounded like a challenge, but Mary had never been one to ignore a challenge. She had a natural love for children, so helping this little boy and his mother was what her job was all about, and she decided to give it a go.

Chapter Eleven

Mary made it her mission to become Laura's friend, as it was clear she desperately needed one. Although Mary was slight in build and height, she was a very determined woman. With her short brown hair, clipped back at the side with a kirby grip, she looked barely out of her teens, but was in fact thirty-five and full of energy.

She visited Matthew at home before he started at the play group, hoping that when he arrived on his first day, because he already knew her, it might not be so traumatic for him and for Laura. Matthew still threw tantrums every morning, but Mary was unconcerned by this as some of the other children also did when they first started.

She had noted what Laura had told her about him; he did not like to be touched, he was very tidy minded, and would fastidiously line up his shoes after changing into his plimsolls and did not like anyone to move them. She knew it was going to be tough. Although she would respect that he didn't want to be touched, it was obvious that whilst being amongst twenty or so other children in a close environment, he would be touched. She was going to have to teach him to bear it.

Although Matthew was only three years old, and had very little to say for himself, Mary felt a rapport with him. She spoke to him as if he was older, and it eventually worked. One day he bit another boy who had fallen against him whilst playing. Mary took him into another room, away from the scene, and addressed him very firmly, saying that his behaviour was not acceptable, he must apologise to Peter, and no matter how much he disliked being touched, he would have to learn to accept it, as it was part of life; people touched one another.

She somehow managed to appease Peter's angry mother when she found the bruise. Normally she would have refused to have a child in her play school who bit others, but Matthew was a special case, and he did respond to her firm words. Although he sometimes bit himself when frustrated, he never bit another child again, so she felt that progress was being made and shared her optimism with Laura.

Matthew watched other children playing, but did not join in or make any effort to socialise with them. Mary wondered if it was because he had spent his formative years with just his mother for company, but she was not a psychologist and could not be sure. The one thing she had no doubt of was Laura's love for her son, and there was no way she would have refused to give him love if he had been able to tolerate it. Did no one understand how unfulfilled Laura must feel, as a mother, to never feel her child's arms around her and the warmth of his little body snuggled against her?

But there were times when Mary could not reach Matthew at all. He would hide himself in a cupboard, with his hands pressed firmly against his ears, and no entreaties would persuade him to leave his own world and come into hers. Mary had not realised just how much patience she had. Mary and Laura shared ideas on how to cope with Matthew, and they both felt they were making headway with him. This became evident when James, a boy of his own age, took a liking to him and followed him around, until eventually even Matthew allowed him to share a very small corner of his life. James was very timid and a bit in awe of the more lively boys, but Matthew, who only spoke when he wanted to, made him feel safe. Very little conversation passed between them, but they sat together most of the time.

Laura was delighted Matthew had a friend, but was very nervous when he was invited to James's birthday party. Could she be sure the afternoon would be incident free?

"Should I let him go, Mary? I can't be sure he won't throw a strop if he is touched."

"You have to let him live his life Laura. He must get used to mixing socially, and if you are as honest with others as you have been with me, people will make more of an effort to understand."

Mary's words made sense. Laura could not keep her son at home all the time with her, one day he would go to school. Different from others or not, he would need to be educated. However, unfortunately other mothers were not as tolerant or understanding about Matthew's condition, so Laura was relieved she had been there to bring him home when he threw a strop because someone had hidden his shoes. Matthew did not understand jokes, or even have a sense of humour, all he understood was that someone had stolen his shoes, which is how he perceived it. After Laura had calmed him down, she made him apologise and took him home, and her heart felt heavy with the knowledge that Matthew's outburst would make him very unpopular at play school; he might be avoided after his display of temper.

Mary took the opportunity to persuade her that a trip to the doctor might help. Agnes thoroughly approved of their friendship and the help Mary was giving them, and added her weight to the suggestion. Laura had been thinking about it herself; after all Ravi was not everywhere, and she was desperate to know why Matthew was different from other children, and how they could all help him.

Her family doctor had no choice but to refer her to a consultant. With her referral letter clutched tightly in her hand, Laura made good use of the Ford Fiesta she had just managed to budget for. It was only a second-hand car, but it made life so much easier; no more train journeys to Eastbourne to visit her aunt, and on this day she found her way to Surbiton in Surrey, where Mr Charles Usher had his private practice.

Matthew had come with her, and initially he was taken away to another room where he could play with cars and be assessed later. Mr Usher wanted to speak to Laura alone and make his own observations, and so she was shown into a small reception room with a desk and chairs on either side of it, and she dutifully sat down, feeling a bit as though she was still at school and had been summoned to the head master's study.

When Mr Usher came in the room, she noted his thick and wavy grey hair, very thick glasses, and the suit he wore was also grey. His white shirt was crisp and without wrinkles, and his tie was pale blue. A pair of charcoal grey shoes completed his smart appearance. His smile was warm when he shook hands and greeted her, which made her feel more at ease.

Charles Usher studied the young woman sitting across the desk from him. As a psychiatrist, it was in the interests of the child he was trying to help to try and make a quick analysis of the mother. He could see from the notes in front of him that she was twenty-one years old, well almost, give a month or so, and as Matthew was three, she had given birth to him when she was only eighteen. She was bringing him up alone, which must have been a daunting task, and although he saw signs of stress in her young face, he also saw a warmth when she smiled; it reached her eyes, which were huge and violet in colour. She exuded naïvety and honesty, and he felt instinctively that he could trust her and she would answer his questions honestly.

Charles, at the age of fifty, had been studying infants and children with this condition for over twenty years now. He had read many books on the subject of infantile schizophrenia, which it had been believed affected children with "refrigeration mothers". This had been a terrible label for a mother to have inflicted on her, so thank goodness modern research had thrown that idea right out of the window.

He had recently read a book by Bernard Rimland, only published this year, in which "Infantile Autism" was now believed to be of biological origin rather than psychological. Looking at Laura, with love in her eyes every time she mentioned her son's name, the new theory made much more sense to him.

Laura had decided to tell him everything, lay bare her heart. This man had kind eyes, she could not see the cruel flashes which had sometimes shown in Ravi's eyes. After three years of trying her best, she needed to know if she was to blame for her son's mental condition.

"When I became pregnant I left home. Matthew's father had been called up for National Service, and my father would not have accepted it, so I was sent away to live with my aunt who has turned out to be incredibly supportive."

"Did Matthew's father know you were pregnant?"

"I never told him. I had no way of contacting him."

Charles hid his surprise, and allowed her to carry on speaking. "I had no experience of other babies, but right from the beginning, Matthew didn't like to be touched, he was angry if I disturbed him."

She then went on to explain that caring for Tasmin had been so different; the cuddling and the interaction, which Matthew had shied away from. Then she told him about the shop and how it had given her a chance to keep Matthew with her, but then she realised he must mix with other children, and so she had been lucky enough to find a supportive friend in Mary, who was also trying to help him to cope with play school.

"How is he doing at play school?" enquired Charles.

"Some days are good, and some are not, he prefers to sit alone and draw or write, he doesn't play with other children much, but he does have a friend called James, who accepts him just as he is."

"Well that sounds very encouraging to me, good."

After a while Charles explained that he would need to go and speak to Matthew and assess him. So in the meantime, if Laura went back into the reception area, she could have tea or coffee, and he would call her back in. Laura went with trepidation, wondering if Matthew would be co-operative, but she chided herself, this man was an expert in his field, he would know how to deal with Matthew.

She read a magazine, and watched the minutes tick by until the receptionist got the call for her to go back into the consulting room. Charles did not keep her in suspense for long. He shuffled the papers in front of him and smiled encouragingly at her.

"Matthew has autism. Contrary to what you have been told, the condition is biological rather than psychological. You are in no way to blame, it is nothing to do with what you have, or have not done, he was simply born that way. But even now, in 1965, we know very little about this condition, much more research needs to be done into it."

As Laura digested his words she felt relief flood through her. It was not her fault, and she felt like a huge burden of guilt had been lifted from her shoulders. Charles continued.

"From what you have told me, you and your support team, Mary and your aunt, seem to be giving Matthew the very best care possible. Children with autism find it hard to make sense of our world, but between you, you are helping him. You are learning in every day life to minimise his difficulties. Bringing him up will never be easy, but you have my highest admiration."

d

"Thank you." Laura was bewildered, she had not expected praise, but she felt hope for the future blossoming inside her.

"I have tested Matthew's IQ. Did you know your son is very intelligent, he is functioning at the level of a much older child?"

"Well I knew he was bright; he can read a bit already, and write his name."

"He is only three years old, but as he gets older we can check him again. It will help him a lot in life and give him confidence. Your son is unique, Miss Clark, don't worry about what anyone else thinks of him, he has the ability to do very well with your support."

"I am so lucky to have my aunt and Mary to help me."

"Yes, families are so important for moral support. Of course, children with autism are not all the same, and although you have told me that Matthew does not like being touched, it's very nice to hear that he hugs you when he feels like it."

Laura beamed. "Oh yes, it's very special, and even Aunt Agnes gets a hug sometimes, but we know that it has to be initiated by Matthew."

"You see, you know even more than our textbooks. Your experiences are invaluable. Matthew could not be in more competent hands."

If Mr Usher was trying to build Laura's confidence, it was certainly working. She realised just how much she had learned in the last three years whilst caring for Matthew. She made up her mind that no matter how hard life would be, she would help Matthew to cope with it. Her son was special, and one day his talents would be recognised.

"Just one thing more, and I hope you will not mind me saying this," he paused, and Laura gave him her full attention, wondering what was wrong. "You were very honest with me today and I respect that. However, I do feel, that no matter how you feel about him, you must tell Matthew's father that he has a son, he has the right to know."

Laura thought about what he was saying. She had been so hurt that Simon had gone away without a word, and then, after Matthew was born, her life had so completely revolved around him, that contacting Simon again had not even crossed her mind. But Mr Usher's frank words made sense, Simon did have the right to know he was a father. No matter what pain it caused her emotionally to contact him, she must do it.

"Well, the truth is I still love him, I always will," she said simply. "But it will be a shock for both him and Matthew."

"Has Matthew ever asked about his father?"

"No, I guess he just accepts that he doesn't have one."

"Well, maybe do it gradually, give them both time," he said kindly, and Laura nodded her agreement.

Later that night she spoke to her aunt on the telephone, and was surprised that Agnes agreed; she had expected opposition.

"It's time he knew. He needs to step up to his responsibilities."

"I don't want any money from him, I can support Matthew."

Agnes knew this was true, the business was thriving, but so far Simon had got off scot free. He should play a part in his son's life in her opinion.

"Well maybe you should pay a visit to him. Writing a letter might not work."

"I wish I could take Matthew to see my parents. I have missed them all, even my brother Sammy, my irritating little brother; he would be nineteen now."

"Leave it with me, Laura, let me give it some thought."

"Good night Aunt Agnes, and thanks for everything."

Laura put the phone down wearily. Her aunt cared and no one else in her family did, but she felt even Aunt Agnes could not fix this amount of damage.

Chapter Twelve

"It's your daughter's 21st birthday and you haven't seen her for almost four years, nor your grandson. Emily, you are a disgrace!" Aunt Agnes, as ever, did not hold back in speaking her mind, and Emily had no defence against her words. She knew it was true, she had tried so hard to keep the peace, and not ruffle any feathers, but it hadn't worked. She wished she had the same sort of courage that Laura clearly did.

Emily had been plagued by her conscience when she sent Laura away to have her baby, but her fear of Trevor's wrath had prompted her to do it. She had not realised just how much she would miss Laura; her smile and sense of fun, their shopping trips together, and even Sam had missed his sister, he had no one to fight with and life was boring.

Trevor was heartbroken when his daughter did not return. Agnes had said she had left her to be independent, but at only eighteen, Trevor thought it was far too young and he had grieved for her loss. He even went as far as visiting Judy to see if she had heard from her, but it appeared that Laura had vanished without trace. Agnes also said she had no idea where Laura was.

Over the next couple of years, Trevor became a broken man. Emily had watched him go from a bullying controlling man to a shadow of his former self. The doctor explained he had suffered a breakdown; he could not work, he just sat at home moping for Laura as though she had died. Emily had so many times wanted to tell him that Laura was alive and well with her son, but she wasn't sure if it would make him even more ill.

But this was the final straw. Life couldn't be much worse than it was now, so when she came off the telephone she told Trevor everything, including how Laura was coping with Matthew, and her shop, and the life she had made for them both; only omitting that Simon was the father. It wouldn't do for Trevor to go off in a temper to seek vengeance on Simon and his family.

Trevor was no longer at the helm of his family; his princess had left them, and life without her was nothing but worry. He had feared she might be dead in a ditch somewhere, or on drugs. After all, some of the current pop stars made it sound cool, she could easily have been led astray. Somehow finding out she was a mother didn't seem that shocking now. He had changed his opinions since she had gone, and just felt sad and angry that whoever the father was, did not consider his daughter worthy to marry, and he felt hurt for her.

" I don't care what she has done. She's had the guts to provide for her child. I am proud of her, and we need to have them both in our lives."

Emily could scarcely believe what she was hearing. The power of the love he had for Laura had brought him to his knees, but who cared, it looked like the family rift could be mended, and they now needed to make up for lost time, as they had already missed the first three years of Matthew's life. Trevor believed that Agnes had only just been told by Laura about her new life, and such was his relief, he was not going to hurl recriminations around. Trevor had changed, underneath all that bluster and bullying, and the need to control, there was a very insecure man.

"We can sort it, Trevor, it's not too late," Emily said, patting his hand with a gesture of affection. At last she was going to get her daughter and her husband back.

Judy was amazed that, after over four years of silence, she had been invited to Laura's twenty-first birthday party. She had been really hurt when Laura had left without as much as a goodbye to her and never a letter either. They had been friends since they were at primary school together, then suddenly she was gone. It was a difficult time for Judy, with no best friend to confide in; her own parents had split, they were now divorced, and her dad had remarried a much younger woman, leaving her mother full of bitterness and jealousy. Judy was glad to be leaving home. She was engaged to the man she had always wanted, and soon they would be living in Guildford, having already put a deposit down on the house they had chosen.

Well, she was looking forward to a happy life, so there was no need to hold grudges. No doubt Laura would explain it all when they met up. All she had to do was reply to the invite and say she was coming. Regretfully it would have to be alone, as her darling was away at a conference and would not be back until Monday.

Simon had never managed to get through one day in the past four years without thinking about Laura with an ache in his heart. He blamed himself for losing her. He had gone away before she returned from her holiday, yet had hoped his note would explain all; and because he felt their love was so strong, she would wait for him.

What a fool he had been. Laura had vanished, no one knew where she was, even her own father didn't know, as he had visited Judy to see if she did. It seemed Laura had gone off to seek her independence, and not only had she abandoned him, but also her own flesh and blood too. He found it so hard to believe she would do that. Laura didn't have a mean bone in her body, not the Laura that he had known.

Her apparent selfishness should have been his reason to stop loving her, but his foolish heart seemed to have a mind of its own, and he continued to cherish the memories of their brief time together. He knew that whatever happened in his life, he would never love like that again; his heart had been given away, and he had wished so many times that they could have had a future together.

He had found life in the army hard, but busy. The endurance courses were tough, so thank goodness he had been able to return home briefly for leave and the comforts that his home life had always provided. His sister Kate was now at drama school and their paths did not often cross, the only person from the old days was Judy, who had always been Laura's closest friend.

The first time he had come home he was full of hope, expecting Laura to be around, or some sort of letter explaining why she was not; but nothing. Judy had needed a friend at that time. Her parents were at loggerheads and she was caught in the middle. So they both turned to each other for solace, and as time went by, he found himself getting closer to Judy, although he knew in his heart she was not Laura, and never could be. They had been together for over three years now. It was clear that Judy adored him, which was balm to his sore heart, but he knew that if Laura was ever to come back, cruel though it might be, he would fight to get her back with every bit of his being, and he would end his relationship with Judy.

But as it was now 1965, and he had not seen Laura since 1961, and even her own parents did not know where she was, according to Judy, he had resigned himself to thinking that maybe she had fallen out with her family in some way and left home, which is why they couldn't trace her.

He had finished his National Service a year ago and was now training to be a lawyer, but his ambition eventually was to be a barrister. The law interested him greatly, and the company he was working for had their chambers in London. As he commuted up there every day, he was renting an apartment in Chelsea and, after they were married, he would travel back to the house in Guildford.

If he was honest with himself, he had been caught out a bit. He had not planned to marry Judy, but when she told him she was pregnant, there was no choice really, he had to stand by her; this is what was expected of him, and whether getting married for the sake of the child was the best idea, well, who knows? If Laura had been here then maybe he wouldn't have even got Judy pregnant, but that in itself had been a shock. She insisted she had taken her pill, but it hadn't worked, and after the lengths she had gone to get it from the doctor by wearing a fake wedding ring, because up until now, the pill was not available to unmarried women, how unlucky she was! He was fond of Judy, and he would stand by her and their child. So the wedding was booked, not the lavish affair his parents wanted, just the local registry office; it was their choice that no one could dispute, as they were both over twenty-one.

Laura was shocked beyond belief when her mother walked into the shop a few days after her conversation with Aunt Agnes that night when she had been filled with despair. Although the past four years had not really aged her much, she saw a new strength in Emily's eyes, she seemed to be more in control of her life, and Laura then found out why.

"Oh Laura, it's been so long. I have never stopped worrying about you and wondering how you are, can you find it in your heart to forgive me?"

Emily held her arms out; there were tears glistening in her eyes, and Laura's memory flashed back to when she was a child; the comfort of those arms, and the warm feeling of knowing her mother loved her. Oh how she had missed that! She ran into her mum's arms, all anger and disappointment was now behind her, finally her mother had forgiven her for getting herself pregnant.

"Oh Mum, of course I do, you have forgiven me. . ." Her tears were flowing now, but they were tears of happiness. Then her voice trailed off ". . .What about Dad?"

"Your Dad has changed. He's been ill, had a breakdown, but he knows everything, and he wants to see you and, is it Matthew?"

"Yes, Matthew, but I have to explain about Matthew; he's very shy with strangers, he is only three and has not yet learned to be sociable."

"Where is he now?" asked Emily, looking around as if she expected him to magically appear.

"He's at play school. I usually shut the shop for about half an hour at lunchtime whilst I go to collect him. But come in the back room whilst I make us a cup of tea, I have so much to explain."

Emily listened intently as she drank her tea. Her heart ached when she realised how tough life had been for Laura since she had left home. But as she looked around the shop, she felt proud when she realised how well Laura had done, she was a true survivor.

Laura prepared her mother for her meeting with Matthew. She explained about his diagnosis and what autism meant, she also explained how she was learning to cope with his needs, and how the family would have to accept him for who he was.

Emily assured her that would happen. The rupture of their family ties had been devastating for all of them, so she knew there would be a lot more patience and understanding in the future. Laura's deep love for her son positively radiated from her whenever she spoke about him.

"Will Dad accept all this?" she asked anxiously.

"Leave your dad to me," said Emily firmly, and this time she felt confident.

Chapter Thirteen

Laura felt a warmth in her heart that had been missing for a very long time. She was getting her family back, and it was all due to Aunt Agnes. They were going to stay for the weekend, and on Saturday her parents had arranged for a few friends to come round to celebrate her twenty-first birthday. First of all Aunt Agnes had declined the invitation, but Laura was determined that the one person who had always stood by her was going to share this weekend with her.

Mary was going to take care of the shop and the dog on Saturday, helped by the new part time assistant that Laura had now been able to employ. In the near future life was going to be easier for Laura; once she had trained Paula, she could leave the shop in safe hands and have time for herself and Matthew.

Ignoring her aunt's protestations, Laura drove to Eastbourne after the shop closed on Friday. Matthew enjoyed riding in the car, he never seemed to get bored, so she knew he would enjoy the outing. They arrived in time for dinner; it was Matthew's favourite, shepherds pie, and Aunt Agnes knew he must have baked beans in it otherwise he wouldn't eat it. They did not go to bed late, as they were all going to be up early the next day to drive to Laura's parents' home in Surrey.

Laura had explained to Matthew that he was going to meet a new grannie, granddad and uncle the next day, but he didn't seem too interested. She had packed his box of Matchbox cars because she knew as long as he had them, something familiar, he would cope. Hopefully in time he would get used to his new family, but she didn't expect it to happen overnight.

When they arrived, Emily opened the door and hugged her daughter, but remembered what she had been told when she saw Matthew.

"Hello Matthew, I am your grandma."

"Hello," said Matthew very woodenly, walking past her, not wishing to be touched. He then proceeded to crouch on the carpet and open his box of cars. Emily would have loved to hug the little boy with the shock of brown hair and very brown eyes who looked so bonny, but his body language forbade it. All she could hope was that one day he would hug her as he did his mother and his aunt. She reminded herself it was her own fault, she had over three years to make up for, and she was not going to spoil the very precarious situation by hurrying anything, so she must just be content to have them both back in the family.

Trevor had Laura back, that was all that mattered to him, and Matthew was her child and his grandson, he wasn't about to frighten the boy away from him, so he would give him time to get used to him. He knew he had been the cause of Laura leaving and he'd cast all his moral principles aside to get her back. What the hell did any of it matter when his princess was still alive; that is what mattered to him. He didn't really understand about autism, but he was not going to mess up again. Whatever it took to understand the boy, he would persevere, because he was his own flesh and blood.

Laura shyly hugged her brother Sam. He was tall and gangly, a young adult really, not the kid brother she remembered. He glanced briefly at his nephew huddled on the carpet.

"I've got some Matchbox cars upstairs that you might like," and Matthew rewarded him by entering his world, and replying:

"Where are they?"

"Matthew, say thank you."

"I haven't given them to him yet."

Laura breathed a sigh of relief. Matthew was being accepted, no one commented on his lack of interest in them. Sam had Matchbox cars, so that would pave the way for a future relationship, because Matthew would remember him as the uncle who gave him his favourite toys: Matchbox cars.

Aunt Agnes was quietly observing everything. It amused her to see that her sister and brother-in-law had changed places. Emily was the driving force, her timidity had vanished, and bullying Trevor was only just getting himself together since the appearance of Laura. One thing was for sure; Laura had proved herself, not only as a single mother, but also as a business woman; at such a young age too, how could they not be impressed? Agnes had stood by her, and would continue to, but she was so relieved that she was back in the bosom of her family, where she should be.

Laura could feel a big bubble of apprehension inside her. She had no way of knowing if Simon was still living at the other end of town, but as her mother knew he was Matthew's father, she was sure he would not have been invited to the party tonight. But Judy was coming. Laura remembered her promise to Charles Usher; she had made up her mind to tell Simon about his son. He might not want to know him, especially with the autism, but he did have the right to know he was a father.

For the rest of the day, Matthew played with the Matchbox cars, and then later he did some drawing, and Trevor and Emily were pleased to see he could write his name. By the time evening came he was ready for bed, which was another relief to Laura, as sometimes he refused to sleep somewhere that was not home, or familiar, but tonight was the exception.

She got ready for the evening, having brought with her a new mini dress she had made herself. It was a polyester material in red, which suited her very well, and it had a zip down the front of the dress, as was the current fashion. She wore white sandals with heels to accompany it, and after she had applied a light touch of make-up, and tried to tame her curls, she felt ready to go.

The party was being held in the large lounge, which was at the opposite end of the house from where Matthew was sleeping, and Agnes was going to sit in the drawing room below, as she wanted to listen to the wireless she said, and she could then listen out in case Matthew woke up.

"But you'll miss the party," said Laura.

"Parties are not for me, but I will come in when you cut your cake," said Agnes firmly, and Laura knew she would not be able to budge her. As long as she was happy; and she did love her plays on the radio.

When Laura saw Judy, all awkwardness vanished, it was as though the last four years had not happened. Tim had come too, but to her relief, Simon had not; because although her heart was crying out to see him, she knew it was something she could not cope with in front of her family.

Judy still wore her very dark hair long and straight with a full fringe, and tonight she wore a black velvet cocktail dress. It was what Laura's dad would refer to as a "pelmet", very short, and tight, and Laura noticed with amusement, which she carefully concealed, that when Judy sat down, she had to do a bit of a sideways wiggle to get onto the sofa. She wondered what would happen if Judy tucked into the food, because there was no room for expansion. The top was low cut with a generous display of Judy's ample curves.

Tim had not changed much. He was still very much the joker, which was something Laura had always liked about him. He could always lighten any party. He hugged her enthusiastically, and she noted he had grown his hair longer, like a rock star. He flapped a piece at her just in case she hadn't seen.

"John Lennon move over," he grinned. "Laura you're looking as lovely as ever. Tell me, as you haven't been around for such a long time, are you still madly in love with Elvis?"

Laura had not had much chance to even think about any pop star since she had left home, her mind had been solely occupied by Matthew and Simon, but she answered lightly.

"Well, I was fifteen then, he was a teenager's dream, but now I am twenty-one and I like all sorts of music, including John Lennon and the Beatles. How about you Judy?" She carefully steered the conversation away from herself.

"Same here. I still like Cliff, but there are so many others. I saw Johnny Kidd and the Pirates at the Orchid, Purley, recently you know, now he's great too, I can tell you!"

"You women don't know a good catch when you see one," laughed Tim, doing a mock imitation of Cliff by curling his lip and speaking like him.

Judy touched his arm playfully. "Tim, can you make yourself useful and get us both a drink?"

"Sure, what are you both having?"

Laura decided, as it was her birthday party, she would have a glass of wine, but Judy opted for an orange juice, which surprised her. Tim brought the drinks back, then went to seek the company of some other males, who were hovering near to the food.

"What's up with you Judy, have you turned teetotal these days?" she laughed.

Judy blushed, not ready to tell her yet. "My stomach's a bit dodgy tonight."

"Well thanks for coming. I need to explain to you why I went away without contacting you." She brought out a photo from her handbag, and said simply, "I was pregnant, my dad didn't know. I had to go away, and I decided to keep my baby. This is Matthew."

As soon as Judy saw the photograph, her heart turned over. She didn't even have to ask whose son it was; there in that photograph was a miniature replica of Simon. Laura had gone away to have his child and he had never known. She was sure he didn't know, because she realised with such a pang in her heart, if he had known, she would not be sitting here with his engagement ring on her finger.

Now she felt such a fear creeping over her. She could lose the man she loved; had always loved and wanted. If only Laura had not returned home now, in two weeks time they would have been married. But then, she reminded herself, she had the upper hand, she was engaged to Simon. Laura had been out of the picture for nearly four years now, she couldn't expect to come home and pick up where she left off. Her best means of defence was attack! So now she must sound convincing.

"What a lovely little boy. I am so glad it's all turned out well for you. Obviously now your parents are OK with it, and why not, he's a child to be proud of."

"I am very proud of him. Matthew is a special little boy."

But Judy didn't want to hear in what way he was special. She knew she had to move fast, or else her relationship with Simon would be no longer.

"I have also got some news for you. After you went away, Simon and I started to go out, then we got really close, and now we are engaged and getting married in two weeks. We were going to marry in September, a big fancy wedding, but we've brought it forward because I am pregnant."

Judy didn't even flinch as she spoke those words; she knew whatever it took, she was not going to lose Simon now. Laura didn't know how hard she had tried over the past three years to make him commit to her, so in desperation she had invented a pregnancy; there had been no wedding planned for September. In a month or two she would have to pretend to miscarry, but right now she had to make it clear to Laura that Simon was no longer available.

Laura felt that knife again, not just being plunged into her heart, but being twisted again and again deep inside her! Simon and her best friend Judy. . . it sickened her, and then jealousy flamed; she could not speak, there were no words to express her anger and disbelief, she sprang up from the sofa and fled from the room not caring if anyone saw her or not.

Judy was alarmed to see her go. After all, it was her party, and everyone would wonder what had come over her, but when she looked around, people seemed to be in groups talking. Judy was hoping no one had seen, and even more worried that Laura's distress might get back to Simon, and worse still, he might find out he had a son. She turned to see Tim beside her.

"Where's Laura? I was going to put on *Yesterday*, just for her, and maybe she might have a dance with me."

"Oh, I think she's just gone to powder her nose," said Judy airily. But inside she was worried; how long before Laura returned? She would not take this news lying down. Even though she hadn't seen Simon for a while, she had his child. But Tim had always had a thing about Laura, although he'd always said Simon was too much in the way and she never looked at anyone else. Maybe Tim could save the day?

"Tim, do you still like Laura?"

"Oh, just a little, about that much." Tim spread his arms as wide as he could.

"Simon and I are getting married in a couple of weeks."

Tim whistled. He hadn't realised they were any more than friends. "I presume you just told Laura, and she still has the hots for him?"

Judy omitted to mention Matthew. Tim might not be so keen to help her if he knew. "Well I had to tell her, didn't I, and now I am not sure where she's gone. It won't look good if she's missing from her own party for too long."

"This wedding to Simon's a bit sudden, isn't it?" and then he remembered she had asked for orange juice, but he refrained from saying, "shotgun wedding". Judy wasn't laughing, so his cheekiness would probably go down like a leaded balloon.

"Never mind me, please go and find Laura. She needs a shoulder to cry on, so now is your chance to get close to her."

He ignored the irritation in Judy's voice. He was getting on her nerves, he could tell, but the idea of comforting Laura, being there for her, really appealed to him. Let Simon marry Judy, he certainly didn't care, and once she knew he was unattainable now, who knows? Laura might actually notice that he, Tim, was a half decent bloke.

Laura couldn't face any of them even though it was her party. When she ran from the room, she had no idea where she was going. The pain of losing Simon yet again, before they had even had a chance to meet, was unbearable. She had made up her mind to tell him about Matthew. Even if he didn't want to know, at least her conscience would be clear if she had told him. If he accepted his son, they might have stood a chance, now they were both older and wiser.

There was a little voice inside, urging her to get her own back on Judy for betraying her; all she had to do was tell Simon about Matthew. Would he still marry Judy after that? But the voice of her conscience was louder. She no longer had a claim on Simon, not even because of Matthew. She had not filled in his name on the birth certificate, and she had been away for four years. In that time he had found love with Judy, was about to be a father again, and she, Laura, had no right to spoil it.

"Oh, damn my conscience!" she said angrily, forcing back her tears.

"What's going on?"

She had not noticed the still figure sitting in the armchair. There was only a side lamp on; and Agnes put down her knitting and looked quizzically over her glasses at Laura.

"Judy has just told me she's pregnant, and she's going to marry Simon in two weeks."

"I see." Agnes slowly digested the news. She spoke gruffly, but kindly to Laura. "It was always going to be difficult coming back here. People change, and some years have passed since you left. I know you wanted to tell Simon about his son, but it seems to me that young man makes a habit of getting women pregnant. How many more have there been that we don't know about?"

Laura had not given that a thought, but her instinct was still to defend him.

"Well, he's known Judy a good few years. I don't think he is a womaniser."

"Maybe not, but he's not for you, Laura. You are still very young and one day the right person will come along."

Aunt Agnes was right, she knew it. Once again she had missed her chance to tell Simon, but at least she did have the love and support of her family back. There was a sound of footsteps coming down the hall.

Her aunt continued: "You need to go back in there and talk to all your guests. Keep your head held high. You can do it Laura, and remember we are all behind you now, even your father."

Tim stood a little uncertainly outside the room; he felt a bit like he was trespassing, this was not where the party was. Then Laura smiled encouragingly at him.

"Excuse me for chasing after you, Laura. Judy was asking where you had gone. Are you OK?"

It was unusual to see Tim being serious. He did seem concerned, and she wondered how much he knew. She put on the widest smile she could possibly muster; time to be a good hostess.

"I'm fine, Tim. Come and meet everyone with me." Then to his delight, she linked her arm through his, smiled at her aunt, and they went back into the party.

Chapter Fourteen

Life for Laura became much easier now. Her family accepted Matthew exactly as he was, and were proud of his quick and intelligent mind. He accepted his grandparents and uncle without question, as he did most things in life, and although he did not show them affection, the bonds were still there. After the grief they had suffered when Laura had been lost to them for four years, as a family they became much more tolerant.

The friendship between James and Matthew was an unusual one. James followed him with the loyalty of a dog; maybe because James himself was a loner. Laura had become friendly with his mother, Valerie, who was also bringing up her child alone. She was in her mid thirties, and had married a man in his mid fifties, who had sadly died of cancer when James was a small baby. So it had been just the two of them, and James felt intimidated by the noisy group of children who played together, preferring to be with Matthew, who sometimes didn't even speak to him, but did allow James to sit next to him.

One day Laura had arrived a little early at play school to collect Matthew, and she felt so sad when she saw the children playing, and Matthew was just watching them intently, but not a part of it. She wondered whether it was the autism that caused him to be alone, or whether, in fact, he wanted to be alone. She could think of nothing worse than being alone, she had always had friends, so to see James with Matthew was heartening, he did have one loyal friend, even if he didn't realise the value of friendship yet. James accepted his ways, and Valerie had no problem with him either. Laura was hoping that when they started school, they might be in the same class.

Laura continued to build on the success of her shop. She now had two staff who ran it for her most of the time. So she did the buying and got herself an accountant, and when the profits for the year were shown to her, she realised she could now invest in her own house and then rent out the flat above the shop.

She knew it would be difficult to get Matthew to move; he just loved that back room of the shop, so she decided to take things slowly. The biggest step of all for him was going to be starting school. At play school Mary had been there to protect him and help him to cope with situations. But now he was five, and he would have to learn to cope at school; and as he grew older, her heart ached because she knew the fact that he was different would be noticed by other children and he would have to learn to deal with it.

Tim had remained her friend for the last couple of years. He frequently visited her and his presence was comforting. She had made up her mind, once again, to get on with her life, to put thoughts of Simon out of her mind; they were just not meant to be, and she must focus on bringing up Matthew. But she sometimes felt lonely in bed at night, and longed to feel a man's arms around her, comforting her, because she could never forget their short lived love affair and how wonderful it had been to know such love.

The night before Matthew started at school, she lay awake; it had been a hard week already. Matthew didn't like the colour green, and the school colour was grey short trousers, with a bottle green striped tie, blazer, and jumper. When she had taken him to the shop to buy it all, he had refused to try anything on, and had such a temper. She could see the lady in the shop was very shocked at what she considered Matthew's "bad behaviour", but Laura knew he couldn't help it. He hated that colour and did not understand that he had to wear it.

So she had returned to the shop without Matthew, and bought all the school uniform in his size. After returning home, she had spent the last week winning him over to wearing it. She had offered to buy him new Matchbox cars if he wore it, and told him he could change as soon as he came home, and never have to wear that colour anywhere else. Eventually, after a great deal of patience, she finally won him round, but was doubtful whether her methods of bribery and corruption would be approved of by the famous Doctor Benjamin Spock, who had written a book about baby development and how to handle your children, but then Dr Spock didn't know Matthew, and she had achieved the desired result without any more confrontations.

She was awake early the morning of the first day, anxious that it would go without a hitch. They were meeting Valerie and James at the school gates, so the two boys could walk in together on their first day, as mothers had been given strict instructions to leave them in the playground, because it was time for their children to learn to stand on their own two feet.

When Matthew got dressed she held her breath, but he had now learned to accept that, although he didn't like green, he did have to wear it. Laura refrained from telling him just how smart he looked in his new clothes; if only she could take his photo, but not today. He still looked a baby, five years old maybe, and over the past year she had allowed his brown hair to grow longer as he didn't like being touched by the barber, and it curled in ringlets round his neck, so he looked less like Simon at this time in his life and more like his mother.

"Let's go then." She would have loved to touch his arm, but was aware as always, that any gestures of affection would not be welcome. She treasured the rare times when Matthew hugged her, but it was always on his terms; he did not do kissing, he only hugged, but to Laura it was a sign that her son loved her, and it meant the world.

The school was only a few yards from the block of shops, within walking distance and on the same side of the road. As they walked along, she saw other mothers, who were familiar because they frequented her shop, excited children running in front of them, little girls in their gymslips, and boys being reminded not to scuff their shoes. She smiled at them all, and Matthew walked quietly beside her clutching the one Matchbox car she had allowed him to bring with him. As they got level with the gate he hid it in his pocket so no one would know it was there.

As they arrived at the gates, Valerie drew up in her Mini. She was dropping off James on her way to work. James was pleased he could walk in with Matthew. He felt very shy on his first day, but walking with his friend made him feel safer. It was a new life unfolding, and a longer day than at play school when he knew his mother would be coming to fetch him at lunchtime.

The two women greeted each other, and James fell into step next to Matthew, who acknowledged him briefly and, encouraged by his mother, tipped his cap in response to Valerie's greeting. When they reached the playground it was alive with children running about and mothers chatting, all waiting for the children to be summoned into school. James clutched nervously at his mother's coat, whilst Matthew just stood, seemingly in a world of his own. If he was nervous of starting school he didn't show it, but Laura felt her nerves were so bad she worried enough for both of them.

The only emotions that Matthew had ever shown, were fear sometimes when in an awkward situation, or anger when he was frustrated and could not understand what was expected of him. Laura understood that was the way he was made, and she hoped others would also.

Then the head teacher came out with a welcoming smile, and explained that usually a bell would go and then all the children would be expected to line up in their class order, but as today was the first day, Miss Robson, who was the reception teacher, would call out the names, and then the children would know where to stand. She finished off her talk by addressing the mothers, and explaining that their children were in safe hands, and they could now leave them and go home.

It was clear by their faces that a lot of the mothers would have preferred to stay and help their children find their peg in the cloakroom, but the ruling was kind but firm. Miss Robson came out, also smiling, and Laura was amazed to see how young she was; she reckoned not much older than herself. Her memory of teachers when she had been at school had been of much older characters, dressed very soberly, but Miss Robson was slim, with long blonde hair, and she was wearing a navy blue mini skirt.

When the whole of their class had been called, the children stood obediently in line, whilst the older children filed into the building. Gradually the mothers filtered away, then stood by the gate continuing to chat. Laura watched Matthew as he slowly walked inside with the rest of his class. Unlike the other children, he did not look back. Laura subdued the pangs inside her, her little boy was now at school, her baby had become a schoolboy.

She knew that he would have enjoyed lining up; his whole life centred on everything being orderly, but in a class of over twenty-five children, how would he cope? She had already met with Mandy Robson, explaining that Matthew had autism and did not like to be touched, and always liked to sit in the same seat, and Mandy had told her they would do their best to help Matthew to cope. So now she just had to wait and see what happened.

Tim was tired of just being a friend to Laura. For two years now he had been a small part of her life, but he wanted more. It hadn't taken a genius to realise that Matthew was Simon's son, although lately he did not seem to resemble his father so much. But Tim didn't mind that at all. The little boy was part of Laura, and as he planned to marry her, he would adopt him if he could, and then maybe they could have more children, at least one more, but first he had to make her realise she needed him.

He admired her so much. She was an excellent mother, a shrewd business woman, and still only twenty-three. He didn't mind that Matthew had autism; he was very quiet, also very intelligent, and he was happy with his own company, being frequently happy to play in his own room. He showed no jealousy towards Tim for his frequent visits. Laura had explained that he had trouble with feelings; he could not show any, but Tim thought in this instance, maybe that was a good thing.

He could see that Matthew was the focus of Laura's life, and maybe he did feel a little jealousy towards him for that, but Tim knew that although he had enough love inside him to last the two of them a lifetime, with Laura the most he could expect was that she would grow to love him. But he knew that nothing in life was perfect, so he felt he could settle for that.

There would always be unfinished business between Laura and Simon, probably on both sides, and he was glad he was not in contact with Simon any more, because not telling him about his son would have been hard. Tim never spoke about Simon to Laura, so she didn't know that his marriage to Judy had lasted less than two years and they had both gone their separate ways. Tim had no idea where Judy was now, but Simon was living in Washington DC; having passed all his exams to become a lawyer, he had set his sights higher, and was now working over there. It was comforting for Tim to know that Simon was so far away, making the chances of their paths crossing very unlikely, which left the field clear for him to woo and marry Laura.

She had discussed with him her idea to let out the flat above the shop and use the rent to finance buying a family home for herself and Matthew. He had even gone with her to view the house and offer his opinion. It was a nice house with a good sized garden, built in the 1930s, with mock Tudor panelling inside, giving it extra character. The only reason she had not moved into it yet was, as she had explained, that Matthew needed to settle at school, too much change at the moment would be detrimental for him.

Tim was a car salesman. He had not been top of the class at school, but he did have a quick wit and a good line in banter. He enjoyed the challenge of selling cars to the public, but the downside to his job was he received a low wage and then got commission on his sales, so when he didn't sell anything, then financially he struggled. His love for Laura was genuine, but maybe if she had not been so comfortably off from her own endeavours, he might have thought twice about marrying her. After all, with his flat rent three months in arrears, what would he have to offer any woman?

He knew the way to Laura's heart was through her son, and as he was good at woodwork, he set to work to make him a garage. Matthew loved lining his cars up, and pushing them about, so he designed an area to park them, and a ramp so they could go to the upper floor, and even a little car lift, so they could go up onto the ramp. He found out Matthew's favourite colour was red; thank goodness he had asked, as if the garage sign was green, apparently he would have flung it across the room maybe? So he varnished the wood and then painted in big red letters, MATTHEW'S AUTOS. He was sure that would endear him to Laura when she saw it.

Tim chose the day that Matthew started school to bring the garage round for Laura's approval. He knew that Matthew would not finish school until three o'clock, and today Laura had asked him to visit the house again with her, to plan furnishings and carpets, as she didn't like what was there and was not ready to move in with Matthew just yet. If he could persuade her to marry him, they could move in together when it was all done; they

94

wouldn't need to have a long engagement, or even a big wedding, as she already had a child, just a quiet little ceremony.

When he arrived at the shop, Laura was having a cup of coffee in the back room, whilst Linda, one of her part time staff, was taking care of the shop.

"Oh great, Tim, lovely to see you. I am just recharging my batteries after leaving Matthew. Would you like a coffee?"

"Why not," he smiled. "I have brought something to show you. It's for Matthew."

He was rewarded by a smile from her. Laura was a pretty girl, but when she smiled, her big eyes positively sparkled and made him feel good.

"How did it go?" he asked whilst she made the coffee. He was planning to show her the garage after that, as it was quite heavy and he had left it in the car.

Laura laughed. "Matthew was fine, it was me! His teacher seemed a very smiley lady; let's hope she is still smiling after he's been there a couple of weeks! How anyone can smile when they look after that number of children in a day beats me," she added.

"Matthew's OK, you know. He knows what he wants; not many five-year-olds do."

He was rewarded with another beam. He was saying all the right things to her. They sat on the sofa slowly sipping their coffee together. He would just give her some time to drink. Up until today, Laura's life had been a whirlwind of activity, it was so nice that she could now delegate her work, and that he had some holiday this week.

She looked great this morning. Dressed in a grey suit and white blouse, with black patent high heels, she looked every inch the business woman. No doubt she had wanted to look smart to take Matthew into school today. Tim could only dream of running his fingers through her blonde ringlets and stroking her soft cheek. Oh, how he ached to take this woman in his arms; but he knew, even after two years of company, rushing it could mean losing her, and he didn't want that.

Laura picked up their empty cups to run them under the cloakroom tap, and Tim used the opportunity to go out to the car and bring in the cardboard box. He was pleased to see her eyes widen in amazement at the sight of it.

"What a big box Tim, what have you got him that is so big?"

"Well, I just hope he likes it. You said his favourite colour is red, but I am not sure it goes with the brown varnish." He laughed, lifting it out of the box.

When Laura saw the garage, and realised that Tim had made it himself, she was blown away. No one had ever taken the trouble to make something like that for Matthew; it meant more to her than any present she could have had herself. She knew he would have hours of play with it. She jumped up excitedly and flung her arms around Tim in gratitude. Her lips brushed his cheek, and as his arms tightened around her, his lips found hers, and without even thinking about it, she surrendered to the passion that flowed from him.

It had been nearly six years since her ill-fated relationship with Simon, and Tim's kiss awakened a need deep inside her. She needed to be loved again; the last few years had been stressful, sometimes it felt like it was herself and Matthew against the world, and she could now see by the softness of his eyes that Tim cared about her. Had she found love again? All she knew was there was a glow in her heart that had been missing for a very long time.

Matthew was a bit scared about his first day at school, and he wished he could tell his mother. He found it hard to show his emotions, so his face remained impassive during the journey to school. The sight of all the other children in the playground was intimidating. He had been told not to freak out if anyone touched him, and just the thought of it made him sweat with fear. No one understood just how hard it was for him to make sense of this world; well maybe one person did, his mother. He could not feel love, but when he thought about his mother, it gave him a warm feeling inside, and although he didn't like his lips to touch anything or anyone, he did sometimes get the need to give his mother a bear hug. And Aunt Agnes when they saw her. He liked going in the car to her bungalow and then staying over. He played with her dog, and he wished he could have a dog, but his mum had said it wasn't fair because they went out a lot. Although she had also said that soon he could go horse riding, and he liked the idea of that, as he liked all animals.

When they met James and his mother at the gate, he

96

remembered what his mum had said; he must speak to people when they said hello to him, or at the very least tip his cap, so this is what he did to James's mother. He didn't feel like talking to anyone right now, James knew that, and he didn't mind him falling into step next to him; he felt protected from all the children who were running around, and some even falling over in their excitement.

It was a relief to him when his teacher got all the children to line up. Matthew liked everything to be orderly, and one child walked behind another into the cloakroom. He also liked the idea of his own peg, his name was on it, and he had a small wooden pigeonhole in which to store his shoes, as only plimsolls were allowed to be worn inside the school.

His teacher was called Miss Robson, she had a high voice and she smiled a lot. He also noticed she had a birthmark on her left arm, which became obvious when she took her cardigan off, after saying how warm she felt. He watched carefully as she put it round the back of her chair.

He was sat next to James, he was sure his mum had asked for that.

"Now, each day when you go home, you have to put your chair on top of your desk before you leave the classroom."

"Yes, Miss Robson," chorused the class obediently, except Matthew, but he remembered what he had been told.

"Now, if you can all write your name on a piece of paper, we will do some spellings."

This was the point when Matthew decided he liked school. He was learning spellings already, and frequently spent his time chanting them both in his head, and at times out loud. His mum always listened with rapt attention, and then clapped afterwards and told him he was a clever boy. Matthew didn't think he was clever, it came easily to him, as did writing, and even doing sums. He enjoyed reading too, and could already read Enid Blyton books and lose himself in the wonderful world of the Famous Five.

When he had finished writing the spellings, he already knew they were right, but then Miss Robson said he must exchange his piece of paper with James, and like the other children, they had to mark each other's work. He didn't want to do that, but it was James, not a stranger, and his mother had told him that when his

e

teacher asked him to do something, even if he didn't want to, if he did it, and told her about it, she would make a chart with points on it, and when the points reached 100, she would take him out to buy some new Matchbox cars. So he did as he was told, and then when the results had been checked, he was the only person who had got all his spellings right, so Miss Robson had asked him to stand up, and the rest of the class clapped him.

Then the bell went again, and Miss Robson said, "OK class, you can go now. No pushing or rushing please," and she picked up her cardigan and left the room.

So it was time to go home. Matthew did not have much awareness of time, but he did hurry into the cloakroom so as not to get mixed up amongst the other children when they came to get their coats. He really didn't like that colour green, it was unlucky; he didn't want to have bad luck, so he carried his cap, jumper and blazer, even though the wind was quite keen. Then he remembered he had not put his chair up, so he rushed back into the classroom, but nor had the others. They were now getting their coats on, so he guessed they would do it afterwards. James was nowhere in sight, so he thought he would have to go on his own.

It didn't worry him that his mother was not waiting for him in the playground. The shop was not that far, so with his satchel over his shoulder, and his jumper, cap and cardigan stuffed inside it, he marched down the road towards the shop.

The shop bell went as he walked in and Linda greeted him as he walked past her. Matthew did not reply, but headed for the back room, and she stared after him wondering why he had not replied. What a strange little boy he was.

Matthew opened the door, totally ignoring his mother and Tim, who were embracing. He had seen the garage on the table, and headed towards it, his face alight with interest, because a garage was for cars.

"Matthew, why are you here now?" said Laura with amazement, breaking away from Tim.

There was no reply; the only thing on Matthew's mind was this garage with his name painted in red.

Laura's voice became louder and she moved over to the garage and stood beside it.

"Listen to me, Matthew, why are you home from school?"

Matthew left his world reluctantly to enter his mother's, and said simply, "Miss Robson said 'You can go now'."

Tim concealed a smile; Matthew had obviously taken her words literally.

"I don't think she meant that mate, she meant go out to play, you don't leave school until after lunch."

Laura saw the confusion in Matthew's face and realised it was a genuine mistake, he had misunderstood his teacher's words; and at that moment the telephone rang. It was a very worried Miss Robson.

"It's Mandy Robson here, I am afraid Matthew is missing, we can't find him in the school or the playground." The anxiety in her voice was evident, and Laura moved to reassure her.

"It's OK, he is here. When you sent him out to play he thought you were sending him home."

Laura and Tim were laughing now, and a very relieved Mandy laughed with them, now that the panic was over.

Tim took control of the situation.

"Tell her I am bringing him back right now," he said firmly. After all, his day with Laura had not even started yet, and he had so been looking forward to it.

Laura repeated his words and replaced the receiver. It might be better if Tim took him. It was his first day, and if Tim was going to be a bigger part of their lives, then he needed to be involved with Matthew too. Everything was going over Matthew's head as he gazed at the garage, so Laura explained to him in the best way that she felt she could.

"Matthew, Tim is going to take you back to school, and I will come and collect you after lunch. If you are a good boy, and don't make a fuss, when you come home you can play with the new garage. Tim made it specially for you, so you need to say thank you for it."

Matthew reluctantly met her eyes. He did not want to go back to school today, but he did want the garage. He had to wear those hateful green clothes again. There were so many things he had to do, and he didn't really understand why, but the one person who could reach him when he allowed her to was his mum. So he allowed Tim to take him back to school, and he promised Miss Robson he would never leave school on his own again. Everyone seemed pleased with him, and when he came home from school he played with his new garage until his mother told him it was time for bed.

Miss Robson had to report the incident to the headmistress. It may have sounded amusing at the time, but the thought that this five-year-old little boy had been out on a busy road on his own, and exposed to danger, was a frightening one. Miss Parker, the head, had been asking the authorities for a safer environment for the children, as there had been reports of an undesirable man hanging around nearby. Now that Matthew had proved how easy it was for a child to slip out unseen, they acted. A security system was set up shortly after, and the gates were kept closed. People arriving at the school during the day had to announce who they were, and no child could escape. Other schools followed soon after, and Miss Parker was proud that her school had been the first to do it.

Chapter Fifteen

"Well, Aunt Agnes, should I marry him? He's kind to Matthew, fun to be with and he treats me so well."

Agnes looked at Laura; her eyes were sparkling, her whole demeanour was happy and that was good because, in her opinion, in her short life Laura had really had a lot to contend with. But was she the one to give an opinion? Single by choice, not keen on any men, preferring to live an independent life. She had not brought up a child alone, and she felt the all too familiar pang of regret. It was amazing it was still there after all these years, but she had learned to live with it, there was no other choice.

"You know my opinion about men; you'd best ask your mother. But I would say if you really love him, and he makes you happy, then do it, but not just because of Matthew, because one day Matthew will be gone to lead his own life."

Laura felt love for Tim when she saw him being so kind to Matthew. Maybe it wasn't the crazy earth shattering feeling that Simon had evoked inside her, but then she reasoned with herself, she had been a teenager, only seventeen, and now she was twenty-four and viewed life in a different way. She hadn't liked being on her own, but felt she had no choice; and Tim, with his easy wit and sense of fun, had at first been a very welcome friend, and then when they became closer, he had proposed. He was the type of man who liked everyone, and was first to buy a round of drinks in the pub. She was sure that both herself and Matthew could be very happy with Tim.

"Well, Mum and Dad think it's great. They have already told

me they hoped it would happen. Matthew didn't seem that bothered one way or the other when I asked him, but that is Matthew, as we know. He is already used to Tim being around a lot so he won't notice much difference."

"Well, it seems to me you know the answer Laura, go for it!"

Laura hesitated, should she mention this or not; Aunt Agnes was already biased towards men. "Tim's biggest fault is he is very generous with his money, but not very good at managing it. I am not criticising him, he's a good man. I suppose it's because I've been on my own for so long, and I have managed to provide a reasonable life for Matthew. . ." her voice trailed off and Agnes had all sorts of thoughts going through her brain about men who take advantage of women by pretending to be in love with them and then emptying their bank account, but surely Tim wasn't like that? She had seen the love in his eyes when he was with Laura, and Agnes had herself taken quite a liking to him.

"If he's not good with money, keep your own separate bank account and carry on managing all the bills yourself."

"Well, the fact that I earn more than him is not an issue. I don't care about it, and he's been honest with me. But for the sake of Matthew in the future, the house is completely in my name, and the business, and my will states it's to be held in trust for Matthew; so if I went first, all Tim would get is half of our daily bank account, which is just spending money. I expect that sounds awful from someone who is about to get married, but I have to think about Matthew when I am not around. It's not a normal situation."

Agnes was impressed. At one time Laura would have been so naïve, she wouldn't have even thought about the future, but she had matured and realised that life is not always as it appears. So if Tim was marrying Laura for her money, he wouldn't get much, and good on her for safeguarding Matthew's inheritance.

"I am delighted for you Laura, you deserve your happiness, you have worked hard for it!"

Now that she had the approval of her parents and her aunt, there was no stopping Laura. She knew Tim wasn't perfect, she knew his failings, but his sense of humour and ready wit were just what she craved. He had taught her to laugh at Matthew's odd behaviour at times; not in a nasty way, in such a way that Matthew knew that he amused them; it was done with love. They were teaching Matthew to laugh with them, as having a sense of humour did not come naturally to him. Laura herself had learned that having a sense of humour took a lot of the stress out of certain situations, and with Tim, who saw the funny side of everything, they managed to laugh their way out of what would have been embarrassing circumstances.

So the wedding was planned for January 1968, some four months after Matthew had started school. It was also a week after his sixth birthday. His teacher was very proud to have such a bright boy in her class, and Matthew appeared to have settled into school. He was also aware that they would be moving into the house, as Laura had explained that the flat above the shop was not big enough for them now that Tim was coming to live with them and be her husband. Matthew accepted that, but Laura had to compromise, and bring him to the shop after school for an hour or so, as he still liked to play with his cars and the garage in the back room. She was hoping over time, as he grew up, he would want to come home and play in his bedroom. She knew everything with Matthew had to be a gradual changing process for him to cope.

It was hard to involve Matthew with the wedding. He only saw clothes as something he had to wear, but as January could be such a dark month, Laura planned to make sure this day was anything but dark. Even though they were just having a small ceremony, with mainly family present, and a few close friends, at the local registry office, and then going back to their new house afterwards, she had chosen to wear a bright red long dress, and Matthew was to have the same colour red shirt, with a bow tie, and long black trousers. He was going to hold her flowers and walk behind her, and he had only agreed because he liked walking in line, and Mary was right behind him, and he knew her.

The house was ready for them to move into after their honeymoon, which was going to be two weeks in the Bahamas, away from the cold chill of winter. Laura had not told anyone that Tim was coming into the marriage with no money of his own. She had made her own provisions for the future, cleared his back rent for him, and even paid for the honeymoon herself. These days money was no problem to her; she was about to open a second shop, and now had a team of hand knitters to back up Agnes. She had realised that having money did not ease the loneliness, but marrying Tim would, and maybe it was unusual for her to earn more than Tim, but who cared? She certainly did not, all she wanted was a happy life for herself and Matthew.

Tim's parents had now moved to the West Country, but they would be travelling up to share their son's special day. Laura had met them and they seemed very happy about it all. Tim also had a brother, Stan, but he was in Australia. He had gone out there on the £10 scheme and by all accounts had made himself a good life. He had a trade, and carpentry was welcomed over there, so he had taken the plunge and left four years earlier, and was now himself married with a new baby on the way. He had declared himself very happy for them, but with the baby due any moment, he could not possibly subject his wife to the trip, and he clearly did not want to come alone. So Tim had asked another friend, Jason, to be his best man.

Laura and Tim had both agreed that if at any time Matthew should freak out, they would make a joke of it. All the family and friends who were coming were aware of his autism, which meant at times his behaviour could be unpredictable. Being upset on her wedding day was not what Laura wanted; she was determined nothing would spoil the day, but she did want Matthew to be a part of it, so they would take the risk, and include him walking down the aisle.

Tim had bought the Beatles new album, *Magical Mystery Tour*, which had entered the charts at number one during the first week of January, and Matthew, who loved music, had developed quite an obsession with it. He kept playing it all day long, and in one of her weaker moments, Laura had agreed it could be played at the reception. Right now she was sitting trying to plan the meal at the reception, and he had it on again, very loudly.

"Turn it down, Matthew," she said very firmly. One could go off the Beatles when they were played incessantly like this! Matthew, of course, did not hear her, and carried on jigging to the music. He was chanting and, as usual, he had memorised all the words to all the songs.

Laura weighed up the possibility of turning it off, or down, and sighed; anything for a peaceful life. It was all about avoiding confrontations with him; he was happy and enjoying himself, so why not work out the meal plan when he was in bed later. So she put down her pen and pad, and made a cup of tea, that was a much better idea. Then afterwards she went down into the shop to speak to Linda about the window display. She noted with relief that in the shop the music was far enough away to be just a faint beating noise.

Whilst they were talking, the telephone rang. It was her mother.

"Hello Darling, how is the planning going?" and then without giving Laura a chance to reply, Emily rushed on: "I just thought you might like to know that Judy is on a couple of week's visit to her mother. I told her you were getting married, and she wondered if you might like to meet up for a coffee and a chat."

Laura's heart lurched. Why did she have to be reminded about Simon just before she married Tim? Could she cope with sitting and listening to Judy talking about him? It wasn't that she still loved him; she had told herself that Tim was now the one for her, and she had moved on. But she still couldn't free her mind from the guilt that she had not told Simon about Matthew. But then Judy had seen a photo of Matthew, and although she had not met him that night, she would have seen the likeness to Simon. Maybe she might have even told him, maybe he knew but just didn't care. The thought of that hurt, so she tried not to dwell on it.

"Yes, that would be nice. She's a mum herself now, isn't she?" Laura reckoned her child would be about two years old, and it was, of course, Matthew's half sibling. Curiosity to see Judy and catch up was so strong.

"She never said anything about that, but her mother told me when I saw her in town, that the marriage broke up. She was quite upset about it, but it was over a year ago now."

This amazed Laura even more, but made her all the more determined to see Judy; and as she was now single again, if she wanted to come to the wedding, that would be nice. She avoided asking if her mother knew anything about Simon, he was out of her life for good now and could no longer cast a shadow over her friendship with Judy.

Emily gave her the telephone number of Judy's mother, which she had known a long time ago, when they were growing up together, but could not now remember. She wrote it in her new address book. When they met up this time she could be completely honest with Judy about Matthew, and she wondered if Judy was surprised that she had found love again with Tim.

After they had put the phone down, Emily couldn't help wondering if Laura was truly over Simon, because hearing news like that just before she got married was bound to be unsettling. She never spoke about him to her these days. Laura appeared to have moved on, and Trevor didn't know anything about Simon being Matthew's father, or if he did, he didn't want to know, so she was not going to risk causing any trouble by mentioning it. Like the rest of her family, Emily had feared that, as Laura was an unmarried mother, she might be left on the shelf, but Tim had taken on Matthew as his own son, and so the whole affair was going to have a happy ending after all.

It was possible that Trevor may have thought that Tim was Matthew's natural father, as they had all grown up together, and having rekindled his friendship with Laura three years ago, he had now taken responsibility for his own son. She might have thought that herself if Laura hadn't confessed to her that day nearly seven years ago. Well, Tim was going to be his father now, and Simon was in America, and unaware he was a father, which was probably the best thing. Emily couldn't see any good coming out of telling him the truth now; his son would be brought up by Tim, and if she felt any guilt about the continuing deception, she brushed it away, because sometimes in life a situation is neither black nor white, but grey, and there is not a clear solution.

She was still sad about missing the first three years of Matthew's life. Attitudes were now changing. Some people even lived together without getting married, and no one appeared to be shocked any more. She just wanted to put behind her those years without Laura and Matthew, with Trevor falling apart and imagining all sorts about his daughter. Thank goodness they had managed to get past all that!

Chapter Sixteen

"Well, Laura, I expect you know that Simon and I are now divorced!"

Judy said this with an air of, "so what, I don't care about it", in her voice, but that was for Laura's benefit. They may have been split up for a while now, but she felt her marriage had never really got off the ground, and the reason was sitting right opposite to her. Laura was her best friend, and Judy knew she had married Simon under false pretences, and unfortunately her lies had forced it to come tumbling down around her. There was no way she could blame Laura for that. She had taken a risk and it had not worked out. Simon was in America, doing very well for himself, and they were now divorced.

"Yes, I am sorry to hear that."

Laura's reply was sincere, she was feeling very happy right now, and she wanted Judy to be happy too.

Judy admitted she had faked a pregnancy to get Simon up the aisle, and then faked a miscarriage. And when he found out, he was so angry, that it had been the end of her marriage. Laura did feel sorry for her, but no marriage could survive those sort of lies.

"Laura, you always think the best of everyone, but living with Simon wasn't easy, you know. His sister Kate once told me that he wasn't as nice as he appeared, and she was right. He was vain, arrogant and very selfish. I am glad to be free of him!"

"We can all be selfish."

She could have said a lot more than that, but she checked herself; it might sound strange if she defended Simon, but even after all these years, she still felt a loyalty to him; maybe it was because he was Matthew's father.

"Well, I have started going out again. There are quite a few men at the Orchid on a Saturday night, but it's no good asking if you want to come with me."

"You've left it too late Judy. Until Tim, I hadn't dated anyone for years. . ." her voice trailed off. Simon had been the only one before Tim, he was her first love, but most definitely not her last, she fiercely reminded herself.

"I know, only kidding! I am still trying to get used to you and Tim, you know. I never expected you two to get together, and here you are now, getting married."

The surprise in her voice was evident, and Laura blushed.

"It wasn't planned. As a single mother I didn't expect anyone to want me, but not only does Tim not care about bringing up another man's child, he also accepts that Matthew is different."

"We're all different, thank goodness, we can't all be the same."

Laura could see that Judy was missing the point. She doubted whether someone who had never had children even knew what the word autistic meant. She couldn't expect her to understand.

Judy had felt justified in criticising Simon. She did not owe him any loyalty now, but she did not understand why Laura had not told him about Matthew. He would have been back at her side like a shot, she was sure. Curiosity made her ask.

"Last time I saw you, you showed me a photo of Matthew. Not only did he look so much like Simon, but the dates fitted with him being his son. You never told Simon, why not?"

Laura blushed. Always that guilt came back to haunt her.

"You were just about to get married and, to be honest, you didn't seem that interested about Matthew."

Judy knew she was right about that. She had not wanted to know about him. She had been so scared that Simon might run to Laura's side and leave her. If their friendship was to continue, she needed to be honest with Laura.

"Laura, I was scared of Simon finding out. I didn't want to lose him, but in all honesty, I never really had him. Our friendship stemmed from his desire to find out about you and where you had gone, and even though I didn't know where you were, it created a bond between us. I was the one who picked up the pieces when you went away. He was devastated. He has always loved you."

There, it was said, and now she felt better. Her conscience had been cleansed. But judging by Laura's expression, it was not what she wanted to hear.

Laura's mind was whirling; none of this made any sense.

"But how could he care? He went into the army whilst I was on holiday, and he didn't even leave me a note. I went round to see him, I even asked Kate for his address so I could write to him, but she said she didn't know it."

"Kate. You mean the Kate that was always bad mouthing her brother? I reckon she was jealous and she wanted to ruin it between you two. Did you tell her you were pregnant?"

"Certainly not. Simon was the one I wanted to tell!"

Laura felt anger rising inside her. It may have been seven years ago, but how dare anyone try to manipulate her life and Simon's! But it was too late now; he had made his life in America, and she was going to marry Tim. She could not help the feeling of regret that swept through her.

"Laura, if you can honestly say you truly love Tim, then marry him, but if you still love Simon I reckon you should write to him and tell him about Matthew; he is missing his son growing up."

"I have such a conscience about that, but it never seemed to be the right time to tell him; and now with my wedding only two weeks away, is it fair to Tim to bring Simon into Matthew's life?"

It wasn't just Matthew she was worried about, it was herself. The thought that not only had she deprived him of his son, but also she had misjudged him, and apparently he still cared for her, made her feel unsettled. She had disciplined herself to put him out of her mind because she believed he did not care, and Judy's revelation was a huge shock.

Then there was also the fear that Simon might reject his son when he found out he was autistic; because deep down she blamed herself for that. She had carried him for nine months and given birth to him, but he was different. And although she loved her very unique little boy, and strived to understand him, and to help him make sense of her world too, it did not stop her from feeling she had failed Simon. But it came to her in a flash; she knew what she had to do and this time there would be no excuses, or turning back, because until she had done it she could not marry Tim, it would not be fair. She had to meet Simon once more, and he had to meet Matthew.

109

"Laura, I need to say what is in my heart. You are my best friend, but sometimes I think you believe everyone is as nice as you are. I know Tim well, but he has not much ambition, he can't manage his money, and I am just worried he may be marrying you for yours."

Her words made Laura bristle a little. How did Judy think she had managed to bring up Matthew alone, and build up her business? Judy had no clue about any of it.

"Do you think I don't know that, Judy? Tim buys drinks for everyone in the pub, then he's broke, and he has a job that pays very little. He knows that I have provided for Matthew in my will, we have discussed why that has to be and he understands. I think he does love me, but more importantly he accepts Matthew willingly!"

"You can't marry him just because he likes Matthew; you have to think about yourself. If you only love him because of Matthew, then it won't last."

First Aunt Agnes had said this, and now Judy, and she knew they were right, but Laura also knew that no one in this world is perfect. If Judy was expecting a faultless man to come along, she would have a long wait. Maybe Simon was vain, arrogant and selfish now, but he had been a good kind person when she knew him, and she was sure if they had still been together, he still would be. Maybe being with Judy, and being deceived so blatantly, had caused him to act in this way.

"I hear what you are saying Judy, and I must admit it's been a shock to find out Simon still cared, and now my feelings are all mixed up. I am going to take Matthew to America with me, and he is going to finally meet his father. I cannot marry Tim until my conscience is clear, and I also need to lay my feelings for Simon to rest."

Judy was amazed, after seven years, and just before her wedding, Laura was off to see her ex.

It was like one of those Hollywood movies, when the bride changes her mind at the last minute. Well lucky Laura, having two men both lusting after her. Judy might have been told lots of times that she looked like Cleopatra, but she had to admit defeat on this occasion to her blonde bombshell friend.

"What about Tim?"

"Tim is going to know everything, he can come with me if he

wants, but if my marriage is going to work, there must be complete honesty with everyone, and Simon can choose whether he wants to have a relationship with Matthew or not."

"Well, for what it's worth, I think you are doing the right thing. Nobody should keep any secrets. I am an example of that!"

Poor Judy looked so downcast that Laura impulsively hugged her friend. She could understand her being in love with Simon, and she didn't blame her for doing whatever it took to get him. It had ended badly for her, but there were other men and she was only twenty-four.

"I was not very nice to you at my twenty-first party. I was so jealous and I ran off when you said he was marrying you, instead of wishing you well. I am so sorry."

"No, you're all right, it was me, Laura, I didn't listen to what you said about Matthew. I knew he was Simon's son, and even then I felt if he knew, Simon would not marry me."

They both hugged again, and there were tears. Emotions had run high, but they were bonded by mutual affection which had started when they first went to school. Two women in love with the same man; but maybe Laura was not any more. She needed to find out if she was only in love with the memory of a teenage romance.

Her main concern, which she kept to herself, was how she would explain to Matthew that he had a father. When he had drawn pictures of his house and family, it had always been just himself and her. He knew all his friends had a father, but he had never asked about his. Did he assume he had died, or she was divorced, did he even ponder on it? She had no idea, but before she booked the plane tickets, she would try and talk to him. Judy had given her Simon's contact details in Washington DC, so first she would speak to Matthew and then Tim. She planned to tell her aunt what she was doing, but maybe not her parents yet. They were looking forward to seeing her married. Although she knew they wanted her happiness, she was also aware that being married with a son gave her respectability, and they would also want that.

"Would you like another coffee, or are we done?" said Judy.

"I will have to go now. It's time to pick up Matthew from school," said Laura, after glancing at her watch. "I can't believe how time flies!"

They walked outside and hugged again, and Laura felt grateful for such a strong friendship that had survived them both loving the same man.

"You must tell me how you get on!"

"Of course. And the wedding; you must come, it's only in the registry office, but we're having a party at home afterwards."

"Of course. It's just before I am due to go back from Mum's. Make sure you invite some spare men!"

They both laughed, then Laura strode over to her car which was parked outside the coffee bar. Judy watched her get in and start it up, before waving as she moved off. She wished she could be a fly on the wall when Laura went to America. What a fallout that might be, and she couldn't help wondering if there would even be a wedding, and if there was, which man would Laura choose? Or alternatively, which man would stick by her, because in Judy's experience, some men didn't.

Well, only time would tell, and now it was time for some retail therapy. She had seen a very nice dress in the window of the ladies gown shop on the way to meet Laura.

Chapter Seventeen

"Did you like your riding lesson, Matthew?"

"Yes, my horse is called Smoky."

"You did very well today, would you like to go again?"

"Yes, Smoky has got a smoky grey coat, that is why he has that name."

Laura looked admiringly at him. Matthew's conversations mainly consisted of yes and no, but Mr Usher had told her that there is often an affinity with animals, and if it encouraged him to speak more, then the riding lessons would continue. Now she had something difficult to broach with him, but whilst he was in a happy and communicative mood was the time to do it. She faced him across the dinner table.

"Matthew, you need to look at me, I have something very important to tell you."

She was ignored the first time, as he was studying the Matchbox car which he had just brought out of his pocket. It was a bright red Mini, and he gently stroked the bonnet of it.

"Matthew!"

He reluctantly met her eyes. His world was a safe world, and right now it was full of cars and horses. Stroking the coat of his four-legged friend had felt very soothing, and feeling the familiar shape of a car in his pocket when he put his hand in was good.

"Do you remember you told me you liked aeroplanes?"

Matthew gave her his attention now. He had made a plane with his Meccano, and enjoyed pretending to fly it. He had told his mother one day he wanted to fly.

"Yes."

"Tomorrow we are going to fly to America; to Washington DC."

"The president lives there in the White House."

"He does. Can you remember his name?"

"Lyndon B. Johnson."

"Well done Matthew! If you are well behaved in America, as a reward, we will go and look at the White House."

Matthew became wary. His mother usually said that when she wanted him to do something he did not understand. Fear swept over him, and he looked down.

Laura saw his distress. She had known this would be hard, but it had to be done. Once she had explained to Matthew why they were going, she had to ring Simon and explain she was coming to America. How would he react to her after all these years?

"We are going to America so you can meet your father. As you know, we don't live together, but he wants to meet you."

She knew that was not strictly true, but she was more concerned about the way he had withdrawn from the conversation. Usually when Matthew didn't meet her eyes it meant he was retreating to his own safe world, and her heart ached for him, how could he make sense of this, even she couldn't?

"I haven't got a father."

"Yes you have, but he lives in America."

Matthew was silent. Suddenly going to America didn't appeal to him. His mother might leave him with a strange man who would be his father. He might not have his cars, or ride his horse called Smoky, or walk to school with James. He felt really scared.

"I don't want to go!"

"Don't worry, Matthew, I won't leave you there. You are just going to meet him and then come home."

Matthew gulped back tears. How was it his mother understood what he was thinking, but he did not understand her, or her world? He could not go anywhere without his mother; she was the bridge between her world and his, she made his life a little bit less confusing. He wondered why his father lived in another country, and not with his mother like other dads did. That was very difficult to understand. He wondered if his mother was going to invite him to the wedding.

114

But that didn't make sense either, she was marrying Tim, so his father would not need to come.

Laura longed so much to hug him to her and make him feel safe; her body ached to comfort him, but hugs had to be on Matthew's terms, and right now he was not in a happy mood, which was when he spontaneously hugged. She left the table, keeping her arms by her side and knowing she had to keep a lid on her emotions.

"It's time to get ready for bed, Matthew. If you get your jamas on, you can read in bed, I don't mind."

After she had settled him in bed, she decided to phone Simon. Hopefully he would be home.

Simon was sitting enjoying a quiet Sunday when the telephone rang. His job as an attorney was very demanding, the hours were quite long, but he enjoyed the challenge of analysing people's characters, and deciding whether he thought they were guilty of their alleged crimes or not. Working hard had been his salvation after a failed marriage and a broken heart. Even though seven years had passed since he last saw Laura, he clung onto the memory of their love and frequently grieved for the loss of her; it was almost like she had died to him.

"Hi! Simon Richards here."

"Simon, it's Laura. I know it's been a long time, but I am visiting Washington tomorrow. How are you? I was wondering if I could pop round and see you."

Was he hearing right? He held the phone away from him in amazement. The woman he had not heard from for seven years, who had simply walked out of his life without any explanation, was at the end of the line. She wanted to come and see him, but why after all this time? Being a lawyer he was naturally suspicious. He tried to keep his voice light, if only to mask his emotions.

"Laura, hi there, long time no see. Where have you been all my life?" then he laughed at his own mock American accent. "Where did you get my phone number from?"

"It was Judy. She told me how well you are doing these days. Congratulations on becoming an attorney."

"Why thank you, but no one has told me anything about you. How are you these days, and where do you live?"

Laura rushed on to explain about the shop, but she omitted to mention Matthew; that needed to be face to face, but she did explain she was engaged to Tim and hoping to marry in a couple of weeks.

Simon's heart turned over, and he felt such a pang of jealousy. Tim had got her, "Mr Ordinary", Tim who didn't have an ambitious bone in his body. Why did she still have this effect on him? He had told himself many times that they had just been a couple of teenagers in love for the first time. She had probably changed now; she was twenty-four, and had obviously moved on. His heart said otherwise; no matter who he went out with, no woman had even come close to the way he felt about Laura. Poor Judy had been doomed, not because of her own actions, simply because she wasn't Laura, and when he had found out there was no baby, there was simply no reason to stay married to her. Well it would be painful to see her and know she was promised to another man, but still he had to do it. She was like an addiction he had to have at all costs.

"Tim, the tickets are booked, we have to leave. I can't marry you until Simon knows about Matthew. I would like you to come with me and Matthew; I am hoping you will stay with him at the hotel when I tell Simon, then we can fix up a meeting between them afterwards. I have already told Matthew. Obviously he is very confused, and I hate all this. . ." her voice trailed off, and Tim's mind was working overtime.

This was the one thing he had dreaded. He had been fairly sure that Laura would never tell Simon about his son, especially as he lived in America now, but he hadn't reckoned on Judy stirring things up. He would have been quite happy to bring up Matthew as his own son; that didn't really bother Tim, he could even live with the fact that he believed Laura was still holding a candle for Simon. What he couldn't live with was being jilted for Simon at the last minute. He loved everything about Laura; her drive and ambition, her bubbly nature, and underneath that he had found a vulnerability which made him want to protect her. She was a woman of character, and he wanted that woman to be his wife.

He knew he had two choices; he could refuse to go with her, but that might put her back into the arms of Simon. The other

116

choice was to go with her, take care of Matthew whilst she was telling Simon about him, and cross his fingers and pray that she would not want to rekindle their love affair again. He knew if he went with her, he would be holding his breath in anticipation until he saw how everything went, but he also knew if he forbade her to go, Laura would not listen. She was a woman with a mind of her own, so he just had to go along with it.

"OK, I will do it, but I don't see how Matthew can see him that often when he lives in America."

"We don't need to think about that yet. I have already promised Matthew we will be coming back. Simon might not want much to do with him after all this time."

That pain shot through her heart; was there no pleasing her? She couldn't bear to see Simon reject his son, and yet trying to establish a relationship across the miles would be virtually impossible. Her only hope was that Simon might visit England occasionally and see Matthew. But that would only be if Matthew wanted it.

She had so many things to explain to Simon. Matthew's autism, the fact he didn't like to be touched, and his brilliant mind, which she was sure was inherited from his father. She had to lay the foundations before they could even meet. As yet, Simon had no other children of his own, becoming an instant father would be mind blowing, and would he be prepared to understand his unusual son?

The hardest part for now had been telling all three of them; that at least was behind her. The packing had been done, their passports were in the carry-on bag, and they were catching the plane from Heathrow in the morning. Tim had gone back to his flat, and the taxi would come for herself and Matthew first, then pick him up on the way. For a while lately, Tim had wanted to move in with her before they got married, but Laura had remained steadfast about that. Maybe it was no longer frowned upon when couples lived together before marriage, but Laura did not want to let her parents down again, so Tim had not even slept with her yet, nor would he until they were married.

She did not expect to sleep well that night, but she was mentally exhausted after what had gone on. So much worry about how Matthew and his father would react to each other dominated her mind; so she was surprised when the alarm went off, and she realised she had in fact slept.

Getting Matthew up was not that easy this day. He was reluctant to go anywhere, so she had to be shameless, and promise him more points on his chart and more Matchbox cars if he co-operated. Eventually they were both ready, the taxi arrived, and then it drove to Tim's flat. He was standing in the entrance with his suitcase, and she felt a wave of gratitude towards him; supporting her like this made it just a bit easier, and leaving Matthew with him when she met Simon, someone who knew Matthew well, was obviously much better for all concerned.

She had tried to make the journey easier by booking first class seats. They were invited to board the plane first, which was just what she had wanted; flying economy was not an option, as if anyone had touched against Matthew when queueing to board the plane, he would have freaked out. Laura knew she was, as usual, treading on eggshells to get him to America, but once they were safely in their seats, she was able to breathe more easily.

Matthew liked the feel of the plane as it took off, and as he had been put in the seat next to the window, once they had reached the cruising height, he looked out of the window at the clouds. He liked the idea of being up so high, safe in space and away from a world that could be very confusing at times.

His mother had promised him rewards if he was polite when he met his father. She even wanted him to shake his hand. He had no desire to hug him; he didn't know him. He didn't even hug Tim; only his mother, Great Aunt Agnes and Emily his grandma. Hugging a man did not seem right; he didn't hug granddad or Uncle Sam. He had seen other boys hug their father, but they lived with him, and knew him, he definitely could not hug someone he didn't know; but because he wanted those new Matchbox cars, he would try to shake his hand.

Later, when they were in their hotel, which had been chosen because it was very close to where Simon lived, Laura picked up the phone to order room service. Most of the choice on the menu involved salad, but seeing green lettuce would upset Matthew, and today they must avoid that.

"How about a cheese and pineapple Pizza?" she asked Matthew encouragingly. He had wanted to try one in America, as it was more well known than in England.

"Well, I fancy a nice bit of steak," said Tim, and she felt a little irritated with him; steak came with salad.

"We can have steak, but nothing green tonight!" she said very firmly.

Tim felt a bit put out. He wasn't bothered about salad, but mushrooms, tomatoes and peas were a nice accompaniment to steak. Sometimes he thought that Laura indulged Matthew too much, the kid should learn that even if he didn't like green, other people did.

But Laura would not be moved. Matthew nodded his head, he wanted a pizza, so she ordered steak for them with tomatoes, chips, mushrooms and sweetcorn. When they had eaten, both Matthew and Tim were ready for a nap. After travelling for twelve hours, including the flight, they felt weary, even though with the time change it was only four o'clock in American time.

So Laura kissed Tim, then she blew a kiss at Matthew, who remained impassive, and she went downstairs to find Elton Terrace, which turned out to be only a couple of blocks away. Simon lived at number two, so she pressed the bell, and then with a thudding heart, she heard his voice.

"It's me, Laura."

"OK, there's an elevator inside. I am one floor up. Looking forward to seeing you."

She drew a deep breath; there was no turning back now, Simon would finally know the truth.

Chapter Eighteen

Simon had not slept at all since the unexpected phone call from Laura. He did not understand how this woman still had the power to get right inside his head and cause turmoil after seven years. And to cap it all, she was paying him a visit just before she was marrying his friend. He could feel anger towards her inside him, but he did not intend to have an argument with her. He would discipline himself to hide his feelings; he had to remind himself he was a successful attorney living a good life in America, and a visit from an old flame was not going to change that.

He spent most of his working life in a suit, so today he was wearing jeans and a check blue shirt which was open at the neck, and it felt comfortable not to wear a tie for a change. He kept his dark brown hair short; it was well cut and groomed as befitted his job. At only twenty-five, with a responsible job, although long hair for men had been made popular by John Lennon, Simon looked stylish and efficient.

Most of the night he had spent wondering why Laura wanted to see him. Was it business? Did she need some advice in a difficult situation? Whatever it was, he would behave in a professional way and help her, mainly because it was Laura. When she pressed the bell and announced herself, he felt it, that surge of emotion which continued to haunt him deep inside, but his training had taught him to hide his emotions and that is what he intended to do.

He held the front door open for her as she exited the elevator, and he wondered if he should hug her or shake hands. After all, they had once been lovers. As she approached, he noticed she had barely changed in the last seven years. She still wore her curly hair long; it framed her petite doll-like face, and she still looked younger than her years. She was wearing a navy blue mini dress and grey long boots. Her figure was maybe a little rounder, her breasts more developed, and her legs were just as perfect as he remembered. With a pang he grieved silently for what he had lost; lucky Tim. But where was the sparkle in her blue eyes? They looked apprehensive, and the carefree Laura he remembered was gone. Over her arm was a red coat, that she had removed, and instinctively he moved forward to relieve her of it.

"Welcome Laura, let me take that off you."

Laura had taken a deep breath as she walked from the lift. What a shock she was going to give Simon, and it was hard to hide her fear and apprehension. Seven years ago he had known her inside out; would he still be able to detect her emotions?

As her eyes moved to meet his, she saw he was in jeans and a blue shirt. He looked taller and had filled out a bit more, but his face still looked very suntanned, and those brown eyes were just as limpid and expressive as always. The only difference was his hair was cut short, so there was no stray lock of hair falling over his brow. Simon at twenty-five was even more handsome than she remembered, and she saw concern in those eyes, which made her gulp with emotion.

"Thank you."

Without even thinking about it, Laura hugged him and kissed him lightly on the cheek. He stood politely, but his body was taut and he did not respond, and she cursed herself for making him feel awkward. Being a naturally warmhearted person, it was normal for her to greet all her friends in this way.

"Can I get you some coffee or tea?"

He had not allowed his body to respond to her touch and that light kiss on his cheek, but inside he had. It took all his self control to keep his arms from holding her, but he was fiercely reminding himself, Laura had not come to him for love, she was marrying Tim. She had always hugged her friends, and that was all he was now.

"Coffee would be lovely, thank you. It's very cold outside."

"It is, but at least we don't have snow. Make yourself comfortable on the couch."

f

Simon smiled at her, and then went into the kitchen, which led off the sitting room, to make the coffee. She glanced around her whilst he was gone; the whole apartment was smart but very masculine looking. The sofas were black leather, the wallpaper was a light coloured pattern with one wall in mock brick effect, and the fitted carpet was in two shades of blue, which added no warmth at all. There were a couple of family photographs but, she noted, no wedding photos of himself and Judy. At the end of the lounge area was a built in bar, which had a shiny top and a display of coloured glasses on the top.

Simon came in with a tray of coffee and a plate of biscuits. He put the tray on the coffee table in the middle of the room, then he poured coffee into the white cups, and enquired whether she wanted milk and sugar.

Laura declined a biscuit, she felt it would choke her, she had waited long enough and needed to say her piece. She picked up her coffee cup, took one sip, then placed it back on the saucer. She felt his eyes studying her and was sure he knew how uncomfortable she felt.

"Simon, I have something I should have told you a long time ago, please forgive me for waiting so long. The reason why I vanished without trace was because I was pregnant, and my mother did not want my father to find out. We have a son."

There, it was said, finally. Relief flooded through her, which was quickly replaced by guilt when she saw the look on his face of total disbelief.

"We have a son?" he echoed. His mind was whirling, as right now all he could feel was extreme hurt that it had taken her all this time to tell him. Being a father was a new experience for him, and he didn't know how he felt about it. Then the pain of knowing that it was Tim who would bring his son up and not himself engulfed him.

"Why didn't you write to me when he was born? Didn't you think I was worthy of knowing?" he said angrily. This was really too much to bear.

Laura bowed her head. She had never seen him angry like this before, and she knew she had hurt him deeply.

"It's all my fault, I know. But I came to tell you, and you had been conscripted. Kate said she didn't know your address, and I was not allowed to come back because I kept my baby. I couldn't

122

face having him adopted, and if my father had known, it might have caused my parents to split up." Her lip trembled and she fought back the tears. She didn't want to break down in front of him, but how could he possibly understand what she had been through?

Simon saw it all clearly; it had been Kate who had ruined things between them, but now he wished he had made it his mission to find Laura when he came home. He did not see his sister now, she was in England pursuing an acting career, but they had never been that close, so he could well imagine that she had deliberately broken them up. But it was too late now anyway, Laura had made her choice.

He saw her distress and spoke gently to her. "It's OK Laura. Kate and her practical jokes. But I did give her a letter for you, asking you to wait for me, and when I didn't hear I assumed you had moved on. It wasn't your fault. I should have tried to find you myself. What is our son's name?"

"He is called Matthew, and here is a photograph of him. He is six years old now and very bright at school."

Simon studied the photograph of the little boy who had curls like his mother and eyes the same colour as himself. He was a bonny child, and there was something unusual about the way the camera had caught him, but he was not sure what it was. He felt pride in his son, and grateful that, although he couldn't have Laura himself, a baby had resulted from their love.

Now that the initial shock had passed, Laura tentatively went on to explain about Matthew's autism and how it affected her life, and Matthew's life. Simon listened carefully and appeared to be undaunted by this news. During his working life he met all sorts of people and they were all different, which he felt made them very interesting.

"I have told him about you. He is back at the hotel, and I was wondering if you could come over and meet him tomorrow."

There was a pause before Simon spoke, and she held her breath, wondering if he would be willing to meet his son, or maybe he thought too much time had gone by?

"Yes, of course I will meet him, I am grateful that you told me."

After she had gone, he sat on the sofa deep in thought. It seemed like there had been intervention from others to stop them from being together. Kate had meddled, and not given Laura his letter. No point in saying anything to her now; she would claim not to remember after seven years. Tim had been with Laura for over two years now but never told him Laura had a son, but then maybe she had asked him not to. He blamed himself for marrying Judy instead of trying to find Laura before Tim did. It was all such a mess, and how could he fight for her now? She loved Tim, and he had to try and move on. But he could, and would, have a relationship with his son, if Matthew would accept him. Keeping that thought in mind he went to bed; tomorrow he would meet his son for the first time.

When Laura left Simon's apartment, she politely declined his offer to walk her back to her hotel. It was still light and only a short walk, was the reason she gave, but the truth was she wanted to put her chaotic thoughts in order before she saw Tim and Matthew. Seeing Simon had unsettled her. He was still the person she remembered, and loved, but his body language when she greeted him had been impassive, so it looked like he was over her.

There was no point loving someone who didn't love her, even if he was the father of her child. Tim loved her and Matthew, so marrying him seemed the right thing to do. She hoped that Simon would keep in contact with Matthew, but knew she had no right to ask; all she could do was see how the meeting went tomorrow.

When she arrived at the hotel, Tim and Matthew were watching *Bewitched*, which had enthralled Matthew, and he wanted to share it with his mother.

"Come and see it, Mum. She's a witch and she doesn't want to be."

"It's very funny," added Tim.

"Matthew, your Dad is coming to meet you tomorrow."

"I thought witches were ugly, but she isn't."

"Did you hear me, Matthew?"

"One, two, four eight, sixteen, thirty-two, sixty-four. . ."

Laura knew that Matthew always started chanting spellings or adding up when he was stressed, and her heart ached for him. She wished she could hug him and make him feel safe. Her little boy was so complex, and he spoke in such a grown up way, because he was so intelligent, that they sometimes forgot he was only six years old.

She decided not to mention it again. Matthew knew, and

124

hopefully things would be all right tomorrow. Maybe she couldn't hug him, but she could take an interest in what he was watching. The idea of a witch had appealed to his imagination.

"Oh yes, the actress is called Elizabeth Montgomery, I have seen this programme at home. She is a pretty lady, not like the usual ugly witch, and she hasn't married a wizard, just an ordinary man, so she wants to be like the other wives."

Laura sat herself on the sofa next to Matthew, and to her delight, he turned suddenly and hugged her.

"Love you, Mum!"

How many times had he said that in his life? She could probably count on the fingers of one hand. No one could possibly understand how much that clumsy bear hug meant to her; and given at this time when she was so stressed about tomorrow. Suddenly life felt so much brighter; her son loved and trusted her, and she knew she would do everything in her power to make this meeting as comfortable for him as she could.

"I love you too. You have chocolate in your hair; we must wash it out when you have your bath."

Matthew gave her one of his special smiles, and she smiled back. He needed a hair cut really, but one thing at a time. Tomorrow it was meet Dad, and Monday it was a visit to the local barbers; if he played up, never mind, they were returning to England and would never need to go in that barber shop again, so whatever was said about Matthew after they went, they would never know.

Chapter Nineteen

Simon arrived at the hotel punctually at eleven o'clock. He had been ready since early morning, but had to bide his time at home. He was amazed at himself; the normally confident, and maybe slightly arrogant person that he usually was, had been reduced to shaking like a jelly inside. Outwardly he had the ability to appear calm, but his insides were quaking with fear and apprehension about meeting Matthew. He had still not quite got over the shock, and was even wondering how he would tell his parents about their grandchild. His mother, for sure, would be sad that she had missed out on the early years of Matthew's babyhood.

"Mrs Carter says to go right up!"

The female receptionist on the desk flashed her very white teeth when she smiled at him, and he felt a wave of jealousy shoot through him; Laura was using Tim's name before they were even married. But his common sense told him why; if they were staying as a family, it was easier. He chided himself for wearing his heart on his sleeve. He was here to meet Matthew, and Laura's life was her own business.

Tim was standing at the open door when he reached it, and they hugged as old friends. Laura stood behind him, and next to her stood the boy in the photo, Matthew. He wanted to get it right, so he politely took Laura's hand and gripped it briefly. The warmth of touching her was somehow comforting yet tantalising, but his self control took over, there was no more Simon and Laura now. He knew he must not touch Matthew, so he smiled and said:

"It's great to see you, Matthew."

Matthew studied the man who was his father. He was tall, and he wore navy blue trousers with a blazer with silver buttons and he had very shiny shoes. Matthew didn't usually like people when he first met them, he had to get used to them, and if they touched him he felt intimidated. But this man, Simon, did none of that, he just stood there, his hands were by his sides and his smile was kind, it reached his eyes, and suddenly Matthew was glad he had a father. It was painful to know that he was different from other children; it was something he could not help, nor change, but it always left him on the fringe at school, with only James being his friend. He had thought maybe it was because he didn't have a father, so now knowing he had a father made him feel he was not such an oddity. Without even thinking about it he held out his hand, giving Simon licence to touch him, and said simply:

"Are you truly my father? It's great to meet you."

Laura held her breath with amazement. There seemed to be an affinity already. Matthew never shook hands the first time, but he had made up his own mind to do that. He must like his father. How wonderful.

"Simon, come and sit down, I am going to order room service. What would you like?"

"Thanks, Tim. Coffee will be fine."

Tim was a bit put out. He had worked hard to gain Matthew's confidence, he knew that without it Laura would not have agreed to marry him, then in comes Simon, oozing big smiles and charm, and totally captivates the usually unsociable Matthew. Well he wasn't having Laura as well. Tim kept his arm loosely around her shoulders whilst they chatted, and his body language warned, she's mine! That was in case Simon was in any doubt.

Matthew brought his Matchbox cars over to Simon to show him; that was something else he only reserved for those closest to him. He allowed Simon to pick them up and study them, and Simon told him about the sports car he had when he was in England.

"Of course, everyone out here has such big cars, and they are not as sleek as English cars. Now I have a very long car."

"Did you bring it with you?" asked Matthew excitedly.

"No, I walked here; it's just two blocks."

"Oh, I wanted to ride in it."

Matthew's face fell with disappointment, and Laura, who was

still recovering from his friendliness towards Simon, hastened to dilute his disappointment.

"We"ll take you into Washington tomorrow. As I promised, we are going to see the White House."

"Well, before you go, I don't mind bringing it round here, and I'll take Matthew for a spin, with your permission, of course."

"That is great, isn't it Tim? We can go into Washington in the afternoon."

"Yes, whatever you like."

Tim felt jealous of Simon; he had always considered he was in his shadow. Simon was more confident, better looking and more ambitious, but he wasn't going to let him charm his way back into Laura's knickers. He had to accept Simon's relationship with Matthew, he was his father, but living so far away like this, once they got home, no doubt Simon would become just a memory. But it seemed Matthew was one step ahead of him.

"Dad, are you coming to England?"

Simon felt the pride of being called Dad. It was such a new experience for him, and it created a warm glow inside him. Matthew had shaken his hand and spoken to him, which is not what he had expected. What amazed him was the intelligence of his son. He seemed much older than his six years, and after listening to him reciting poems and spellings he was impressed. He didn't have much experience of children, but those six year olds that he did know were certainly not that advanced.

But with the brightness came the downside; the autism, the isolation it caused, the loneliness, and the attitude of others towards a child that was different. It hurt him to think that even as young as six years old, his son had to suffer in this way. He had dealt with a case recently, when a young man had autism, and because he was different he had been arrested and accused of all sorts, including the rape and murder of a young girl. The cops had bullied him a bit to try and make him confess, because his autism was such that he couldn't really explain himself, and his desperate parents had hired Simon to help them clear his name. He had done just that, because there was no real evidence against the young man, he had been judged because of being different, and it had been Simon's greatest relief afterwards when the cops had arrested the girl's boyfriend, who had thought he had managed to avoid suspicion, and it was later proved to be him. He could still remember the joy of the parents when their son had been cleared.

"Yes Matthew. I will be visiting my parents soon, so if your mother and Tim are OK with it, maybe we could spend some time together."

"Of course we are," said Laura, and Tim nodded assent; he didn't really have much choice. He would be glad when Laura was safely married to him, just in case Simon had any ideas, but it did seem most of his attention was taken up with his son, luckily.

Laura thought better of explaining that Matthew had a complete new set of grandparents as well, there had been enough for him to take in today. She was so delighted that he had accepted his father so readily. She had been expecting much worse; tantrums were part of their life, but she excused him because she understood that her world was very confusing for him at times, and he preferred his own safe world.

There was a tap at the door; room service had come to take the empty tray and crockery away, so Laura opened it to let them in. As soon as she saw the girl with the bright green apron on, a warning light came on inside her.

But the young dark haired girl, who was probably no more than seventeen, was oblivious to anything. She stepped into the room past Laura, and Matthew turned from speaking to his father just in time to bump into her. Enveloped in the green apron, he screamed loudly, then ran under the table, blocking his ears and sobbing.

"I am so sorry, it's not your fault. My son doesn't like green, he thinks it's unlucky," explained Laura as she showed the bewildered girl out.

She took a deep breath, wondering what Simon would think of this display. It was going to be hard to coax Matthew out from under the table, it would have to be bribery again. She went over and bent down, speaking calmly to him.

"Matthew, there is nothing to be frightened of, the lady with the green apron has gone now."

"The devil is outside. Green is unlucky," muttered Matthew.

Simon was watching intently. He wanted to understand his son, but with the best will in the world, it would be impossible to spend his whole life avoiding the colour green. If this was a

129

regular occurrence, he could see how hard it must be for Laura, and he admired just how well she had coped.

"Matthew, that is a superstition and it is not true!" Laura spoke firmly. She was dreading that this might change Simon's mind about keeping in contact with Matthew. This time he did not answer his mother, but just peered out fearfully from underneath the tablecloth.

"If you come out now, to say goodbye to your dad, you will get some more points."

Simon wondered what that meant, but Laura hastened to explain.

"We collect points for Matthew every time he copes with a difficult situation, and when the points reach the target, he gets new cars."

This gave him an idea.

"Well Matthew, if you come out now, not only will you have points from your mother, but also, when we go for a ride tomorrow, I will take you to a model car outlet where they have models of cadillacs, and you can have one to take back to England."

He wondered afterwards if he had overstepped the mark, but the temptation of this offer was too much for Matthew to resist, so he scrambled out from underneath the table, and stood up. Laura's relief was evident, whilst Tim was just a shadowy figure in the background, who seemed quite content to let it all go on around him.

As they stood at the door to say goodbye, Matthew once again shook his father's hand, but then disappeared back to his cars whilst they were all talking. Simon resisted the urge to ruffle his curls; they sprang defiantly round his face and he brushed them back impatiently. Laura explained that the next day, when they went into town, his hair was going to be cut.

"He doesn't like being touched by a barber, or even a ladies hairdresser, so I grew his hair longer, but now he sometimes gets mistaken for a girl." She laughed.

"Well there's a good barber in the centre of town, I think the name is Kelly, and yes they are Irish." Simon laughed too, aware of Tim hovering uncertainly in the background. Laura smiled back.

Thanks for that, Simon, that is a great help. If you can come round about eleven tomorrow to take him out, it doesn't need to be far, that would work for us."

"Yes, I'll be glad to."

130

Laura glanced over at her son, now busy lining up cars. Thank goodness he had come out from under the table, and also, thank goodness Simon's car was not green! One had to have a sense of humour at times. Simon had seemed unperturbed when Matthew had thrown a fit. She was used to Tim keeping out of a confrontation, and she understood that he didn't quite know how to deal with it, but in that short time, and after, when they had joked about the barber, she had felt a rapport with Simon, and she guessed it was because they both shared the same son.

Tim was glad when Simon had gone. He didn't feel safe with him around. All past friendship was now forgotten in his mind, and he didn't like to see Simon and Laura getting cosy as Simon left. But when they got home, it was such a short time to their wedding. He just had to get through tomorrow and they would be heading back to England. By the time Simon visited his parents, they would be married, and Tim intended to get Laura pregnant as soon as he could, then they would have their own child to create a bond.

As Simon walked back to his apartment he relived the meeting with his son. So much had changed in his life in the last twenty-four hours. He had suddenly been plunged into fatherhood, and he liked it. Laura was doing a fine job in difficult circumstances bringing up Matthew, but Tim, in his usual weak way, was doing nothing to help her. Maybe his criticism of Tim was fuelled by jealousy, but it was clear to Simon that it would be quite a challenge to raise Matthew; it needed lots of patience and a strong will, and he didn't think Tim was up to it. But it didn't matter what he thought, Laura loved Tim and not him any more. He so dearly wanted to bring up his own son. The first thing he would do was get him used to green; expose him to his phobia and let him see it didn't harm him. But maybe it wasn't that simple, maybe Laura's way was better, but if only they could bring him up together.

He was glad they had not invited him to the wedding. It would have been very difficult for him to keep a polite smile on his face whilst he watched Tim marry the woman he loved. He would wait for the dust to settle, then he would be over to visit and maybe he could build some sort of relationship with Matthew. In the meantime, he had already taken a couple of days off work, but after tomorrow he would plunge himself back into it, because helping to get justice for people was very rewarding to him.

After Matthew had gone to bed, Tim and Laura sat in the room next door to where he was sleeping. It was just a small sitting room, so they spoke quietly just in case he was still awake.

"I am glad Simon knows, and he took it very well after missing out on Matthew's early years. They seemed to get on well, didn't they? Matthew rarely shakes hands with strangers, as you know."

Tim wasn't sure he was glad now she had Simon back in her life, but in all honesty he knew it could not have gone on like it was. Simon had a right to know about Matthew, and he was being selfish, but that was because he wanted Laura so much.

"Yes, it's done now. Maybe later Simon might ask him to come and stay with him."

"What, in America?"

"Why not? It will give you a break, or us a break."

Laura had never thought of it in that way. She had not spent any time away from Matthew since he was born. She had spent her life trying to protect him and help him cope, but the thought of Simon caring for him didn't bother her. After seeing them together today, she somehow felt that Simon would cope; after all, he was Matthew's dad.

Chapter Twenty

"You look so beautiful Laura, and look at Matthew in his red shirt!"

Emily clasped her hands with excitement. It was such an emotional moment to see Laura in her long red velvet dress and bolero, maybe an unusual choice for a wedding, but it gave her such a glow. She had never seen her daughter look so happy.

"Are you sure it's OK, not too full on!"

"Look at my shirt, Mum."

Laura knew her choice of colour would please Matthew, and she had found if he was happy, then so was she. But being of pale complexion, red had always made her feel bright and happy, and it complemented her golden hair, which usually cascaded down her shoulders in ringlets, but today had been straightened and dressed in a chignon on top of her head, with a big wide hat and a discreet veil; and she felt ready to go.

"Time to go, princess."

Trevor was ready to do his bit at the registry office and give her away. He thought Tim was a fine bloke, he was taking on Matthew as his own, and that alone endeared him to both Emily and Trevor. He wasn't going to have it easy with Matthew, but it didn't seem to worry him, and for that Trevor was grateful.

When Laura had broken the news about Simon being Matthew's father, it was just as well for him that he lived in America, because Trevor wasn't happy. That upstart had left her high and dry was what he believed. But then Laura had explained everything, and it seemed he had only just found out he was a father and he wanted to have a relationship with Matthew, and within a few weeks he would be visiting his family in England.

Laura's revelations changed his opinion of Simon. It seemed he had misjudged him. He did care about his son, and although he would always blame him for getting her pregnant at such a young age, he had promised Laura he would never take him to task or cause any trouble over it.

Since his breakdown, when he truly believed his beloved daughter had come to such harm, Trevor had become far less aggressive. There was no way he wanted to lose his daughter again, or Matthew, his very bright grandson. These days he preferred to let Emily make a lot of the important decisions. After all, nowadays women were going to work just like men, and they had strong opinions; too strong to be ignored.

Laura put her arm through her father's, thankful that their relationship had been restored. She preferred her dad now, he was a lot less fiery than he used to be and, with a bit of charm, both she and her mother found it easier to get through to him. At one time he would have slaughtered Simon when he found out he was Matthew's father, but when she told him not to cause trouble, he had not argued with her. Now she was an adult, with her own business, Daddy had finally conceded that she was a grown up independent woman with a mind of her own. Even her mother had come out of her shell and taken the reins in recent years, and Laura was pleased to see that.

When they arrived at the registry office, Mary was there, she was wearing a very sophisticated grey velvet dress and her hat and shoes were red, so she blended perfectly. Matthew had long grey trousers, with a red shirt and bow tie, and he was walking just behind his mother. Well that is if no one upsets him, thought Laura, it was best to be prepared for the worst.

Emily was all in blue, but her dress was a discreet knee length, as she felt she was too old for a mini length, and Aunt Agnes wore a greyish tweed suit, as she always did, with a white blouse and low heeled shoes. Not that Laura minded what she wore, her aunt would always have a special place in her heart because of the support she had given her at a time when she was at her lowest. Laura would never forget that, and also the way she had helped her to set up her first shop. She would shortly be opening her third and business was booming, all thanks to Aunt Agnes.

There were just a few guests: Tim's parents, who were a similar age to her own, they had travelled up from Devon and would be staying with her parents that night. Judy was there, wearing another clingy black number, she was full of smiles as, since Laura had last seen her, she had managed to find herself a new boyfriend, who was tall and good looking, and they were sitting behind immediate family members. Laura suppressed a smile when she saw her brother Sam. Tall and gangly as he was, his trousers were not quite long enough and they showed a glimpse of his black socks. That was Sam; he hated wearing a suit.

It was only a short walk up to the registrar, where Tim stood with his friend Jason, who was in charge of the ring. Tim turned to look at her as she walked towards him, he was wearing a very smart charcoal grey suit, a crisp white shirt and, in keeping with everyone else, a red tie. His hair had been sleekly styled; he still wore it in a similar style to his idol, John Lennon, with a fringe, and his eyes shone with happiness. Laura had never thought of Tim as handsome, he was just Tim, but today he looked perfectly groomed, and she felt proud to be standing by his side and marrying him.

Matthew followed his mother. He liked his shirt and tie; red was such a vivid colour. He was careful not to touch against anyone, and he didn't mind Mary walking closely behind him, because she had been in his life ever since he started play school. When his mother stopped, and took her place next to Tim, granddad Trevor said to the registrar he was giving Laura away, and then he stepped back, taking Matthew's arm and steering him to sit down with Emily at the front. Matthew didn't mind his granddad touching him, he felt safe because his mother had explained that this is what families did, and he could accept that. He had tried really hard to please his mother by accepting that being touched was part of his life. Sometimes his teacher touched his shoulder when he was in line at school, so he had learned to accept it as normal.

After the marriage ceremony was over, Tim turned to kiss his bride. He had done it; Laura was now his, Simon could not have her. He could see his son, that was only right, and Tim would never get in the way of that, but this was now the beginning of his life with Laura. Maybe she was the stronger person in their partnership, the wealthier, and the more successful, but she never made him feel inadequate, so he could live with it.

Laura felt very happy. Not only had Matthew done himself proud as a page boy, but also the ceremony had gone off beautifully, she had felt really elegant in her red dress, and Tim had told her she looked beautiful. He had just presented Matthew with a set of Matchbox cars. Tim was great, he never forgot Matthew, and knowing that gave her a warm glow inside. She had been right to marry Tim; he cared about Matthew. Knowing he cared about Matthew endeared him to her even more. Anyone who could take on another man's son as his own must be something special. She was a lucky woman.

Now they were off for two blissful weeks in the Bahamas, where the sun would shine, and they could laze in front of the swimming pool and spend time being just the two of them. Her parents and Agnes between them would be looking after Matthew, as they had all agreed to come to the house so his routine would not be disrupted. Matthew did not appear to be anxious about being separated from her, although deep inside her she knew she would miss him; it was their first time apart.

Laura had plenty of staff to run her shops now, so she knew she could leave them in safe hands. Tim had finally left his job as a car salesman. He was going to be more involved with running the business, hiring staff and buying stock. Laura planned for them to work together. Tim was easy going, with a great sense of humour, so it seemed a much better idea to bring him into it than to get someone new. For the first time for a long time, Laura felt content with her life. There were no more secrets; Simon knew about Matthew and there was already a bond, and she was looking forward to a happy life with Tim and Matthew.

Simon was glad when the day was over. He might be thousands of miles away, but his heart was right with Laura. He pictured her marrying Simon, and it hurt. All the people would be celebrating, Matthew would have a new father figure. . . that hurt, too! What a fool he had been for letting her get away. There had been one last chance when she visited him, but after seven years apart, he just wasn't sure how she felt about him. The usually very confident person that he was had become a mess inside, and he had been so scared of rejection, but now looking back, he wished that he had risked it. Maybe it wouldn't have been fair to Tim to try and split them up, but loving her made him feel very selfish. He still wanted and loved her, he always would love her, she was the mother of his child and that love would bind them forever.

But now the deed was done, she had married Tim, so Simon had to accept it and live with it. His trips to England were going to be more frequent now because more than anything he wanted a relationship with Matthew. He needed to make up for losing his first six years. Maybe one day Matthew might come out to America and stay with him. That would be great.

In the meantime he knew what he had to do; pick up his life and get on with it. He could not allow his feelings for Laura to dominate him like this, he must move on. He had not had anything more than a couple of casual flings since his marriage to Judy had ended, but he was only twenty-five. He vowed he would get out there again and lead a more social life outside the courtroom. Maybe the right person had not come along yet, but they would. He had to believe that, because if he did not, then he would have to admit his ship had sailed without him. Had he really missed the boat?

He decide to telephone his parents and tell them about Matthew. This would give them a couple of months to get used to the idea before he visited them. Then there was Kate. He had thought about it and decided that she needed to know what she had done. Her meddling had not helped the situation, but most of all he blamed himself for not making more of an effort to track Laura down, he should have realised she still cared at that time.

His mother Elizabeth was very startled to find she had a six year old grandson, and he explained about the autism as best he could, but she confessed it was not a subject she knew much about.

"With the right help at school Matthew will be fine. He's very intelligent!" he said firmly.

"That's good, but what a shame you live in the USA, that makes it harder."

"Well, Mother, that means you will see more of me."

"I won't argue with that. We don't see enough of you as it is. Tell me when you are next coming and I'll get Kate to come and stay too, you haven't seen each other for a while."

Simon refrained from telling her what Kate had done. It was between them, and maybe his rather spoiled little sister might have grown up now.

"That sounds great. How is her stage career going?"

"Not bad, considering what the stage school fees were. She's with a touring production of *My Fair Lady* at the moment. She is in Scotland, but after next month she'll be taking a break until the next project comes up." There was a short pause and then she said: "Simon, I am still in shock about being a grandmother, and sad we missed the first six years."

"I know, Mother. I am sad too, and Laura has now married an old friend of mine, Tim, do you remember him?"

"Of course I remember Tim; the tall lad who was always very amusing."

"Yes, you've got it."

Elizabeth had not missed the tone of regret in his voice, and she felt for him. He hadn't said he still loved Laura, but was it mother's intuition? She felt he still did, and it must be hard for him to see her marry his best friend. Well, poor Simon had certainly paid for his teenage mistake. First of all missing the early years of Matthew's life, and then also losing the girl he loved to someone else.

"How are you finding the American girls?" she asked lightly, trying to steer the conversation away from the painful subject.

"Oh, they are great!" said Simon, and his enthusiasm was especially for her; let Mother think he was doing fine.

"Well, don't forget, if you meet a nice one, bring her over to England when you come. All your friends are welcome."

"I certainly will!" Simon replied, and the more he thought about it, it seemed a great idea.

Chapter Twenty-one

"Hello Matthew, did you have a fun time with Grannie, Granddad and Great Aunt Agnes?"

Laura gulped back the feeling of wanting to hug him, he was busy lining up his cars in the toy garage.

"Yes."

"He's been very good, and his teacher says he's working very hard," said Emily encouragingly.

Matthew made sure the cars were lined up properly, then gave his mother his attention. Her face was very brown, and so was Tim's, but that was because they had been to a very hot country. He had not been allowed to go with them because he was not allowed to miss school.

"I got a gold star."

"Well done son!" said Laura warmly, and then he came over, and spontaneously his arms went round her in a bear hug which left her breathless. He would never be able to say he had missed her, but that hug spoke volumes and it meant the world to her.

"How are you doing, mate?" enquired Tim. It was pleasing to see him playing with the garage still, that had been such a good idea of his. Matthew studied him thoughtfully, and then remembered what his mother had told him.

"You are my stepfather, a step is something that helps you to get up, and I have a real father who lives in America."

"That's right, you got it!" laughed Tim. Matthew was such a quaint little boy.

Laura hugged her parents and Aunt Agnes. Matthew was well

and happy, so between them they had done a fine job. The honeymoon had been all about being just the two of them to start their married life. She had taken her mind off Matthew, as he was in good hands, and concentrated on Tim. It had been a long time since her love affair with Simon and, once she was in her husband's arms, she banished all thoughts of Simon.

Tim was a considerate and gentle lover; it was so unlike the passion that had made her pregnant, but it was a very safe and satisfying love. For Laura, being loved again was what she had been yearning for, and Tim had risen from friend, to husband, to lover during the last two years, so she felt safe and sure with him. He had always found Matthew's eccentricity amusing, and she had learned to laugh with him and not take life too seriously. She felt they were a great team, and with three shops now being run for her by staff, she had more spare time than she had ever enjoyed before.

Her biggest dream would be to have another baby, a sister for Matthew, but that in itself was a risk. Would another child be born with autism? If so, could she cope with another child with such challenges? Tim spoke warmly about having another baby, but she was worried that she might let him down in the way she had felt she had let Simon down.

It was not that she was ashamed of Matthew, it was the opposite, she was very proud of him. But life was tough for him, he had to try and make sense of her world, and so how could she blame him for retreating into his when it all got too much for him? There were twenty-nine other children in his class, but none of them were affected by autism. Deep inside she felt life was unfair to him, but she would never let it show. She would just continue to encourage his talents and minimise his difficulties.

But life was a risk, and she didn't want Matthew to be an only child, so she agreed with Tim that they needed to have a baby of their own to make their family unit complete. So they were just going to let nature take its course, and this time she could afford to have a private doctor and hopefully the best care available. Not that even the best care would stop a baby from being autistic; the fault was biological and not due to lack of care at birth. But at least she felt if she did this, she was doing all in her power to help her baby.

Later that night, when Matthew had gone to bed, Laura

checked through all the post that had arrived when they were away. Tim sat in the chair with the TV on and a glass of whisky in his hand.

"Some of these letters are spam. Could you help me to open them, then we can throw the rubbish ones away?"

Tim felt slightly irritated, but hid it. Laura was a workaholic, and they had only just got home.

"Tomorrow, my love. I am shattered, and so are you."

"OK, tomorrow then, but there is always so much to catch up on when you take time off."

He got up and stood in front of her, grinning widely. He had thought of another way to stop her from trying to plunge straight back into work.

"How about an early night?" he whispered, gently winding her curls round his finger.

Oh, he's not too tired for sex! Was the thought that leapt into Laura's mind. They had done a lot of travelling, and that was the last thing her poor weary body wanted. She had just wanted Tim to give her a bit of support with the mail, was that so much to ask? He had wanted to leave his car salesman job and share the business with her, but now all he wanted to do was drink whisky and go to bed early.

"If I have an early night, it's to sleep."

If her voice sounded sharp, she didn't mean it. Now she was home, Matthew was OK, and tomorrow she needed to catch up on work. Was she just being a grizzler? Whatever was wrong with her. She didn't know, but she needed everything to get back to normal, and after a good night's sleep, she would feel more in control.

Tim flinched. This wasn't like Laura, she was usually sunny and bright, but when he looked at her face, she really did look very tired. He would have to make a bit more effort to help her tomorrow; his little wife clearly needed him.

"Of course honey, let's go up and cuddle, then tomorrow we can tackle the mail."

Then he put his arm round her and steered her out of the lounge and up the stairs. Laura didn't know why she felt like this, she could not explain it, but she felt soothed when they lay in bed together. Now the honeymoon was over.

Tim stroked her hair gently until she fell asleep. He was well aware that Laura was the driving force in their relationship. She was a very driven woman, and some men might find it intimidating, but he liked that about her. It was obvious though, that even this strong woman needed his support, even if it was opening a few letters, and tomorrow he would.

He gently slid his arm out from behind her. Laying on her back, with her eyes closed and her curls framing the pillow, she looked so vulnerable. Marrying Laura had given him a comfortable lifestyle, and now he needed to get her pregnant. This child would bind them together, he thought fiercely, as an image of Simon, tall and handsome, rose up inside, threatening to choke him. She might even be pregnant now, that would explain her mood. With a sigh he turned over and was soon also asleep.

Simon was caught up in a very intense court case, which lasted for over six weeks. The guy was a drugs baron, and he had been dealing drugs to young women. One of these poor unfortunate women had died, and it was clear to see the man had no conscience. He also had an attorney who was very skilled and was trying all sorts of loopholes to get him off. But Simon was determined he would not succeed. Simon might be younger and less experienced than the other attorney, but this jerk was the scum of the earth!

Those thoughts were circulating in his mind, but outwardly he was able to maintain a necessary calmness, and this calmness, coupled with determination and a very strong resolve, eventually helped him to achieve a conviction, and the criminal with the sneering smile was put behind bars for a long time.

After the case was over, he had time to think about himself and Matthew. He planned to fly to England at the beginning of the next week, and when he told his associate Marcus, his daughter Susy, who was blonde, bubbly and quite outspoken, couldn't help herself from remarking.

"Wow, England, I have always wanted to visit!"

"What a good idea," remarked Marcus. "Twenty-one years old and never left DC."

Simon laughed with them. Marcus was always grumbling that she was still at home, but he was very proud of his strong-willed daughter, and Simon suspected that both Marcus and his wife

Diana, would be lost without her. And when he thought about it, why not? She would be an entertaining companion for the flight, someone to take up to London to see the sights, and he wouldn't feel quite so alone. He could also work out something for when he spent time with Matthew; if Susy didn't want to come, his mother could take her shopping or somewhere she wanted to visit. Susy might only be a friend, but that suited him well, he didn't want any strings attached and her company would be a welcome diversion. He would explain all to Mother, so she didn't put her foot in it.

"Well Susy, if you want to come with me for three weeks, I am staying with my family in Guildford, and I can show you the sights of London."

"Gee thanks, Simon." He was rewarded by seeing her eyes sparkle, and her face light up with a smile.

"Buddy, I was only jesting," said Marcus. He knew Susy had taken quite a shine to his handsome new associate, but he hadn't meant to push them together. Of course she would love it, but it might put Simon in an awkward position. He was so polite, as English people always were, he could not really refuse her without causing embarrassment.

"No truly, I would be delighted with Susy's company, really I would!"

Well that was his chance to back out politely, and he hadn't. Marcus was pleased for his daughter, whose eyes were shining with happiness. Maybe Simon liked her; he hadn't particularly spotted any signs, but he knew only too well, after all his training to be an attorney, Simon had learned the art of hiding his true thoughts and emotions. This is why he was so good at his job. Susy was a stunner, not just because she was his daughter; everyone said so, and if he could have chosen a boyfriend for her, then he couldn't have chosen anyone better than Simon, who had a great future ahead of him. This trip would be great for all of them.

Chapter Twenty-two

Laura did not understand herself at all. She was only just back from a wonderful honeymoon, with her whole life stretching in front of her, and she should have been as happy as she possibly could be. But she had discovered already that the Tim she had married was totally unlike the Tim who had just spent the last two years getting to know her.

When he had not lived with her, he had always been bright and happy when they met; indeed it was his zany sense of humour that had first attracted her to him. But every morning he wanted to laze in bed instead of getting up and working. She bit her lip against saying anything, but wished he had stayed at his job selling cars. He had to get up then.

Eventually, when he did present himself, he was more interested in having lunch out than buying stock for the shop. She was in despair; she could run her business without him, she had done before he even came along, but with their marriage came the partnership, and by adding him in, she had wanted to show him she loved and trusted him.

Then there was the way he addressed the reps when they came in one of the shops. He referred to it as *my* shop, and made no reference to Laura whatsoever, it was like she didn't exist. She felt he was taking over, and she didn't like it.

And the worst thing was his attitude towards Matthew had changed. When he had visited, and Matthew came home from school, he had taken an interest in him, but these days, after a liquid lunch most days, he took himself off for a lie down, and didn't resurface until late afternoon, almost dinner time. It wasn't the easiest thing to build up a relationship with Matthew, but now he didn't even try, and that hurt her even more than the way he was acting. She turned to Aunt Agnes for advice because she knew she would be completely honest with her.

"Well, Laura, it's true you never really know someone until you live with them, and I have to confess to you that Tim fooled me too. He is clearly after the prestige and money he gets from being married to you, so you either have to file for divorce, or speak to him and give him the opportunity to change after you have told him the way he is acting is not acceptable."

"I know, but I have to give him one more chance. Can you imagine my parents if we split up? I have already given them a lot of heartache."

"Well you've been married for six months now, how is Matthew coping with his loss of interest in him?"

"I am not sure he notices that much, and Tim always told me that he would bring up Matthew like his own son, but now he barely sees him."

Agnes said nothing, she had always feared that Laura had mistaken her own real love for Tim's supposed love for Matthew. She had felt love for him because of her son. She had even asked Agnes if she should marry him, and they had both thought he was a good man at heart, but just not very good with money, and Laura had taken care of that. They had neither of them expected him to be perfect.

"And what about Simon?"

Laura felt herself blushing. She had wished so many times that she was with Simon, Matthew's real dad, and not Tim. Simon had a much more positive nature, and a strong work ethic, but she needed to put all that firmly in the past and move on, just like Simon had.

"Well, Simon comes over quite often to visit him, about every eight weeks. The first time he brought his girlfriend, Susy, but the last couple of times he's been on his own. They seem to get on really well, and Matthew has taken it in his stride about having a father."

Agnes noticed her colouring up; so this Simon still affected her, maybe that was why Tim had turned all balky, maybe he was jealous, especially if Simon was visiting that often. She had never

g

been one to meddle with other people's lives, but Laura at twenty-four still seemed very vulnerable and naïve where her love life was concerned. She had proved herself to be a brilliant businesswoman from such an early age, but her love life was an absolute mess.

"I think Tim may be jealous and feel pushed out, have you ever thought of that?"

Laura thought about it. Tim was acting like a spoiled child, in her opinion; lazy and selfish, so she would speak to him. If he didn't change his ways they would have to separate, but she didn't really want that, her heart ached at the thought of it. She hated to fail at anything, and it was her fault too.

"Yes, he might be, I know, he was so keen to have a baby of our own."

"Well, I would hold fire on that until your relationship settles down."

Such wise words from Agnes, but spoken a little too late. A couple of days later, Laura missed her period, and then came the sickness which was relentless. She didn't need to have it confirmed; the only time she suffered like this was when she was pregnant. At first she tried to fight it, but it was impossible, and the nausea and dizziness lasted all day, she could keep no food down, and after seeing the doctor, he advised her to stay in bed until it passed.

Tim was absolutely delighted that she was pregnant. He had hoped once they were married, she would conceive immediately, but six months had passed, and during that time he had seen more of Simon than ever, when he visited because he came round to collect Matthew. He didn't like the way Laura's face lit up when she saw him. He had tried to encourage her to adopt a more relaxed attitude towards the business. After all, she had staff to run it for her, and he felt they could spend more time together whilst Matthew was at school.

But finally she was pregnant; the baby was due in April of 1969. Matthew would be seven, quite an age gap, but maybe he might not be that interested in a new baby, who could tell with Matthew?

When he found out that Laura was confined to bed, Tim was secretly elated. Now she would have no choice but to leave the running of the business in his hands until she was able to take up the reins again. Now he could prove himself to her. Laura had explained that he needed to bank the takings every day, and then do the wages and put them in the little brown envelopes, and the staff were always paid on Friday. Every other Monday he needed to go to the warehouse and stock up, and from her sickbed she made a list to make it easier for him.

Tim had become more attentive since she had announced her pregnancy, and Laura was now hoping that giving him this responsibility might work. She had no choice, she could not leave her bed, the vomiting lasted most of the day and she kept very little food down. Her mother had brought round some Lucozade to help her replace the energy she had lost.

"You look very peaky, but never mind, you have Tim to help you whilst you are laid up. Would you like me to cook dinner tonight, for Tim and Matthew?" she added hastily, seeing Laura heave at the mention of food.

Emily and Trevor were so pleased that Laura was now married, and Tim was so charming. When the new baby was born they would be a proper family, just as they should be. Emily thought that Laura was lucky that she could leave Tim to run the business whilst she was ill, as not all husbands would have been willing to step in like that, or even know how to run it. Emily herself wouldn't know; she was so proud of Laura, and what she had achieved, but Emily knew she couldn't take the credit for Laura's business sense, it had not been inherited from her. It was a long time since Emily had worked; just a couple of years after leaving school, typing in an office, and then along came Trevor and they had married, and she had devoted her life to her husband and children.

"Thanks Mum, Tim will only make a sandwich, he doesn't cook, I am grateful. Hopefully in a week or so things should settle down and then I will get back to normal."

"Yes, it's three months usually. Now what would they like tonight do you think?"

"There's some sausages in the fridge, they both like sausages, and mashed potato."

Emily watched Laura heave again at the mention of food. Her face was full of sympathy, poor Laura! Then she remembered something.

"So it's carrots for Matthew, but what else? Virtually every vegetable I can think of is green."

"He likes sweet corn, but you can do peas for Tim, he doesn't like sweetcorn, and I can't expect him to miss out because of Matthew."

She didn't tell her mother, because Emily had no idea anything was wrong between them, but when she had dished up a meal without any green vegetables recently, Tim had complained bitterly, and when she thought about it afterwards; maybe she had been unfair to him. It was such a little mistake, but it had become a huge argument, and she realised that she was putting Matthew first, because after all their years on their own it had become a habit, but now it must stop.

"Of course, but however do you manage in life? So many things are coloured green."

"I know, and you wouldn't believe how hard it is sometimes. If I take him to the park he doesn't want to walk on the grass, he uses the path only, and he won't play football at school; he thinks green is a cursed colour, all because of a stupid superstition."

"Couldn't he have some sort of therapy for it?" suggested Emily.

"Maybe, but at the moment, Simon, his dad, is trying to help him with it. He believes that exposing him to his phobia might help to cure it, and I have every faith in him."

Laura didn't often mention Simon by name to her parents, she knew it was a sore subject, but he had given her a lot of support with Matthew, and had even suggested getting him a dog to take to the park, and the more she thought about it, the more it would make sense. Matthew loved all animals, and playing in the park with a dog just might make him forget his phobia of grass.

When Emily left her to rest, she sank back against the pillow. This sickness was such a curse, she felt so helpless stuck up here, and she kept wondering if Tim was coping. Every time she asked him, he kept saying it was all fine. Matthew always came into her room every day when he came home from school. But she hated both of them seeing her like this, and she couldn't wait to reach three months, when she had convinced herself that her sickness would fade away.

Tim had enjoyed getting his teeth into the business, and really feeling he had some power. He couldn't stay round Laura when he saw her in bed. Tim didn't do illness, she had told him when she reached three months the sickness would settle down, and that was good enough for him.

When Simon came to collect Matthew on one of his visits, Tim was delighted that he had to deal with him, and not Laura, and he was even more delighted to tell him that Laura was pregnant. Simon's face gave nothing away. If he was jealous, he hid it well.

"Congratulations to you both!" he said warmly.

"Thanks, unfortunately Laura has bad sickness, so she can't get out of bed right now, but it's OK, I am taking care of everything."

Simon expressed his sympathy, but couldn't help wondering how the business would fare in Tim's hands. For as long as he had ever known him, he doubted whether Tim could organise anything, but maybe he had changed, and it wasn't his business to say anything. Now Matthew was going to have a brother or sister, so they would become a closer family unit. He squashed down any pangs he might feel; all he needed to do was make sure Matthew could cope with the change.

After Simon had taken Matthew for a visit to his parents' home, Tim sat down and poured himself a whisky. In the beginning he had dutifully banked the takings every day, and shown the paying in slips to Laura. After the first week, she had not asked to see them, so he hit on the idea of how to make more money very quickly. It was obvious really, money made money, so he went to the local bookies and put the money on Firebrand. That horse was like its name but, to his great disappointment, it didn't win.

Not to be thwarted he tried again, and again; the gambling fever had such a grip on him he couldn't stop. Now there was no spare cash left, he could not buy any stock, so had to tell Laura that he had, and she believed him, thank goodness.

The next problem was he had no money to pay the staff. He had managed to keep them happy last week by promising them a double amount this week, but it had only been a way of stalling them and now he had run out of options, and he knew the only person who could save him was Laura, for only she could sort out this mess.

Tonight he had been able to down a few whiskies, unlike that evening when Emily had stayed and cooked them sausages. He'd been a model husband that night, but tonight with Matthew out of the way, and Laura in bed, he didn't have to hold back, he could indulge himself, and it helped to take his mind off what he had to do tomorrow. He didn't like to go to Laura cap in hand. He had enjoyed a taste of wearing the trousers in this relationship, and he liked it. It was such a bloody shame that his horse had let him down, otherwise he could have increased the money very quickly. By the time he laid down to sleep in the room he was using temporarily whilst Laura was ill, his head was spinning, and he just didn't care because tomorrow was another day.

But the next day, nursing a very bad headache, he chickened out of telling her. He didn't even go into her room to see her. She would find out soon enough when news reached her that her staff wanted their wages. He went downstairs to make some black coffee and take some aspirin, hoping that would help his king-sized hangover.

Then he had a thought. What about the money the shops had taken this week? He could pay them out of that. All he had to do was pull himself into shape, then he could drive over and see how much money there was in the till. Why had he not thought about that before; the money was coming in every day? Eventually Laura would know because her accountant would query it with her if the takings did not add up, but it got him more time right now. He felt bad about backing the horse, and when it was the right moment he would confess what he had done, but not right now, she was not well.

Having drunk the coffee, he went upstairs to wash and shave. Today he must dress smartly, he was, after all, a senior member of this business, so he put on a light grey suit, a blue shirt with a striped tie and some black shoes. As he dabbed on the aftershave, he made a mental note to himself not to go near the bookies. Once he had picked up the money, he needed to bring it back home and make up their brown envelopes, then everyone would be happy.

The shop he was visiting was the first one that Laura had opened. Paula was now the manager and she usually did the banking, but Tim explained that he needed the money to make up the wages. As far as he was concerned, he thought all three managers were only puppet managers, and he pulled the strings. Paula did not question that, but he could tell by her manner that she felt a bit taken over. Laura trusted all her managers, and

150

normally gave them some freedom, but he had explained that whilst she was out of action, this was how it had to be.

After he had collected the cash, he jumped back in the car. He would just have time to make up the wages before Valerie dropped Matthew home from school. She was helping out quite a bit whilst Laura was laid up. Simon would have taken him to school this morning and then he was going to have him again next weekend, so he would pick him up from school on Friday. That meant Tim wouldn't have to see him that day. As far as he was concerned, Simon was an unnecessary thorn in the flesh. He had often rued the day Laura had told him about Matthew. Tim had no idea the contact with his father would be this often.

The first thing he spotted as he drove up the drive was the ambulance parked on the left hand side. It was a wide parking area, so he pulled up next to it, and he could feel such a panic inside him. It was Laura, it must be, there was no one else in the house. Whatever could be wrong with her?

When Laura woke up this morning, her nausea seemed to have passed. She sat up in bed and she didn't feel dizzy. Did that mean she could finally leave her bed? It was almost three months, so maybe at last her insides had settled down. Usually Matthew came in to see her every morning before he went to school, but today he was with Simon, he had spent the night there, and tonight Valerie would bring him home.

She wondered if Tim was up yet. It was all very quiet, but he must be around somewhere, the doctor had said she must not be left alone at any time just in case she fainted, but now hopefully the fainting period of her pregnancy was over. Right now she was planning to try and drink a cup of tea as she hadn't fancied one for a while, and then with Tim's help she could bath and dress, and then find out how well everything was running.

"Tim, where are you? I feel a lot better today."

But the only sound that greeted her was complete silence, so either Tim had got up and gone out earlier, or he was still asleep. She very much doubted he would have got up early, and she felt her irritation rising that he just couldn't get up. Would he ever change?

She got out of bed slowly. She felt OK, then she put her towelling robe on. Sheer curiosity led her to the door of Tim's room. She actually felt fine, and was sure he would be pleased to see her up. But his room was empty. The bed was ruffled, so she could see he had slept in it, but it looked as though he had gone out in a hurry.

Now she felt mean for thinking the worst of him. He was working hard, obviously, and soon it looked like she would be able to take up the reins again and get back to work with him. As she turned to leave the room, she failed to see the slipper which was sticking out from underneath the tumbled heap of bedclothes on the floor.

As she tripped, Laura tried to save herself by grabbing the chair next to the bed, but it wasn't stable, it came with her, and she crashed to the floor, still clutching it and banging her head on it. As she lay on her front, her last coherent thought was that she was glad the floor was carpeted.

When Agnes came in later to see Laura, she was horrified to find her unconscious on the floor. Her stomach was somehow all caught up inside the upturned chair, and she had a big bruise on her head with blood dripping from a cut also on her head. She wasted no time in calling an ambulance, and she kept calling frantically for Tim, but the house was empty.

The ambulance man helped Laura to come round, after gently removing the chair from underneath her.

"Wake up Laura, you have fallen over. Does it hurt anywhere besides your head?"

"She's nearly three months' pregnant," said Agnes anxiously.

"I see, well we had better take her in and make sure the baby is unharmed, as she must have fallen on the chair."

Agnes stood back and let them do their work. Both the man and his female assistant seemed to know exactly what they were doing. Although now conscious, Laura seemed very sleepy and not quite with it.

"I will take care of Matthew," Agnes reassured her, and she saw Laura's face light up at the mention of his name. She watched as they put her on a stretcher and made their way towards the ambulance. And Agnes fully intended to do just that. She had arrived on the train and then got a taxi; she was staying for the week as they had arranged. She would not step on Tim's toes, but where was Tim when he was needed? Already her opinion of him was changing, he never seemed to back Laura up when she needed him.

152

She followed them outside to see Laura into the ambulance, and was just in time to see Tim running towards the house in a blind panic.

"Oh my God, Laura, whatever has happened? I only popped out for a couple of hours to collect the takings."

"I found her on the floor of the spare room, unconscious, they are taking her to check the baby is all right!"

The baby, of course! Tim felt a wave of anguish course through him. His first thought was that it had taken him over six months to get her pregnant, and if she lost this baby they would have to start all over again. His second thought was for Laura; he hoped she was not in pain, seeing her like this was very distressing to him. He addressed the ambulance man.

"I am her husband, can I come with you?"

"Of course, in you get," said the man, as they carefully lifted the stretcher into the ambulance. He was short and stocky, as was the young woman helping him, they looked strong, and he remembered thinking that they probably had to be because not every patient would be as light as Laura was. He had very short blond hair cut in a crew cut, which made it look very spiky. His companion had her long brown hair tied back in a ponytail.

"No, I will follow you in my car," said Tim. Aunt Agnes didn't drive, so he was glad he had the presence of mind to remember this. He had no desire to stand around waiting for a bus later, or rely on public transport in any way.

The ambulance did not put its siren on, so he comforted himself with the thought that it wasn't life threatening, but then he reminded himself, it was if she lost the baby. He followed after them until they reached the county hospital. The ambulance drove up to the main entrance, so Tim quickly put his car in the car park, and then followed them in.

By the time he got to reception Laura had been taken into casualty, and he was pointed in the right direction. He was glad he could sit with her whilst they waited for a doctor. She had been dozing, but then woke up with a start, moaning.

"Help me, the pain!" and she was thrashing about on the narrow bed. Tim tried to soothe her. He wiped her hot brow; there was sweat pouring off her and she was panting. Whatever could be wrong?

After what seemed an age, but was probably only a few

minutes, the white coated doctor appeared. Laura had drawn herself up the bed and was in a sitting position, her screams of terror rang all around.

Then Tim saw the blood gushing down her leg, which was outside the sheet, and the doctor gave a huge groan.

"I am so sorry. You are losing your baby, and there is nothing we can do to save it."

Chapter Twenty-three

When Simon heard about Laura's miscarriage he was devastated for her. If he had been closer, he would have cherished her, bought her flowers, anything to put a smile back on her face, but it wasn't his place, it was up to Tim. He told himself he would have felt the same if it had been his own sister Kate; it was a cruel thing to happen to any woman, and Laura would always have a special place in his heart because she was the mother of his son Matthew.

He figured the best way to help her would be by supporting Matthew. After all, he had just lost a sibling. Matthew came to stay for a week at his mother's home whilst Laura was recuperating. Luckily it was half term, so they could spend some time together. He explained in the best way that he knew, about the baby.

"Your Mummy had a baby growing inside her tummy, but it didn't grow properly and it wouldn't be able to cope in this world, so Jesus took your baby to live with him in heaven, where it would be safe."

Matthew listened carefully to his words. Recently he had been learning about Jesus at school; he was the son of God, just like he was the son of Simon. When Christmas came they were going to celebrate his birth because he had been born in a stable. They were doing a play at school, and Matthew had been chosen to be a wise man. He didn't have to speak to anyone, just walk up to the crib with long robes on, and give a gift to the baby. James was also a wise man, so he would do it, but he would stand next to James, because he wasn't keen on the other boy, Robert, who had teased and bullied him and thrown his cap at times.

"Does Jesus take care of babies that are not well?"

"Oh yes, and when we die, at the end of our lives, he takes care of our spirits too."

Matthew seemed happy with that, and Simon breathed a sigh of relief. If any of his friends could hear him now he would lose all credibility. But he wasn't exactly an atheist, and that seemed the best way to explain things to Matthew.

"Now, Mummy has said you can have a puppy, so as long as Granny Elizabeth agrees, we can go out and choose one."

His Mother entered the room, catching the last part of the conversation.

"You can bring the puppy here, but it has to be kept out in the kitchen until it's house trained."

"Thanks Mother, that's very fair."

Matthew watched his dad hug his grandmother. He did that sometimes to his mum, but unlike his dad, he didn't let his lips touch his mum's cheek. He couldn't, but he didn't know why that was.

Elizabeth beamed. It was so nice to have Simon visiting; and after she had got over the shock, it was nice to have a new grandson. Kate didn't seem to be in any hurry to marry, so Matthew was the first, and very special. As she got to know him better, and his unusual ways, something had clicked in her mind about the past. It was something she had never understood as a child, but she did now. One of these days she would tell Simon too.

Simon took Matthew to a local pet shop. There were cages with all kinds of animals in: cats, dogs, hamsters, even mice and rats. There were also fish swimming around in tanks. But when he saw the black and white collie in a cage with a golden retriever, he knew this was the dog for Matthew. It was only young, so its tail was still just a stump, but that didn't stop him from jumping up at the cage and wagging his whole body in delight. Retrievers were lovely too, but collies ran around all day, and were quite demanding, if any dog could stimulate Matthew, a collie would.

Simon's idea was a good one, as was proved over the next few weeks. Whilst Laura was trying to pick up her life and get over the loss of her baby, Simon and Matthew managed to get Toby house trained, and also, the biggest break through ever, cure

Matthew's phobia of green. He was now running on grass and throwing the ball for Toby. One morning, he had completely forgotten himself, and ventured out into the garden to retrieve the ball in bare feet; so he had even touched the grass with bare feet.

Simon thought it was a shame he had to scold him for not having shoes on, but it was the end of October, and he had no wish to send Matthew home to his mother with a bad cold.

Eventually Simon had to return to America. He didn't really want to go, as it was becoming increasingly hard to leave his son behind. Matthew meant everything to him, and he was even considering returning to England and setting up a business there. After all, people always wanted lawyers. He planned to discuss it with Marcus when he returned to Washington.

Laura recovered physically from her miscarriage quite quickly. All nausea and sickness had gone and she started to eat again, which was just as well, as she had become pale and thin with all the stress that constant vomiting causes for the body. But emotionally it was going to take much longer. For three months she had thought about the tiny life growing inside her, a sibling for Matthew, and then suddenly that little life had been extinguished.

She felt she had let Tim down. He had been so thrilled about the pregnancy; they both had, and she was sure being a father would have been the making of Tim, but sadly it was not meant to be. She cursed herself for being so clumsy and falling down, but the doctor at the hospital had told her the foetus had been abnormal, it had not developed properly, and he felt with or without her fall, she would have miscarried as it was nature's way of preventing imperfect pregnancies from continuing.

So she threw herself back into work with more energy. Even the knowledge of how Tim had misused the company money didn't really affect her too much. It wouldn't take long to make up that shortfall. She had given him the chance to prove himself, but he had blown it, so she wouldn't make that mistake again, it was as simple as that. But she was going to make sure he didn't have access to anything more than their joint account of spending money. In the case of Tim, she had to save him from himself, so there could be no money available for him to waste at the bookies.

Deep inside Laura realised that being married to a man who was so hopeless at managing money, and also could not be trusted with it, did not work, but at this point in her life, she had neither the strength nor the energy to do anything about it. All she wanted was peace right now, and time to grieve for her baby. The doctor had said she must not try again for a baby for at least six months as she had lost a lot of blood, and had to have her womb scraped afterwards, which was an unpleasant experience. She was relieved to hear this. He had put her on the pill, and although she said nothing, the fragile state of her marriage made her think that having a baby might not be the answer.

One thing she did find heartening was how much Simon was making headway with Matthew. During her three months in bed, she had felt she neglected him, but Simon had sensed how much he was needed, and he had stepped up by buying Matthew a dog, and curing his phobia of green. Matthew listened more to what his father said than anyone, ever, and although he didn't live with Simon, she could feel his strength and support at all times.

Toby the dog was a delight; he seemed to sense that Matthew was special, and was at his side at all times. He even slept in his room, and although Laura tried to stop him from sleeping on the bed, in the end she had to concede defeat. Toby's devotion to Matthew was very touching; he could reach him without the benefit of speech, and it was remarkable to see Matthew responding so much more to situations outside his own lonely world, and interacting with people. What a great idea of Simon's it had been.

Tim was relieved that Laura had not said much about the misuse of the money whilst she was laid up. He guessed that just like himself, her grief over the failed pregnancy made everything else pale into insignificance. He just didn't know how to move forward. A baby would have bound Laura to him forever, and that is what he needed, because with Simon now back in her life, and taking an active part with Matthew, he felt he could not compete. It wasn't as if Laura saw Simon; when his car appeared Matthew ran out to greet him, or sometimes Tim himself followed after him to speak to Simon, because Laura was usually at work.

But when Matthew arrived home after a visit, he seemed to be very stimulated, and spoke to them more than he ever had. Laura was convinced it was that dratted dog. Tim didn't like dogs, they were nasty, dirty noisy creatures, but now because Simon had got it for him, they had to have it in the house, and even on Matthew's bed, and he couldn't see why it couldn't have a kennel in the garden.

The more Tim heard about the wonderful Simon, the more his hostility towards him grew. Sometimes in his mind he had a fantasy that some kind person came along and shot Simon, so he would be out of their lives forever. But it was only ever going to be a fantasy, because Tim knew that it was not something he was capable of.

If he heard Laura speaking on the telephone to him, which they sometimes did to discuss Matthew, he became convinced they were getting back together again, and he had accused her of such. Laura's response had been to tell him he was being ridiculous, and to remind him they had both agreed that Simon should know about Matthew, and now he was taking an interest in him. He knew this was true, but he had thought, with Simon in America, there could not be much of a relationship; but damn it, Simon seemed to be over in England far more than he was in Washington!

Six months had now passed since Laura's miscarriage. It was now April 1969, and Tim tried to forget that this was the month their baby had been due. He felt anger towards the world in general, but tried to follow the example of John Lennon, who had married Yoko Ono on 20th March in Gibraltar, and then had a Bed In honeymoon in Amsterdam, all in the name of Peace. Tim wanted peace, but he also wanted his love life back, as there had been nothing between them except the occasional embrace since the miscarriage.

That night, in bed, he stroked her hair and kissed her gently. Laura's response was to hug him, with his head on her chest. He knew the way to rouse her, but tonight it didn't seem to work; her body tensed when he tried to touch her breasts, and something inside him snapped. A wild idea came into his mind, and he had no control over it. All through their marriage, Laura had been the dominant partner, she had proved her character to be as strong as any man, and because it gave him an easy and cosseted life, he had welcomed it. But not any more, he felt he must at least assert himself in the bedroom.

He had spent the evening drinking whisky, trying to get up the courage to make love to her, and now she was refusing him. Drunken anger coursed through him, and he felt himself pressing her body down, and she was pleading with him.

"No Tim, no, I don't want to!"

This only made him more determined, and he ripped her cotton nightie away in disgust. In the past this would have excited her, but not now, she was sobbing with distress, but he no longer cared. He grabbed hold of his penis, but to his absolute disgust it was small, flaccid, and totally unresponsive to the situation. Feeling thoroughly humiliated he rolled away from her, and she fled into another bedroom, locking the door behind her. Oh my God, what had he done? He couldn't even get a hard on when he needed to.

The next morning he could not face her, and he stayed in bed until well after she left for work. He should have taken Matthew to school, but he guessed as he was not up, she would have arranged something. He didn't care really, as his bond with Matthew was no longer close, and he blamed Simon for that. He didn't play with that garage Tim had made so often now, every waking minute was spent with that filthy dog!

After lunch the telephone rang; it was Laura, asking him if he could meet Matthew from school. She made no reference to the night before, and even suggested if he didn't want to drive, he could walk the dog to meet him. As he had already enjoyed two whiskies, maybe that was not such a bad idea; he had nothing else to do that day, so he set off with the hound on the lead, and then stood with the other parents in the playground whilst the teachers brought their classes out and lined them up in readiness for their parents to collect them.

Matthew came up to him without a glimmer of a smile, and grabbed the dog's lead from him. He watched Toby licking him, and saw Matthew laugh. My God, this boy was so rude, he'd rather take notice of a dog than him!

"Come on, let's get you home," he said curtly.

As they walked towards the school gate, Matthew stiffened. Robert was standing there, with a sly smile on his fat puffy face. His mother, equally fat and puffy, was talking to someone with her back turned. This time he couldn't hit Matthew as he had in the past, because Tim would see him. He felt glad.

But Robert had other plans to wind Matthew up. This boy was not like the other boys. He always played alone, he had only one friend and that was James, but tonight James was not with him, and that would have been a great opportunity to smash his face in. Robert didn't like his face, or his brown curly hair, and he wanted to spoil it. But today he could not, so he did the next best thing, in full view of Matthew, but not Tim, because he was busy opening the gate, he kicked Toby full in the face.

Matthew didn't really understand what love was. His mother had told him that love created babies, and he knew they grew in their mother's stomach, and it was the same with dogs; Toby had also grown in his mother's stomach. Ever since Toby had come to live with them, his life had changed. Toby was with him all the time and he made him feel safe. All he knew was that Toby's loyalty and presence created a very warm feeling inside him and made him smile. Toby could be really funny when he jumped in puddles and frolicked with other dogs, and he made him laugh a lot, so if those feelings he had were love, then that must be what love was.

But when Matthew saw Robert kick Toby, and heard his dog whimper, he felt a blinding flash of anger and a red mist descending on him. Forgetting his fear of the bigger and stronger boy, he leapt at him, his fist catching him full in the face, and Robert's mountainous bulk toppled to the ground with blood pouring from his nose, and him blubbering at the top of his voice: "Mum!"

"Oh, you animal! What have you done to my boy?" screamed his mother, rushing over.

Matthew said nothing, but put his arms round Toby, checking to see if that kick had caused any blood. He couldn't see any, and Toby grovelled over to him, which made him sad, he would never hurt his dog, but that big oaf had!

Tim was mortified. Matthew was nothing but trouble to him. The kid was bad news; fancy attacking the other boy like that! His one thought was to calm the situation.

"I am so sorry. Matthew has autism, and it makes his behaviour strange sometimes!"

The big woman, who looked just as threatening as her son, was not convinced.

"Oh, what an excuse to hide behind!" she sneered. "He's out of control, look at my poor Robert's face!"

They were standing just outside the school gates. Probably most women would have taken their child home and stopped the nose bleed, but Brenda Pratt was no ordinary woman, she was the mother of a boy who had a weight problem because he ate too many cakes, which had been inherited from her, and if she thought anyone was taking advantage of her poor boy, then she wanted the whole world to know about it.

"I am going to call the police. This is common assault, and you are no fit parent, your breath stinks of whisky!"

Tim groaned, thank god he was not driving the car. This stupid woman had turned something that was admittedly Matthew's fault into a high drama, but the last thing they needed was the police.

"There's no need for that. Matthew is very sorry. Matthew, say you are sorry!"

Matthew looked at Robert, who was sitting on a wooden seat by the school entrance with a handkerchief pressed up against his nose. He was still blubbering loudly, and by now curiosity was causing people to stand and look. Tim had asked him to say sorry, but he couldn't; he wasn't sorry, and if he said he was, then that would be a lie. So he remained silent.

Tim was feeling desperate now. He was way out of his depth, not only with Matthew, but with the whole situation. Without thinking twice about it, he grabbed Matthew's shoulder: he would do as he was told! And repeated his words.

"Say sorry, Matthew!"

Suddenly nothing in Matthew's world made sense any more. His world contained a dog, this dog was his closest friend, and he knew he would protect him with his life if he had to. For no reason whatsoever except spite, Robert had kicked his dog, and Tim wanted him to apologise; he just didn't get it. So he did what he often did when the world got too tough for him, he ran towards the school railings sobbing, and curled himself up in a heap on the ground trying to shut out everything; but not everything because Toby was with him, licking away his tears, and crouching on the ground with him.

When Tim eventually managed to smooth over the situation by giving Brenda a ten pound note to treat Robert, to make him forget he had been attacked by a "psycho", everything calmed down. His next task was to persuade Matthew to leave the railings, stand up and come home. He could get no words out of Matthew to explain why he had attacked Robert, so he gave up trying; maybe later his mother would find out.

"Matthew, we need to get Toby home, he is hungry and wants his dinner."

Matthew stood up. His dog had been hurt, and now he was hungry, so they needed to take him home, he could see that. He walked home very soberly; he felt drained, and he knew even his mother would be upset with him. But sometimes his problem with communicating made his life so much harder, and he couldn't change.

Laura felt her relationship with Tim was really breaking down. Last night he had wanted to make love to her, and she knew that was perfectly reasonable after abstaining for six months, but her body had let her down. Her fear that it might hurt, meant she was still not ready, and then for one awful moment she had thought that Tim was going to force himself on her, but he had stopped, and she had run away from him into the spare room. They should have talked about it, but this morning he had not appeared for breakfast and she knew he was upset. Then she remembered she had a meeting with the buyers this afternoon, so she had dropped Matthew at school, hoping Tim would pick him up later. After she had asked him, she wondered if she had done the right thing. Tim was a bit too dependent on whisky lately. She knew he used it to block out his grief, but she didn't want him to drive the car to get Matthew, that was putting them both at risk. Luckily he had agreed to walk Toby round there, even though he didn't seem to like dogs much.

She spent much of the day on edge, and was relieved when she came home to find everything peaceful. They all sat down to dinner together; it was shepherd's pie, an all time favourite of Matthew's, and then suddenly her son spoke.

"Robert kicked Toby right in the face and made him whimper."

Laura looked at Tim for some sort of explanation. He felt really irritated by the whole thing; Matthew's scene in public had created quite a stir, and made him feel ridiculous.

"I wasn't going to tell you in front of Matthew, but he gave another boy a bloodied nose, and his mother was livid."

"Matthew!" said Laura, in amazement, she had never known him to be violent before, but in a flash she saw it all; he had hit the boy because he hurt Toby, and he would have had such strong feelings at the time, he probably wouldn't have been able to explain himself.

Matthew was busy eating his shepherd's pie, with his head down. It had taken him a while to feel ready explain what had happened to Toby, and now he retreated back into his safe world, away from his mother's accusing stare.

"I gave her ten pounds to buy the boy something. It was all I could think of to calm the situation."

"I know Robert, he's a big boy, and he picks on the others quite a bit, doesn't he Matthew?"

Matthew made no response, he was busy patting Toby. He wondered how his mum knew about Robert. He had never told her that Robert bullied him, he had never stood up to him before either, but he hadn't hesitated when it was Toby; no one was going to kick his dog!

Chapter Twenty-four

"I can't expect him to take responsibility for Matthew. It's my duty. Matthew is hard work, and Tim can't cope."

"But he knew that when he married you. You need some sort of support, you are not superwoman!"

"Well maybe he didn't realise because he only visited us. It's not until you live together you get the full picture."

Laura didn't really know why she was defending Tim. She felt he had let her down, and gradually their marriage was falling apart. They were leading separate lives now. He was always out, he drank too much, and they didn't even share the same bedroom. He had blamed everything on Matthew and Simon. Matthew he said was impossible, and Simon was always around, coming between them.

"Laura, you have carried that man right from the beginning. He doesn't work, he drinks too much, and he lives off you. How much more proof do you need to divorce him?"

Agnes shook her head in disgust. It's funny how a person can change their opinion of someone, and she most certainly had with Tim. Gone was his charm and wit; it had all been a cover for a very shallow man, and she had no sympathy for him at all.

Laura shook her head helplessly.

"I know, but this is not a normal situation, and he has always come second to Matthew. It is my fault, and now he no longer cares for Matthew; he considers him a nuisance."

"Well then he needs to go, Laura. I know he's jealous of Simon, but look how Simon's helped Matthew. You have to put your boy first, Tim always knew that, but he's a man who needs someone to spoil him, just like his mother did."

"Did she?"

"She certainly did; and if you separate, he will go trotting off to her in Devon. Don't worry, Tim will always fall on his feet."

This gave Laura something to think about, but Agnes was glad she had not probed her further. She had never forgotten what Tim's mother had said to her on the wedding day. She wondered if he was doing the right thing in marrying Laura because she had "baggage". Agnes had wanted to tell her to butt out; the woman was clearly jealous, and she was relieved that no one else had heard. Her reply was to say it was their lives and no one else's, and then she had made sure she was nowhere near that woman for the rest of the day. Looking back, she now wondered if his mother had known her weak son wouldn't be able to cope, but had made it sound as though Laura was to blame. However, there was no doubt that when he ran home to her, she would say, "I told you so!"

Tim had only stayed in this marriage for as long as he had because of the fact that Laura was a rich woman. He had believed he loved her at first. She was a strong woman and he was very attracted to her, and he had felt he could deal with Matthew; after all, the boy barely spoke and spent a lot of time in his room, and he didn't feel he was any threat to their happiness. But a lot had happened after he was introduced to his father.

He had not expected Simon to be in his life much, but he was, and Matthew was changing. He was not always in his room; he had the dog now, and he played with it a lot. Then there were his obsessive habits. He liked music, and whichever was his favourite song of the moment, would be played incessantly all evening, until he couldn't stand it any more, and had to tell him to change it.

He couldn't tolerate what he considered was Matthew's rudeness; he was not at all sociable, and Laura just made excuses for him saying it was part of his autism, but Tim felt that manners could be learned, and he was surprised that Laura had not insisted on it, because Matthew had only one friend who would put up with him, James, the spineless wonder. What a strop Matthew had thrown when he found out they were moving soon, and he was starting middle school without anyone. Well, life was tough, and it was getting tough for Tim too, having to put up with all this nonsense!

When 1970 came, he realised they had now been married for almost two years, and it was two years too long. The most notable part of entering another decade, although not a particularly inspiring one, was the end of the Cold War, which had lasted since 1945; half a crown ceased to exist, and on 26th January Mick Jagger, lead singer of the Rolling Stones, was fined £200 for being in possession of cannabis.

Rock and roll was still going strong, and it looked like Paul McCartney was going to leave the Beatles. The newspapers were full of, will he or won't he stories, all trying to compete against each other to be first with the news.

But to Tim, none of this was as notable as the fact that he met Leanne, and this time he fell in love with someone who could truly make him happy. Leanne was just a barmaid living in one room, with barely enough money to get by; she wasn't very bright, but she was very pretty. Her long blonde hair was completely straight, she was tall and very slim, with amazing legs. Although unlike her in appearance, something about her bubbly nature reminded him of Laura when they first met. She was always up for a laugh, and he vowed to cut down on his drinking, get a job and be a more responsible person. Leanne was more than happy for him to share her bedsit, and now that he had somewhere to go, he packed all his things and left one morning whilst the house was quiet. He wrote a short note to Laura, as he felt she did deserve that, but when he left the house in the car she had bought for him, all he could feel was relief that, when he closed that front door and posted his keys through the letterbox, he had become free of Laura, Matthew and Simon, and their very complicated lives.

Laura was so glad to be home. It was a cold wet night, the rain was pattering loudly against the window pane, and she undid her boots and thankfully slipped her feet into her warm slippers. Matthew was due to start his new school soon, and Valerie and James had moved to another area, so he would no longer have the company of James. Laura was trying to get him used to it. He was eight now, and didn't like her taking him to school, and had asked to ride his bike. She wasn't sure what to do; she didn't want to wrap him up in cotton wool, and he would be nine in the New Year. The school was not far away, and he didn't have to cross any main roads, so she intended to check with the school and see if any other children were riding their bikes.

One thing she didn't have to do was remind Matthew to take off his muddy shoes and put on his slippers when he came in. Ever since a small child he had always lined his slippers up by the front door, ready to change into when he came in, and woe betide anyone who moved them! Once a cleaning lady had put them in his bedroom under the bed, and that had not gone down well, so now they all knew to leave them by the door.

" Come down, Matthew, if you want a drink and a snack."

She didn't expect an answer, he would just come. After all, he had hollow legs; he was always hungry, and dinner would not be ready for a couple of hours. She put a couple of muffins on to toast, then as she moved towards the kettle to pick it up and fill it with water, she saw the envelope propped up against it.

It had her name on it, and now she was curious. It was Tim's writing, so she slit it open quickly.

Dear Laura,
I am leaving you. I think we both know it's for the best, our marriage could never work out with so many obstacles to climb. I hope you and Matthew will be happy. I am sorry that Matthew was just too much for me. Part of me will always love you, but not enough to continue like this. I have found someone else, please be happy for us. I will contact a solicitor later to start the divorce.
Tim x

When she read it she felt sadness and relief all at once. She was trying to find the courage to end it herself, but didn't want to cause him unnecessary pain. She felt to blame for the failure of her marriage, and now that Tim had done it for her, there was the relief that he had found someone and would be happy; she had not ruined his life. It became clear at that moment that she was not a good marriage prospect to anyone, and she vowed she would spend her time helping her son to grow up happily, because there

168

would be a time one day when he didn't need her, and that is when she might find her own happiness.

She brushed away a tear, grieving for their doomed marriage. She had loved Tim, but he had changed so much, and maybe that was her fault, she had expected too much of him. Moving over to the grill, she turned it down, and picked up the muffins to butter them, just as Matthew came in the room.

"Do you want some jam on them, Matthew?"

She kept her voice bright and smiled at him; he wasn't really looking at her closely, he was seating himself at the table. Instead of replying, he opened the fridge door and got the jam out. Laura decided she would tell him later, when she had got her head round it, how it would affect him she had no idea, but they would cross that bridge when they came to it.

As it happened, when she told him later, Matthew showed no emotion whatsoever, he just commented, "Tim made me a garage." He then proceeded to resurrect it from the toy cupboard and spent some time playing with it. Laura guessed that was his way of remembering Tim, and she felt a little sad that Tim had tried with Matthew in the beginning, but it just hadn't worked.

Simon was sad that his only communication with Matthew right now was by letter or telephone. Communication on the telephone was not good, as mostly Matthew just said "yes" and "no", but he was much more forthcoming in letters, telling his father where he had been and what he was doing.

He had returned to Washington with a mission, that was to sell his half of the company to Marcus, but Marcus didn't want to own it completely, so he needed to find a buyer. It had not taken too long, but now he was obliged to keep working to keep the books in good shape, as it appeared the whole legal transaction would take about six months. He really did not want to miss out on seeing Matthew for six months, as he had already lost the first few years of his life, so he wrote to Laura asking if Matthew would like to come and stay for the whole of the summer holidays. He was aware he would be starting a new school and losing a friend in September, and he really hoped all the business would be settled by then, so he could go to England and start looking for a new law company to join, and a new

h

home too. Clearly Matthew would need extra support at this difficult time.

A letter came back from Laura; Matthew did want to come, and Simon was overjoyed. He got himself a new housekeeper, who was also prepared to spend time with Matthew when he had to go to work. Kim was very nice, she had short hair, and was very attractive in a boyish sort of way, with her big green eyes and happy smile. She reminded him a little of the film star Kim Novak, which was probably why she had her hair in that style.

He explained in great detail about Matthew, his autism, and his unusual needs, and it did not faze Kim at all, because her own brother suffered from autism. But, as she explained, he also had brain damage, so he had to live at home with her parents, because there was not a school that would take him, and they didn't want him to go into a home.

"He would just get left in a corner, and my poor Mama doesn't want that. She spends all day trying to stimulate him," she explained.

"Oh, that is sad, let's hope one day there will be schools for children who have special needs," said Simon, inwardly counting his blessings, that although autistic, Matthew had no brain damage and could easily cope at school.

With everything set up, Simon booked the plane ticket for Matthew. As he was still eight years old, he would have a companion to accompany him on the plane, and then he would be taken to a meeting place, where Simon would take over. With his son so soon to come over, Simon set to work with renewed enthusiasm. If he had a choice, he would rather be in England now with his future to take care of, but Matthew coming over to spend time with him was the next best thing.

When he met him, he noticed how tall he was getting. He looked about ten, and was taking after himself in height. His sister Kate had yet to meet Matthew. She had been mortified when she realised what she had done that day, and as it happened, she was coming to stay for a bit whilst Matthew was there. She had just finished a run in a musical, and Simon had invited her over. Her next one started in September, so she would be with them both for about ten days. He hoped Matthew would take to her, because it would be nice for him to spend time with his aunt.

170

"Did you bring your car?" Matthew asked. He had enjoyed riding in it. He still remembered even after two years or so.

"I certainly have, it's in the parking lot."

"We say car park in England."

" 'Course you do, and so will I when I am there, but over here no folks would understand what I am talking about."

Matthew spotted the car before he had even reached it, and he ran over and stood beside it, waiting for Simon to catch up.

"Let's put your case in the boot."

They got in the car and drove towards the entrance, where Simon paid the bored looking man who was sitting inside his booth. As they drove towards his apartment, Simon felt content, he was looking forward to the next six weeks, and he would make Matthew's stay as enjoyable as he possibly could.

Chapter Twenty-five

1970 was probably the worst year of Laura's life, and one she would never forget. The recession was affecting sales in her shops. Home knitted garments were now becoming less popular, as shops such as Mothercare were springing up everywhere and selling knitted baby clothes at a cheaper price than she could, because she had to pay the knitters as well. Neither did many people sew.

Socks had become much cheaper to buy, so nobody darned holes any more, and the number of people dressmaking diminished as off-the-peg clothes for adults and children became much more affordable. People no longer stopped to come inside a little local shop, they went into the towns where the big stores always flourished. One or two local dressmakers still frequented her shops to buy buttons, zips, and general sewing needs, but it wasn't going to be enough to keep her afloat; she knew she would have to take a backward step, and sell off one of her shops to finance the other two.

So she put the one she had acquired last up for sale. It was a bit off the road, and there was nowhere to park outside because of yellow lines, which seemed to be springing up everywhere. It was bought by a man who wanted to set up a tanning salon. He was full of ambition and enthusiasm, and Laura truly hoped it would work for him.

Then the bombshell came. A letter from her solicitor confirmed that Tim wanted to divorce her on the grounds of mental cruelty, and he also claimed she had made him so ill with worry over

Matthew, that he would be applying for a fifty/fifty share of all her assets. His reasoning being that he gave up his job as a car salesman to help her expand her business. It was at that point that Laura stopped blaming herself for everything; Tim was proving to be very unreasonable and greedy. She took the letter and went to see her Aunt Agnes.

When Agnes read it, she frowned. "How could he do this to you after all you have been through? He's totally and utterly selfish!"

"I didn't honestly think I had inflicted mental cruelty on him; but no doubt he needs money. Tim always does, he spends it just like water."

"You mean he spends *your* money like water, he's never had any of his own."

"True, and Mary knows the girl he is living with, Leanne. Apparently they got thrown out of the bedsit because they couldn't pay the rent, and now they are back in Devon, as you predicted, with his mother."

"Well, she would have put them up to this!" said Agnes darkly, remembering what Tim's mother had said at the wedding.

"Maybe, but you know, they are not going to get away with this. I wanted to keep the situation amicable, but Tim knows how hard I have worked to give Matthew a secure future, and he expects a slice of it when he did very little at any time to support me! I am struggling right now and will have to lose one shop, so my assets are vanishing, and I am going to sue him for adultery, and then let him try and get his hands on half of the money! No way. I will get a good solicitor; I intend to fight for our future!"

"Well I am glad you've got your mojo back. Couldn't Simon put you in touch with a good solicitor?"

"I don't want to bother him. He has Matthew staying there right now, so he's not in the country, he's busy winding up his affairs until he returns to England."

Laura didn't want to add, that from the little that Matthew had told her, Simon had a new girlfriend called Kim, and so if Laura had entertained any hope of a future with him when he came back to England, it had been dashed once again. It seemed that even though they had a son, they had no future together.

"But he knows that you and Tim have split up?"

"Well, I haven't mentioned it to him. His offer to have

Matthew came just at the right time for me; it has given me a chance to try and get back to normality. I will have to concentrate on finding something else to sell in my two shops and, if Tim is successful in his claim, I could well be back to only one shop again, and the house might have to go."

"We won't let that happen!" said Agnes very firmly, and she meant it. She had watched Laura build up her business, and now she felt very sorry for her. The recession was affecting lots of people, with empty shops appearing in secondary parades in town, and supermarkets, who sold everything, taking over.

Laura went for a walk around her nearest town. She noticed that the busiest shops were the ones that were selling food. It seemed that whilst out shopping, if people got hungry, they would pop in for a hot drink and something to eat. This gave her an idea; she would rather be busy than sit and worry about how much money Tim could claim from her, so she put her thoughts into actions. She found a solicitor and left him to sort out the divorce.

First she moved all her stock into the shop she had first set up near the bus stop. She set up a big sale sign, and instructed Paula to sell off all the items that were slow moving at half price, and then to make a note of what customers were asking for, so Laura could buy that from the warehouse.

Then she applied to the council for a change of use, and was granted permission to change the other shop into a snack bar. She applied for a licence, and got some catering staff in. Her plan was to sell hot and cold drinks, snacks and sandwiches, and as there was a huge office block nearby, one of her staff was going over there to build up a sandwich round.

Her new venture took off very quickly. People filled the shop continuously, which really heartened her, so she had some shelves put up, and bought small items of giftware, such as posy vases, ornaments, china boxes, anything that caught her eye, and arranged them on the shelves. They were to be sold and then gift wrapped free of charge. The display shelves were positioned right next to the till, and it worked, people liked the idea of a free gift wrap, and gradually she could see things improving, and she had made enough money to replenish the shop.

She could feel her confidence returning. Her life was calming down now. She had missed Matthew, so keeping busy had helped her to cope. By the time he was due to return home, her finances were stable again. The solicitors were still fighting it out regarding her divorce with Tim, but she tried to look beyond that.

Simon had put Matthew on the flight home with his companion, and already he was missing him. Matthew had only a few days before he started his new school, and he wished so much he could be there with him; but it was going to be a couple more weeks before all the legal stuff had been completed. In the meantime he was also losing Kim, who had certainly proved her worth, and he had been grateful for her help with Matthew. He could imagine how much support she gave her mother. She had tolerated Matthew's silences and occasional strops, and understood his obsessive habits, like clutching always at least one car in his hand, and playing the same music over and over again. They had both made allowances for the fact that he was missing Toby, because Simon knew that ever since Matthew had Toby, his cars had taken a back seat.

As he drove back to his apartment he reflected on their time together. It had been six weeks of finding out more about his son. He didn't have another child to compare him with, but he could see how hard Laura must have worked with Matthew to help him make sense of the world. In his eyes she was an amazing woman, because right now he felt mentally and physically exhausted. Although there was a warm glow in his heart put there by Matthew; his son had hugged him when he said goodbye, and that meant everything to Simon because he knew Matthew's hugs were not freely given.

Kim had told him about how her brother had suffered brain damage at birth and now had epileptic fits, each one was so frightening, they could never be sure if they would lose him. Her mother had worked hard with him, and he could walk, but he could not speak, and there was no place for him except home, so as a family they helped him as much as they could. Simon realised then how tough it must be for this family, and he counted his blessings that Matthew had not been damaged at birth. His health was good, and he was extremely bright, so he did have a future. All he could do as his father, was to support Laura, especially when Matthew was struggling to cope. His lack of social skills would always be a challenge for him, and his reactions to situations he didn't understand were sometimes very negative, so Simon was glad he would be around in England to help him cope. Soon he would be on that plane too, and then the house hunting would begin. He could stay with his parents whilst he was looking around. Money wasn't really an issue, and where he lived would depend on where he worked, and he was even thinking of taking Matthew with him when he viewed properties, because he felt if Matthew was involved, it would be easier to choose somewhere knowing he was comfortable with it too.

"Matthew, would you like a drink?"

Matthew shook his head. He was thinking about his dog, Toby. He had not seen him for six weeks, and he couldn't wait to take him for a walk. He was sitting clutching his car; it made him feel safe, although the lady who was taking care of him had a nice face and a warm smile. Her name was Lorna, and he knew she would take him to the meeting point when they landed, and his mother would be there to meet him. On the way out to America, his mother had taken him to the meeting point, and a man called Joe had taken over, and he remembered Joe was wearing a navy blue suit and he had glasses, and during the flight he had fallen asleep and snored. Matthew hadn't minded that because then he didn't have to talk, because sometimes he didn't want to talk, he just wanted to sit and think about other stuff.

When the food came round, Matthew had chosen chicken; he liked it, and there was mashed potato and carrots with it. He surveyed the small container of salad next to it, peeping out from underneath the tomatoes was some lettuce and cucumber, and they were green. But his dad had said that green wasn't unlucky, it was something called "an old wives' tale", which he had said meant it was not true; and Matthew believed everything his dad told him, so he used the fork, and ate it all. Then he drank the orange juice, whilst Lorna smiled approvingly and praised him for eating his food. It was getting late now, and it would be at least seven hours before they landed, so Matthew pulled the blanket around him and settled down to sleep. When he woke up he would be home with his mother and Toby, and soon his Dad would come to England too. He felt safe.

Chapter Twenty-six

"You've got even taller since you've been away. What has your dad been feeding you?" laughed Laura. She was so happy to have Matthew back. Six weeks was a long time to be parted from him, and the only reason she had not worried was because she knew he was with the best person he could be. Simon got him, he understood his unusual ways, and he was proud of him, which made her feel very happy.

"Dad is coming to England soon. I am going to help him choose a house."

"Oh, that is nice, then you can go and stay with him and Kim maybe?"

Matthew eyed her with surprise. Why did his mother think Kim was coming?

"Kim's in America, with her mother and her brother."

"Maybe she's coming on later," suggested Laura, ignoring the fluttering of her heart inside her chest. Simon would never be on his own, he was far too good looking and kind.

Matthew shook his head; now bored with the subject, he retreated into his own little world. He had asked his father why he didn't live with his mum like other dads did, and that had made his dad sad, so he wouldn't ask again, but he still wondered why. He hadn't told his dad about Tim going, as it was something that made him feel uncomfortable. He had seen his mother crying and he didn't like that. He liked it when his mum was strong and happy, and usually she was. Today she was; he knew she was pleased he was home, and in two days he was going to his new school.

"I've bought your new uniform. The jumper and blazer are royal blue." Laura's eyes were twinkling now; it was their joke, the colour green.

"I ate lettuce and cucumber on the plane," volunteered Matthew.

"Well done, I knew you could."

She was so impressed about how Simon had cured him of that phobia, because it had been so difficult in the past. It was surprising how many things were coloured green, but it no longer mattered, and what a relief that was.

Toby was ecstatic to see his young master; jumping at him and licking him, which made Matthew chuckle. They both disappeared on a walk, and Laura let Matthew go without her for the first time. The park was nearby, with no main roads to cross, and he was nearly nine. She had explained to him about not talking to strangers, but in the case of Matthew that was highly unlikely.

She had enquired about him riding his bike to school, but it seemed pupils were not allowed until they reached eleven, so she was going to do the next best thing, come rain or shine, she would walk Toby to meet him every day. Maybe seeing Toby might take away the disappointment of not being able to ride his bike.

Matthew arrived back from his walk tousled but happy, and Toby was panting and ready for a big bowl of water.

"Did you throw his ball for him?"

"Yes, he ran all over the place, and there was another collie, and they played together."

"That's nice."

Since Matthew had Toby, he had been more willing to have a conversation, and every day Laura silently thanked Simon for his good idea about having a dog. She didn't tell Matthew that Toby had missed him whilst he was away, because there were going to be other times in the next few years when Toby would not be able to accompany him. But although she had seen he was walked and fed properly, every evening Toby had laid by the front door waiting for his young master, and his devotion had been touching to see. Laura wished more humans were like dogs, then Matthew could be accepted for who he was; a unique little boy.

Before he went to bed he dropped the bombshell.

"Aunt Kate came to stay. She took me to Washington and bought me some new cars."

178

Laura stiffened. She had bad memories of Kate. But it was in the past now; they had all just been teenagers, and now Kate had met her nephew. No doubt that had been a shock! She smiled at Matthew, he had, in the last couple of years, suddenly acquired lots of family members; two sets of grandparents, an uncle and an aunt, and he had coped with it all. At one time all he had in his life was herself and Aunt Agnes, but this was how it should be, these people were his roots.

"That was nice, I used to go to school with Aunt Kate, many years ago. "

Matthew rushed on excitedly: "She is an actress. She goes all around the country singing and dancing."

"Yes, I can believe that, she always wanted to be an actress."

"She lives in London, and dad said when they were young they used to argue a lot."

"All brothers and sisters argue; it's normal," said Laura, remembering how Sam used to wind her up, and then feeling the pang of sadness deep inside her that Matthew was an only child and would not know about sibling love.

When Matthew was in bed she came to say goodnight to him. Toby had already slunk up the stairs in the hopes of being undetected, and currently she could see a lump under the duvet, which she ignored. The dog was his life, and it was his first night home. Matthew had not hugged her at the airport. She knew it was because there were too many people around, and she had restrained her feelings of wanting to hug him, she knew she must, it had to be on his terms so he felt in control. But now in his own bedroom, as she bent towards him, his arms came out in his usual clumsy bear hug.

"Missed you, Mum!"

That was the closest he would get to "I love you." Her eyes filled with tears of happiness, it was so special to her.

"I missed you too, but I am sure you had fun with your dad."

"I am glad he's coming to England."

Laura wanted to say "Me too," but didn't want to confuse Matthew. It was bad enough that his parents were not together like parents of most other children, but if he had any idea that his mother still loved his father, then that would make life more difficult for Simon and Kim, and Laura didn't think she had the right to spoil anything between them, especially as Matthew

179

would be visiting. She was finally admitting to herself she still loved Simon, and probably always would. She had hoped when she met him in America and told him about Matthew's existence, that she would find he had changed. He was a successful and rich lawyer, but when she had met him there had been no trace of the arrogance his sister had accused him of when they were young.

He had never been ashamed that Matthew was different, he had accepted him totally as he was and helped him so much, and even though she had deprived him of the first six years of his son's life, he bore her no malice and showed how grateful he was to be in his life now. Neither had he shown any animosity towards Tim for marrying her and becoming Matthew's stepfather. If he was jealous, he never showed it. She wondered if Matthew had told him about Tim leaving and the pending divorce. Somehow she doubted that Matthew would have found that easy to put into words.

"Did you tell your dad about Tim?" She tried to keep her voice light, so as to not upset him too much.

Matthew did not reply, so she knew the answer; his face looked uncertain and frightened. She patted his hand, not wanting him to go off to sleep with worries on his mind.

"It's OK, Matthew, Tim and I were not suited, and we are getting a divorce because he has a new girlfriend."

Emotions were something Matthew could not get his head round. He knew when he saw his mother's tears she was sad, but sometimes when she had tears she said it was because she was happy. When he had tears it was because he was in despair, and unable to cope with a situation. But as his mother was speaking now, she was smiling, there were no tears any more, so if she didn't mind about the divorce, and Tim had a new girlfriend, it must be all right. He smiled back at her, and she tucked him down, pretending to scold him when Toby's guilty face came into view.

"Don't worry, I will write and tell your dad; and as for Toby, he can stay for tonight, on top of the duvet. I hope he's not been jumping in any muddy ditches."

"No," said Matthew settling down contentedly with Toby's head against him. Toby made him feel safe, and now he was home with mum again, and nothing in his life had changed except Tim, who often used to get very angry with him, and then he shouted

180

at Mum, and Mum got upset. Well that wouldn't happen now, so he felt glad that Tim had gone.

Laura decided a letter was a bit impersonal, so she would telephone Simon, and whilst it was on her mind, there seemed no time like the present. She glanced at the clock, and calculated it would be about three in the afternoon now in America. All she planned to say was to thank Simon for giving Matthew a great holiday, ask after Kate, and then casually mention about Tim and the divorce.

At this time he would be at work, so that might not be good. But then she remembered he was winding up the business, so he might be at home. She dialled his home number, but it rang out without being answered, and she felt disappointed; she was all set to tell him and he wasn't there. There was no way she would ring him at his work place, even though she had the number, so she would have to wait at least three more hours before she could speak to him, but she would do it just before she went to bed.

With this thought in her mind, she put on the kettle to make herself a coffee, and whilst she was in the kitchen her telephone rang. It was Emily.

"How are you, darling? Dad and I thought we might pop over on Sunday to see Matthew before he starts his new school, if that is OK."

"Of course, Mum. You'll be amazed at how much he has grown."

"He enjoyed America then?"

"Oh yes, but right now he's snuggled up with Toby; he missed him."

"Well we missed him, and I am sure he's going to shock his teachers when they find out just how clever he is!" said Emily proudly. It had been a huge shock to her and Trevor to find out about Tim. They had not realised he was such a weak man, who drank too much and gambled. He had always been so charming, and when he left Laura, they had both suggested that the pair should have tried harder at the marriage, just like they had with theirs at times. But although Laura had been loyal to Tim's memory, Agnes had put them straight about him and his mother. When they realised that the only person who had tried in that

181

marriage had been Laura, they felt so sad for her. She deserved to be happy; she worked so hard. So keeping in touch was essential, and supporting their unique grandson Matthew was all important.

"I hope he will be OK at his new school. He needs to be understood, and he's getting older now. I just have to let him take the rough with the smooth."

"I know you do, but you know, Laura, children get teased for all sorts of reasons, being fat or thin, wearing strange glasses, having red hair; anyone who looks different from the crowd will get teased. It's a cruel world out there."

"Yes, I know Mum, and knowing his dad has helped a lot, he's becoming tougher and more resilient. Did I tell you Simon is returning to England soon?"

"Well that is great for Matthew, he can take a more active part in his life."

"Yes, bye Mum, see you all on Sunday. Maybe we could all go out for lunch."

Was it her imagination, or had Emily detected a note of happiness in Laura's voice when Simon's name was mentioned. It's funny, in the eyes of Trevor and herself, Simon had been the bad influence who had got their daughter pregnant, then abandoned her, and Tim had been the knight in shining armour who had come along and made them into a family. But now she knew they had got it so wrong. Tim had proved to be a very weak man, who took more from Laura than he ever gave; yet Simon, as soon as he found out about his son, could not be faulted in any way. He cared about his boy, and made sure he was a part of his life, even giving up his life in the USA to be near to Matthew. If only Laura and Simon could get back together, but that looked like the fairy tale ending that could never happen.

Chapter Twenty-seven

"Hello Simon, I just wanted to say thanks for giving Matthew such a lovely holiday."

"No worries, we had fun, and Kim was great with him. Her brother has autism too."

Just for a moment, Laura's heart turned over. Maybe Simon had been attracted to Kim because of her own experiences; supposing he married her. Would she be better than Laura herself at caring for her boy? But then she chided herself for being ridiculous. She was his mother, she had carried him for nine months and given birth to him, and Simon would always respect that. She was in no danger of losing him to Kim.

"Oh, I am sorry to hear that, but her experience must prove useful."

"I wanted to make sure he was all right on the few occasions I had to work."

"He came home very happy, and is currently asleep with Toby as close to him as he could get. The dog did miss him, but I never told him."

"Of course. When I am in England, and he comes to stay, I am happy to have Toby too."

Laura thanked him, then there was a pause, as she kept her voice calm for what she had to say.

"Just before Matthew came to stay with you, Tim left me. Our marriage had been over for a while really, but now he has a new girlfriend and is very happy. We are in the process of divorcing."

At the other end of the phone, Simon's jaw dropped with

amazement. How many times had he wished that Laura was with him and not Tim? In his eyes no one could equal Laura, so what type of brainstorm had Tim had to leave her? But more importantly, had the bastard broken her heart; because if she had loved Tim, Simon's love for her was so strong, he could have put up with losing her if he knew she had found happiness.

"I am so sorry, Laura, are you OK?" His words were sincere, and his heart ached for her.

"I am fine. It seems that Matthew was just too much for him, he didn't seem to want to understand him."

Simon bristled with indignation. Tim had known what he was getting into when he married Laura. He'd always been weak, even when they were children, and how his mother had spoiled him!

"So he blamed Matthew, how dare he! Who's the child, and who's the adult?"

Laura suddenly found herself pouring out the whole story. Tim's gambling, his inability to cope with money, his drinking and his unreliability, and once it was all out she felt so much better. To the rest of the world she felt she owed him a loyalty, but to Simon she could be herself, because they still had that closeness and connection that had always been there.

"So you can see, I am well rid of him, and soon we will be divorced. But I am not saying much about it to Matthew; he starts school on Monday, and I want to keep him calm."

"Of course, I get it; and as soon as I can finish off here, I will be over to England. Then maybe I can take a more active role as his father."

"You already have, Simon; but we'll keep in touch."

"Yes, I will ring him after his first day."

As Simon put the phone down, his heart felt lighter than it had for a while. Laura was free of Tim! Was there any hope for him now? All these wasted years when they should have been together, and all he could do was become her friend again and support her with Matthew, unlike Tim, who had let her down. This time he was going to fight for Laura, and he would not give up unless she told him she didn't love him. But he squashed that thought right down, it must never happen because Laura was, and always would be, the love of his life.

On Monday morning, Laura and Matthew set off for his new school, with Toby walking beside them on his lead. Toby's presence helped to keep Matthew calm, and Laura was glad to have him with them. She hid her misgivings from Matthew, but she knew that as he was approaching his ninth birthday, teachers would not be so understanding and protective of him. She had tried to make him realise that some of the things he found abhorrent were normal in life, such as being touched by other boys; as up until now he had avoided boyish pursuits like fun rough and tumble. He did it with Toby, so she had tried to explain it was quite normal to do it with other boys, as long as he didn't hurt them, and if someone tried to engage with him in this way he must not overreact.

She wondered how he would get on with playing football. He hated sport that involved physical contact, and when the players on the television all locked together in a scrum he had eyed them with distaste. Then there was the hugging of each other when they scored a goal. The only men Matthew had ever hugged were his father, and sometimes his grandfathers, according to how he felt that day, and somehow Laura couldn't see that ever changing.

As far as his school work went, she had absolutely no worries. He shone at every subject, and next year he would take his 11-Plus, and then hopefully go on to Grammar School. He could swim adequately, but not good enough to be in a swimming team; he went for long walks with Toby, and he enjoyed horse riding, but that was as far as his sporting ability went. His main love was reading. He would spend hours with a book. He preferred books to people, and was now reading adult action packed stories. The James Bond stories really gripped his imagination. Right now 007 was his hero; he could achieve anything, and Matthew admired him so much.

Matthew would not allow his mum any nearer than the entrance of the school gates. He didn't think that James Bond would have let his mother take him to school. In two years he could ride his bike he had been told, but two years seemed to be a lifetime away. Some of the other mothers dropped their children at the school gates and then drove off to work, not many walked these days, as most women had their own cars. With women now familiar figures in the workplace, and contributing towards the mortgage, which was now based on joint wages, rather than just the man of the house, the need to be a second car family had arrived, as most couples needed to go in separate directions during the day.

Robert Pratt was also at the middle school. He lived only a couple of roads away, so it was inevitable that he would end up at the same school. Ever since the day when Matthew had given him a bloody nose, he had never tried to bully Matthew again. He was a typical coward, inflicting misery on others because he was jealous of them, but when Matthew had stood up to him, he had shown just what a blubbering coward he was.

Although he now steered clear of Matthew, Robert and his mother had given Matthew the nickname of "psycho", and Robert used it as freely as he wanted to. Because of this tag, and also because he had no social skills, this had made Matthew an outcast from the other children, who viewed him with suspicion; and it was going to be worse at this school, he knew, because James and Valerie had moved to Gloucester, so now James had become only a pen friend. Robert was going to do his best to alienate everyone from him; he seemed to have some sort of power, and other children were frightened of crossing him, so Matthew would be ignored, just like at his last school. Matthew knew that and so did Laura, but they both also knew it was something he had to learn to deal with, because life would always be full of bullies.

When the bell went, Matthew filed through the door with the other children. Girls, he found, were kinder to him than boys. His dad had laughed and said it must be his unruly curls and brown eyes. He had an interesting face. He looked like both of his parents; with his mother's curls, and his father's bronzed looking complexion, and eyes that often looked so far away because he was often in his own world. He was gentle towards girls, and some of the other boys were not. At this age it was not done to sit next to a girl in class but, if you were misbehaving, sometimes the teacher moved you there as a punishment. Matthew didn't mind if they did this at this school; it had only happened to him once at his last one. He had been in his own world, and had not responded to the teacher's question to him, so he had been put next to Sarah, and all her friends had giggled; she looked happy, and afterwards they all kept smiling at him. Maybe they hadn't believed he was a "psycho".

First it was assembly, and then they were called into their new classes. Matthew had already met his new teacher, his name was George Potter, or Mr Potter, Sir, as the children had to refer to him. He was a burly man, with a big stomach, which fascinated Matthew; it made him look like he had a shelf beneath his chest, and although not more than about thirty years old, he had prematurely lost his hair and now sported a shining head. Privately the pupils called him baldy, which if he had known would not have gone down well with him. His eyes showed that he was short tempered, so it would not do to get on the wrong side of him. He was also head of sport, and anyone who was good at football was in with him.

Matthew often wondered during his time at the school why he was head of sport, because all he did was blow the whistle and shout encouragement or derision, according to how the game was going, from the side of the field. Never once did he see him on the pitch encouraging others. Needless to say, he did not appear to like Matthew. It did not bode well for his future, but whilst he was at this school, he knew he would have to try and keep on the good side of Mr Potter.

Unfortunately for Matthew, Robert was in his class, so it seemed the label of "psycho" would continue to dog him. He decided to let Robert do his worst, he didn't want school friends anyway, his friends were at home, his mother, Dad, Toby, and all the rest of the family. He had the ability to switch himself off from what was going on around him, so he imagined he was James Bond in his sleek sports car. When he thought about his hero, he realised that in the films not many men liked him, some even wanted to kill him, but women did like him and he always had a girlfriend, and Matthew could understand that.

Maybe it was because right from the start of his life, he only remembered his mother and Great Aunt Agnes caring for him, so with women he felt safe. His father, his two granddads and Uncle Sam were the exceptions to this, because they were family. James had been like a brother, but he was now gone, although Mum had said they might go and visit him and Valerie at half term. They had been invited to stay for the whole week, but Mum said she could only spare three days from work. Valerie had told his mother there was a very nice swimming pool near to their new house. She had even said Toby could come, and Matthew had promised his mum that at their house Toby would sleep in the kitchen.

Half term came and went, and the two boys met up and had fun together. This was mainly because of Toby. Throwing the ball for him and running around together they found fun, and Laura was delighted to see Matthew was engaging with James. Never in the past had he played with anyone, and James had been like his shadow, but romping in the local park with Toby saw them interacting together, and Laura was so pleased to see this, even if it was only going to happen occasionally when they met up.

It took another few months for the divorce to finalise. She had not been able to prove Tim's adultery; he would not admit it as they were now living with his parents, so it was granted on irreconcilable differences, and the judge did not think Tim deserved half of her assets, as he felt she had done a fine job in supporting her son, and Tim would have to learn to make his own life, because there was absolutely no proof that when he joined the company, his presence had ever built it up in any way.

Being a mere woman, Laura had not expected the judge to rule in her favour, but times were changing, and women such as herself, who could prove they were independent, and had a voice, were listened to and respected. She could feel a little compassion in her heart for Tim, so she agreed to let him keep the car he used, and as a token of goodwill, but without admitting any sort of liability, she gave him a thousand pounds, which she explained to her solicitor was to help him and tide him over until he got a job.

She regretted the end of their marriage, and realised a lot of it was through lack of communication. Neither of them had taken the time to tell each other how they felt, and share their problems together. It was too late now because the love had gone, but if she ever found someone else, she vowed not to make the same mistake.

With Matthew, his condition made it impossible for him to communicate well and share his fears, but there had been no excuse for her and Tim, and between them, she felt, they had destroyed their own marriage. All she could do now was the same as Tim had; put it behind her and move on.

Simon returned to England in early November. All his loose ends were now tied up, and he was going into business with another man in a law company in Guildford. Then came the house hunting, and as promised, he involved Matthew. Eventually he settled on a spacious three bedroomed flat, near to Laura's main shop and their house, he had purposely kept away from London; after all, lawyers and solicitors could operate anywhere, and being near to Matthew and Laura was of paramount importance to him.

Then came furniture, carpets and making the place his home, and it was finally ready for occupation just before Christmas 1970. To his delight, Laura was happy for Matthew to spend Boxing Day and a few days afterwards with him. She was very amicable towards him, so he nursed the hope that in time they might get back together; it would be the most natural thing in the world if she still loved him.

When Simon arrived in England alone, Laura had finally found out that Kim had been nothing more than a housekeeper and child minder. Matthew had explained that to her when she expressed surprise that he was alone. Her heart skipped a beat to think he was single, but then she chided herself; he was such a handsome and charismatic man, there was no way he would be single for long. Could she risk having her heart broken again, or should she be content with the friendship they had? They respected each other, and they both had Matthew's best interests at heart. But when she thought about it, it was nowhere near enough, she wanted Simon back, and all his love.

Chapter Twenty-eight

Christmas was now over, and 1971 was celebrated. Matthew was now nine years old. He was allowed to choose what he wanted to do for his birthday. Laura wished he would be like the other children of his age, and ask for a party, but she knew that wouldn't happen. Matthew hated parties, so she had stopped holding them on his birthday after he was five years old. Parties involved interacting with other children, and even now he struggled with that.

He rarely got invited to parties either. Only twice had it happened, and then he made an excuse not to go; so it seemed it bothered Laura, but not him. But Laura couldn't bear to see him isolated; she should have got used to it by now, but her heart ached at the thought of him leading a lonely life. Maybe he would never marry or have children, because it took a special person to understand him. Even though he didn't have a mean bone in his body, he was different, and a target for people like Robert Pratt to sneer at and ridicule.

Matthew chose to have a day in London. He wanted to visit museums; unusual maybe for a nine-year-old, but he was intensely interested in how things worked, and Laura was sure if there had been a James Bond museum, he would have loved it. Matthew insisted that Simon came too, he wanted both his parents, and Laura didn't argue. Simon was impeccably dressed that day in a blue suit of very good quality material. He had a crisp white shirt with it, and a blue striped tie. As the January weather was grey and rainy, he had over the top of it, a dark raincoat and black shoes.

Laura felt her heart flutter when she knew he was coming with them, and she wondered how she could look her best on such a rainy day. In the end she opted to wear a grey woollen dress with a black shiny belt and long black shiny boots. Over the top she wore a royal blue hooded coat, which really accentuated her eyes, and Simon noticed that even the greyness of this day could not dim the radiance that seemed to shine from her every time she smiled. He doubted if he could love this woman any more than he did, and silently thanked Matthew for inviting him to share his special day too. They travelled to and from London by train, and Matthew was allowed to choose where to eat. He loved fish and chips, so they managed to find a fish bar. It was quite crowded, but they found a table in the corner, as Laura was aware that Matthew could not sit at a table that was amongst the crowd, where he might get jostled and touched.

They travelled home on the train. It was getting dark now, so when they reached the station, Simon ordered a cab to take them home. Laura invited him in for a cup of tea, and he ended up staying until Matthew went to bed. Laura felt so comfortable with him; it was like the years had never passed in between, but she had to remind herself it was because they were Matthew's parents, they would always have that in common, that was their bond.

On 15th February 1971, Britain and Ireland decimalised their currency. For Matthew, he found it easy to understand, but for Laura, like many people born in the 1940s, and used to pounds, shillings and pence, it was a struggle in the beginning to make sense of it. Laura noticed too, that when she went shopping, everything suddenly seemed to have gone up in price, because tuppence in old money, was not the same as two pence in new money. But after a while, the British people got used to it, as they were now in line with the rest of Europe and America.

A new James Bond film was released entitled *Diamonds are Forever*. Matthew wished he was twelve, because then his parents would take him to the cinema to see it; three years seemed such a long time to wait. He had been curious about the fact that James Bond kissed women, he actually let his lips touch theirs, so maybe it was something, when he grew up, that would happen to him.

James had told him one day in the playground that babies came out of a man's willy, and he had to put it inside a woman's part where she did wees to give her the baby, but that seemed very far fetched to him. It sounded dirty, and he could not imagine his mother doing something like that. He had never asked her if it was true. It was a subject that had never been mentioned, and until he felt comfortable to talk about it, he was not going to ask.

He had been at his new school for a few months now, and as was expected, all the teachers were impressed with the easy way he learned things; all except George Potter, who frequently complained about his disinterest in football. Matthew knew he was right and he did hate football, so he managed to let Mr Potter's moaning go over his head; it was safer to retreat into his own world, he knew he had no defence, what the man said was true.

But George Potter was determined that Matthew would make an effort, so one evening he told him to stay behind for football practice after school the next day.

"You can tell your mother to pick you up forty-five minutes later than usual!"

Matthew's heart sank, he couldn't get out of it this time. Potter had a bullying manner about him. He was like an older version of Robert Pratt, he thought, only this time Matthew could not fight back; he could not hit his teacher, he had just to put up with the bullying and sarcasm so frequently directed at him, much to Robert's delight. Matthew was silent.

"Answer me, boy! Did you hear me?"

"Yes."

Potter bellowed at the top of his voice, this young upstart had a way of getting under his skin, "Yes who?"

"Yes sir."

So the next day, Matthew presented himself with some other boys on the pitch, which was near to the school gate. He was wearing shorts with long grey socks that had a royal blue band round them, which was the school colour. It was a very windy and cold day, so he was running on the spot to keep warm. The other boys were already kicking the ball around, but no one called him up to join in.

Potter arrived on the field to supervise, and Matthew envied him his warm tracksuit with long trousers, and the sweatshirt and overcoat he was wearing to protect himself from the wind.

"Come on, Clark, join the others!" he said impatiently. The boy was hopeless, he didn't have a clue!

Matthew attempted to join in without physically touching anyone, which didn't really work, as he did no tackling, and basically just ran around the field getting as near to the ball as he dare.

Potter's anger rose. The boy was a joke, he was making a mockery out of the game of football! Then Matthew moved to the back and that faraway look came into his eyes, and something inside Potter snapped; the little upstart wasn't bothering any more, he wasn't even concentrating.

Potter went over and grabbed Matthew's shoulder in rage, but Matthew broke away from him. So the boy was defying him now, there was only one solution.

"You insolent young pup, come with me!"

Potter shouted instructions to the rest of the boys, and with a sinking feeling, Matthew knew he was going to get the cane. He had tried so hard to avoid it, but he could feel this man's hatred towards him. If he ran away from Potter and went home, his mother would be angry with him, so he followed meekly behind him towards the locker rooms where he had got changed.

When he entered it, Potter was holding a cane, his eyes were glassy and staring, beads of sweat ran down his face, and he looked a terrifying figure to Matthew. He felt such fear running through him, and he did what he always did when he was in a situation where he couldn't cope. He ran up against the wall with his back to Potter, and curled his hands together, resting his head on them to try and shut everything out.

Potter was loving this; he liked having boys at his mercy. This is why he had chosen to be a games teacher. He couldn't play football, but he could stand on the sidelines admiring all their youthful limbs, and watching them play. He could feel himself hardening, so quickly he locked the outer door, just in case a curious boy should come peeping.

He walked up behind Matthew, who was now sobbing. Oh, didn't he just love having him at his mercy, and pushed his very hard erection against Matthew's back, his voice thick with lust, he said softly.

"Take off your shorts, and arch your back boy, I think you are going to enjoy this!"

193

j

Matthew didn't mean to be a coward. He knew this man was evil, and he had to accept a beating, but no one had ever hit him before, and his bullying attitude had reduced him to tears. But then all comprehension deserted him when he felt the hardness of this man's penis digging into his back. He did not understand what was going on, didn't even know a man would do such a thing, but he knew it was wrong, it was revolting, it made him feel sick to be touched by this man's penis, even if his clothing was in between!

He left the safety of his own world. He knew that no one except himself could save him from this vile human being; there was no way he would let Potter's penis touch his bare skin, the man was deranged and evil!

"Get off me!" he shouted, turning suddenly to see the teacher had now dropped his trousers, and he was confronted by a very large penis, which was pointing right at him.

"Hold it, go on, hold it!" gasped Potter, and Matthew stared with horror, momentarily stunned by the sight which greeted him. Potter had such a strange look on his face. Matthew did not understand this monster of a man who stood before him. His only thought was to escape, and for the first time in his life he wanted to be with people, where he felt he would be safe.

He ran towards the door, and Potter had a disadvantage, as he tried to pull up his trousers over his bulging erection. Matthew was sobbing as he wrenched at the door, then remembered it was locked. As he turned the key to open it, Potter had by then done his trousers up, and he shouted threateningly after him.

"Don't think about telling anyone boy, no one would believe you over me, they all know you are a psycho!"

Matthew just kept running over the sports field where the boys were still kicking a football, then he saw the gate was not locked, so he ran through it. It was too early for his mother, so without thinking, he just ran for his home. By the time he had reached home, he had stopped crying, but he vowed to himself he would never go back to that school again! He didn't understand that sordid incident, but he never wanted to be anywhere near that man again. There was no way he could tell anyone. Communication was difficult for him at the best of times, but he just could not describe that incident to his mother, so it would remain locked away inside him, and he would go to his bedroom, away from the world, and the only companion he wanted to keep him safe was Toby. His dog must be out with his mother right now, so when he came back, they would shut themselves away from this frightening world with evil men in it.

Laura was surprised that Matthew was staying after school for football practice. He hated football, and in the summer Simon was going to play cricket with him. That was a better sport for him. As he was so studious, sport was not really his thing, but he must at least try. She had been told to come and meet him forty-five minutes later than usual, so she set off with Toby, and prepared to wait for Matthew by the school gate. But as it was later, the gate was open, and she saw one or two other boys being collected by their mothers.

She waited patiently until the last one had gone, but no Matthew. She was beginning to worry, but then out came his teacher, and spoke to her.

"If you are looking for Matthew, I am afraid he went early. It seems football is not for him!"

Laura could tell by his tone of voice that he had found Matthew difficult, but there was something about this man she did not like. He seemed brash and hard, and although she knew Matthew had to get used to that, because it was a tough world out there, instinctively she knew there was no chance this man would even try to get through to Matthew. His voice sounded hard, and almost threatening, she definitely did not like him.

"Thank you for telling me. Matthew has autism, and needs a lot of understanding. I am sorry if he has given you any trouble. I expect he is at home."

Potter watched her go off with the dog. If that boy told anyone, it would be his word against Potter's, and he was a well respected teacher at this school, having been here for over five years, whereas that little runt was only on his second term, and was not liked by any of the children.

But Potter hadn't been able to get him off his mind; those curls, that innocent face, he had wanted him from the beginning. But now his lust had turned to hate; the boy had spurned him, and for that he would pay. There was no room for both of them at this school and he, Potter, was going nowhere. So he would make Matthew's life miserable, and he would be glad to leave.

For the next few days Matthew just lay in bed staring into space, and refused to talk to anyone, or answer Laura when she spoke to him. She thought he must be ill, because Matthew never stayed in bed normally. He got up early every day because he wanted to spend as much time playing with Toby as he could before he went to school.

He barely touched any food, and Laura guessed something was troubling him, but whatever it was, it was tucked away inside him and there it seemed it would stay. She had telephoned the school to say he had a tummy bug. She felt a bit guilty, and when it got to the end of the week, she made up her mind it was time for him to return to school; the situation could not go on like this.

Simon was away on a business trip and she didn't want to bother him. But after four days, in desperation, she phoned the hotel where he was staying, to ask him what she should do. For once in her life she could not cope with Matthew. He had retreated into his own world, and she felt like there was a big thick curtain between them. She could not believe it was just over football; it was like he had suffered a trauma, and her gut instinct as a mother told her something was seriously wrong.

Simon's advice was to take him back to school on Monday, and then speak to the head. He suggested that maybe the teacher had caned him and it had upset Matthew, but Laura pointed out she had already examined him and he had no marks on him. Simon cursed that this was happening whilst he was away from home, because Laura had said that maybe he could get through to Matthew, and find out what was troubling him, as she had not been able to.

So Simon left the conference. There would be other conferences later, and right now his distressed son was more important to him than any work, and he hated to hear Laura so stressed. He planned to talk to Matthew and get to the bottom of whatever it was troubling him.

When Laura went to tell Matthew he would be going back to school on Monday, some sixth sense stopped her. She was going to let Simon do that. He really looked up to Simon, and would listen more, she was sure. So instead, when she saw he was out of bed and dressed, she suggested that he take Toby to the park to get some fresh air before dinner.

"We have chicken today, and I'll save some for Toby if you eat yours," she said encouragingly. Matthew's lack of appetite had been a huge shock because she had always thought he had hollow legs!

Matthew was tired of his bedroom, and tired of seeing that man's evil face and bulging eyes. He was haunted by him in his dreams, and the idea of running free in the park with Toby appealed to him. Maybe it might help him to forget that dark day.

His mother made him wrap up warm because the wind was blowing, but once he got out of the house, it was amazing how much better he felt. Toby barked enthusiastically and ran ahead of him. As they reached the park something seemed to disturb Toby, he ran on ahead barking, and then disappeared into the public toilets. Matthew wondered how he knew which was the men's one, as he disappeared into it.

Curious to see what had distracted his dog, he ran towards the toilet, but as he got to the door, he was pushed out of the way by a youth in a hooded grey jacket, which was pulled over his face, hiding his features. Matthew saw he was wearing dark glasses and he had jeans on, but the hand that pushed him had a tattoo on the back of it, and he noticed that it was a tattoo of an eagle.

Matthew continued into the toilets where Toby was whimpering, and concerned for his pet he went over to him. Then he saw the figure sprawled on the floor; there were stab wounds all over him, and blood just about everywhere. There was a knife embedded in his chest, and the figure was spluttering, and trying to remove it. Without even thinking, Matthew put his hand on the knife to try and help, then he met the bulging staring eyes of Potter. Matthew screamed, and with one last convulsing shudder, Potter took his last breath.

Chapter Twenty-nine

Robert Pratt had a burning curiosity to know why the psycho had run away from football training the other evening, and had not been seen at school since. Maybe Potter had caned him. The thought of that gave him a sense of malicious satisfaction. Clark was everything that Robert would have liked to be; normal size, very brainy, tall, girls seemed to like him, even though he appeared to be oblivious of them. Of course, he was very anti-social and had no friends, unlike himself, Robert, he swelled his chest with pride, he had such power in this school; nobody crossed him, or fought back, and he liked that. He reigned supreme.

His mother was going to the bakers to get some fresh bread and she said he could choose a cake for teatime, so Robert accompanied her today. The doctor had told his mother that they both needed to lose weight, and to cut out the cakes, but it was a pleasure they both enjoyed, and so they still ate them. Robert had once been called Billy Bunter; but only once, he had made sure that boy never said it again. His mother puffed when she walked, and they both had faces where their eyes disappeared into the folds of fat, so as they crossed the park today, they were both puffing with exertion.

As they came close to the public toilets, Robert heard a scream, and he recognised the dog standing by the entrance, it was Clark's dog, the one he had kicked, and made it yelp with pain. It had been so great to wind up Clark that day, and then get a ten pound reward after. His mum would have reported it to the school, but she had said, as she took the money to spend on them both, maybe

198

she shouldn't. But there was no doubt about it, Clark's stepfather had bribed his mother to keep quiet.

Brenda stiffened. "What's going on?" she enquired.

Robert's curiosity got the better of him, so he puffed up to the entrance to the toilets, and the sight that greeted him was truly mind blowing. He had never seen so much blood before, it was everywhere, and a body was sprawled across the floor, with wide staring eyes, Potter's eyes, and sitting on the floor next to the body was the Pyscho, his hands over his face, but those hands were covered in blood, and the Psycho was sobbing.

Terror gripped Robert. Everything was so obvious here. Clark had killed Potter, no doubt in retaliation for being caned. He really was a psycho, but right now he was sobbing like a baby, and Robert knew he had to get out of here, away from him, and call the police. The psycho was a murderer!

He ran back out to where his mother was standing, and gasping with fear he shouted:

"Quick Mum, get the police. The Psycho has murdered one of my teachers; he's in there and he's very dangerous!"

Brenda went white; this was not what she had expected, and over the other side of the park there was a red telephone box, but as she puffed her way over to it with Robert in tow, PC Peter Griffin was passing on his bicycle. She gasped out what Robert had seen, and without wasting any more time, Peter called for a police car to come, and then went over with them to survey the scene of the crime.

When he entered the toilets and saw all the blood he felt quite sick. He was new to the job, and so far had cycled around his beat and done a bit of traffic control but not been involved in major crime. It was clear to see the man on the floor had been murdered, and the boy sitting next to him, with his face covered, had his hands all covered in blood, too. He tried not to panic; the squad car was on its way as well as an ambulance, but sadly it was too late for the victim.

The boy in front of him seemed traumatised. He was not going to assume anything, but it seemed a wise thing to take him outside, away from the horrific scene. He touched his shoulder, saying kindly:

"Would you like to step outside with me sonny? It will all be OK."

There was no response, the boy did not even look at him. But Robert butted in eagerly.

"I came in and he was holding the knife, he stabbed him."

"Why do you think he did that?" asked Peter patiently.

Robert was so enjoying this. "Well, he's a master at our school, and the other day he caned him for misbehaving. It's obvious he was getting his own back."

By then the ambulance and police car had arrived. The area was cordoned off so the forensics and police could do their work. A couple of ambulance men managed to get Matthew to come out. He said nothing whilst they checked him over to see if he had any injuries, but it appeared he just had Potter's blood on his hands. One of the senior police officers addressed him.

"What is your name?"

Matthew did not respond, and Alan Gould spoke patiently.

"I know this has been a terrible shock to you, but I need to know your name, telephone number and address, so I can call your parents to come and get you."

Matthew was shutting it all out. What a frightening world he lived in; people were speaking, but he only saw their lips moving. All that blood, and Potter's staring eyes, he could never forget that scene. Suddenly he felt very sick, and he leaned over the side of the car park, where the ambulance was standing, and vomited.

Robert was full of his own self importance, so he gave the policeman Matthew's address. Who could forget that he lived in a great big house with double gates and a big driveway? That family were so rich. Because the house was so near, Peter went round to tell Laura what had happened, and to ask her to attend River View Police Station where her son was being taken care of.

When they arrived at the police station, Matthew was taken to a small room. A police lady sat with him, and Alan made another attempt to speak to him.

"Well son, we find you next to a man who has been stabbed to death, you have blood all over your hands, and your fingerprints are on the knife. Maybe you need to start talking."

Reluctantly Matthew returned to the real world, scary though it was. They made it sound like he had killed Potter.

"My name is Matthew Clark, I live at Meadow Croft, Langley Way. . ." He then went on to quote his town, county, and phone number.

200

After that Alan was amazed because Matthew was chanting sums and then he went on to chanting poems. He felt angry; this boy was making a mockery out of him. He was not that old, maybe ten or so, and he appeared to have knifed someone then treated it as though it was a joke! He held up his hand.

"Enough!"

Matthew then proceeded to carry on with his chanting, but this time they could not hear him, but just see his mouth moving. Alan had never met a youngster like this before; he was certainly odd, but if he thought distracting him would put off the questioning, then he was very much mistaken!

"Did you kill your teacher, Mr Potter?"

"No."

"Why did you have his blood on you?"

"I saw him trying to pull the knife out, and I went to help."

"So he was alive when you saw him."

"Yes."

"Was anyone else at the scene."

Matthew hesitated. Of course, he had nearly forgotten, the youth in the hood.

"My dog led me over there, and just as I got to the door, there was a boy coming out."

"Describe him."

"He was wearing dark glasses and jeans, with a grey hooded jacket."

This was hopeless. What sort of description was that? Alan was fast losing patience with this boy!

"Right, so you tell me that someone was running away when you got there. You don't know his age or height, whether he was dark haired or blond, white or black. Is that right?

"Yes."

Alan faced him across the table. With that shock of brown curly hair, this boy was so innocent looking, but his eyes never really met you, and he fought against keeping his head up and looking you straight in the face. He clearly had something to hide.

"Matthew, I don't think you realise just how serious this is! How old are you by the way?"

"Nine."

So he was only nine years old, and according to the other boy, he had a grievance against his teacher because he had given him the cane. But could a boy stab and kill a fully grown man, who clearly would be stronger than him? It was a mystery. He tried again.

"According to your friend Robert, you didn't like Mr Potter. Is that true?"

"Yes."

"Was it because he caned you?"

Then Matthew remembered that day in the changing rooms, and he felt nausea swirling around him again; that secret would stay locked inside him forever!

"Robert is not my friend, and he did not cane me."

After that he refused to speak any more. Probably this had been the longest conversation that Matthew had ever had with anyone, but he felt the sense of danger all around him, and he didn't want to be blamed for killing his teacher. He just sat staring into space, and stayed like that until Laura and Simon arrived.

When Simon arrived back from his business trip, he went straight round to Laura's house. He was concerned about Matthew not leaving his bed, but when he got there, he was relieved to find he had gone out with Toby. Laura was sitting in the conservatory, looking through her post, and she made him some coffee, and then sat down to drink it with him. He noted her anxious expression, when she told him that today was his first day up and out of bed; he didn't appear to be ill, but had not eaten properly for days. They both knew this was so unlike him.

"He usually goes horse riding on Saturday, but he didn't want to go today. He's out walking Toby," she explained.

"Maybe it's something at school that has upset him," suggested Simon.

"Well it might have something to do with his games teacher. He has a bullying attitude. I didn't take to him at all that day he told me Matthew had gone home."

"Would you like me to have a chat with him, and see if I could find out anything?" asked Simon. He would not have done it without asking, as in the case of Matthew all parenting had to be in harmony, or it just wouldn't work.

Laura looked relieved, and smiled. "Yes please, Simon, man to man might work."

She was so grateful for his support, especially now Matthew was getting older. Maybe in a few years his dad could explain better than she could about girls, and how he must respect them. Girls seemed to be drawn to Matthew, but he was as yet unaware of it. But right now, they both wanted to get to the bottom of what had been troubling him.

When the doorbell rang, Laura went to answer it, and her heart turned over with fear when she saw PC Griffin holding Toby on the lead, and no sign of Matthew. All sorts of scenarios flashed before her eyes; she opened her mouth to speak, but no sound came out.

"Can I come in Madam, I have some news about your son, Matthew?"

Simon came out just in time to see her holding the door open and the burly figure of PC Griffin entering the house, whilst Toby was whimpering, clearly for Matthew.

"Whatever is wrong?" asked Simon, putting a protective arm around Laura's shoulders. She was shaking with fear.

"Sir, Madam, you need to come to River View Police Station. Your son Matthew was found crouched next to the dead body of his teacher, in the toilets of the local park."

Chapter Thirty

"Max, can you meet me at River View Police Station in about thirty minutes. My son is being held there, and I need someone present for his interview."

"Certainly Simon, how old is your son?"

"Nine."

At the end of the telephone Max Harris raised his eyebrows in surprise. Maybe the young whipper-snapper had been stealing from Woolworths, it couldn't be much else at nine, and of course, as he was his father, Simon could not represent him.

"It's serious Max, but I know my son, he wouldn't have killed anyone. He has been found next to a dead body, and he has autism, so it's hard for him to explain himself."

Max knew about autism, as a solicitor he was used to representing people who had all sorts of difficulties, and he was paid to help them.

"Does he also have learning difficulties?"

"No, actually he is very bright, we are lucky in that aspect, but interviewing him will be difficult."

"Don't worry, Simon, I am on my way."

Simon thanked him and put the phone down. PC Griffin had now gone to collect his bike and continue cycling his beat, and there was just Laura left sitting on the sofa, twisting her hands together with a look of complete bewilderment on her face.

"Matthew's not violent. The only person he ever hit was Robert when he kicked the dog. Even when he has a strop, he has bitten himself, but never hurt anyone."

"I know," said Simon quietly, and without even thinking about it, he bent towards her and put his arms around her. "We are going to the police station to sort it out, and I have the best solicitor I know coming to represent Matthew."

Laura found his arms comforting at such a time. Simon wouldn't judge Matthew, he was his father, and just like herself, he loved him, and together as a couple they would do everything to help him. Her heart ached for Matthew right now, he was with strangers, however would he cope with that?

"I am so grateful," she said. This time she was totally out of her depth. She had fought all of his life for her son, and would continue to do so, but right now she was so glad of Simon's strength; as independent as she was, having him there was helping her to cope.

When they arrived at the police station, Max was already there. Simon explained to the duty policeman about Matthew's autism, and said that being interviewed would be hard for him, and as parents could they be present; he was only nine years old, and they would sit there and not interfere. Eventually Alan came out, and it was all explained to him again. He had heard of autism, but this had been his first experience of a child with it, and he now realised that Matthew not meeting his eyes might not be because he was shifty, it was maybe because of his condition.

Alan hadn't really liked the fat boy or his forbidding mother, and they had clearly wanted to make sure that Matthew got the blame here. Maybe the reason he was called Psycho was because he was different, not because he was violent.

"Well, as you know, Matthew has to agree to it, and right now he is not saying much. We have not arrested him, we are just holding him for questioning."

When Laura and Simon were shown into the interview room, Matthew was sitting on a wooden chair at a table, and there was a police lady sitting nearby. He was hunched over the table, his head in his hands, and Laura knew straight away he was shutting the world out because he was under so much stress. Her heart ached for him; she shared his pain, and to see him like this was so distressing.

"Matthew," she said softly.

"How are you son?" said Simon, also softly.

Matthew was so scared, he didn't know what to say or do. He

had not killed anyone, but they thought he had. When they had asked him if he wanted his parents in the room, he had nodded, he had no desire to speak to anyone, he just wanted to stay quietly in his own world. When the door opened, and he saw the familiar faces of his parents, and heard their calm voices, something inside him made his heart lift, and without even thinking about it, he left his seat to run across the room to them.

Matthew had never acted like this before, but today he hugged both of his parents, and stood between them; it was here he felt safe, with the people whom he knew loved him. After a while he was persuaded to sit down. They sat with Laura next to Matthew, Max, the solicitor, was the other side, and they faced Alan over the table, whilst the police lady hovered unobtrusively in the background, near to the tape recorder.

Alan asked Matthew to describe again what had happened that morning, and he also asked Matthew to once again give details of the person running away. Matthew repeated what he had said earlier, and once again Alan thought how hopeless this was, a description like that could fit any young person. Simon tried to explain to Alan why Matthew's description was so sketchy.

"Matthew sees people in a different way to us, you know. He sees the clothes they wear, if they have glasses or any imperfections, he does not see height, hair colour, or age."

Something clicked in Matthew's memory when Simon said that, and he knew he must tell them.

"This person had a tattoo of an eagle on the back of his hand."

Alan brightened, this sounded interesting, maybe that would help. There couldn't be too many people around with a tattoo on the back of their hand.

"Well done, Matthew. That could help a lot. "Turning to Laura and Simon, he said, "You can take Matthew home now, we have more investigations to make, so please don't leave the country."

It was with huge relief that Laura and Simon took their son home. Once she got in the car, Laura's eyes filled with tears of relief, and Simon kept telling him how well he had done. After they got home, Matthew went to his room with Toby, and they didn't stop him. He had endured a terrible shock today, and he needed time to cope with it. Resting in his room with Toby was the best thing for him they both agreed.

Later that day on the local news, the police appealed for the man with the tattoo to come forward and help them with their enquiries. They also asked anyone who knew of a person with that eagle tattoo to contact them.

Simon stayed with them. He asked Laura if she minded, and she told him not at all, she was so glad of his support. It was about nine o'clock when the telephone rang. Matthew was by now asleep, and Simon was just thinking maybe he should head back home. Laura picked up the phone, wondering who it was likely to be. Alan' s voice sounded very triumphant.

"We've got him. A sixteen year old boy. He says he was a former pupil of Potter's and he had been abusing him for years. He had not seen him for a long time until recently, then Potter saw him in the toilet, and tried it again."

Laura could feel such nausea sweeping over her again. Maybe he had abused Matthew, but how could she ask her son such a thing?

"Has he admitted it?"

"Yes, he came forward, that will work in his favour."

"Why was he carrying a knife?" asked Laura wonderingly, looking at Simon, who was wondering what had been said.

"He said it was for his own protection. He lives on a very rough estate, where there are drugs and prostitutes and all sorts."

Laura thanked him and put the phone down, and then went on to explain everything to Simon, including her fears that Potter might have raped Simon; and her voice shook with emotion when she said how she was worried about her son, and doubted he would tell her anyway. Apart from embarrassment at having to admit such a thing to her, he would be so traumatised.

"Don't worry Laura, let him have a good night's sleep, and I will come back and talk to him tomorrow?

"Simon, you are my rock where Matthew is concerned, thank you so much."

"No need to thank me, I am his father!" said Simon with feeling. If only Laura knew just how much they both meant to him. He would happily take care of them both for the rest of his life, but it might not be what Laura wanted.

After a sleepless night, he returned the next day, and was relieved to see Matthew didn't look so pale, and Laura was pleased that he had eaten a little for breakfast. Simon had spent all night trying to formulate the best way to find out if Matthew had been abused. With Potter dead, there would be no charges against him for such vile acts, but Matthew might retreat even more into his own safe world, away from them, and it would continue to cause him stress.

He spent time with Matthew in his bedroom talking. Simon was doing most of the talking, and suddenly Matthew explained in his rather awkward way how Potter had frightened him in the changing room, and he had run home. Simon realised at that moment just how naïve Matthew was, he had not understood what Potter was trying to do.

Relief flooded through him, and he explained to Matthew how twisted some men are, and how wise he had been to run away. Matthew didn't mind his dad talking about personal stuff, so he asked him:

"Dad, do babies really come out of your willy?"

Simon hid his amusement, and then went on to explain a bit more to him; as much as he wanted him to know at nine.

"Matthew, forget what that man tried to do to you, he's dead; and they have a boy now who killed him, thanks to your description of the tattoo."

"Do I have to go back to that school?"

"Your mum and I will talk about it. But remember, he won't be there any more, and in a year you will be taking your 11-Plus, your teachers say you will be ready at ten and there is no doubt you will pass it."

Simon left him to think about their conversation, then went to tell Laura that it wasn't quite as bad as they thought. She was filled with relief, and felt with their love and support, Matthew would recover from the trauma in time.

"I even gave him a little talk about the birds and the bees," grinned Simon. "He had heard some stuff in the playground, so I tried to make it a bit clearer for him."

Laura blushed. "I was wondering about that, you have saved me a hard job."

"Well he's only nine, I knew nothing at that age. That school playground has a lot to answer for."

"I feel sorry for the youth they arrested. He comes from a very dysfunctional background," said Laura.

Simon had been thinking the same thing, and was so relieved that it had not been Matthew. In his opinion, Potter had got his just desserts, and it meant that Matthew would never have to testify against him in court, even if he could have done. Matthew would not be put through that, but from what he had heard about the lad arrested, Potter had provoked him to do what he did. He shared his thoughts with Laura.

"That youth, Graham Kerr, I am so grateful that we have been spared, I am going to do my utmost to get him the lightest sentence possible, even if they can't afford to pay me. He's had a shit life up until now!"

Laura realised at that moment what a waste all these years had been without Simon. She was bursting with love for him, but too afraid to tell him, in case she put him off visiting them. When he was with her and Matthew, she felt so safe, and his strength and loyalty never wavered. She didn't want even to try and find another man, Simon was her love forever.

Later, at his mother's house, Simon explained everything to his mother and Kate, who just happened to be there, and they were appalled at what Matthew had been through and concerned about how it would affect him.

"I have something to tell you about our family, Simon. It's something that was locked away in my memory, but now I can recall it," said Elizabeth.

Simon was mystified, whatever was his mother talking about?

"My Aunt Tilly was my mother's sister, and I remember my mother telling me she had a baby daughter, I even went to see the new baby, and then I was told she had died. Her name was Esme."

"Go on." Simon was intrigued.

"After that she had twins, a girl and a boy, Jack and Jill, and they grew up and got married and had their own children. . ."

"And then what happened?"

"One day when I was about ten, we went over for the day, and whilst we were playing hide and seek, I went right to the top of the house to find the twins. We had always been told it was not used, and just full of old boxes, but I heard a noise from one of the rooms. Thinking it was them, I flung open the door and said 'Found you.' Inside the room was a nurse with a girl about three years younger than me; but she didn't speak, she just screamed, then fell on the floor and had a fit. I was so shocked, I just stood there, and after the nurse had tended to her, she told me to get out, and never to tell anyone what I had seen. I was shocked, but did as I was told, never quite understanding. Since I have known Matthew I now believe that little Esme was autistic, and her mother hid her away because she was ashamed of her. The reason I am telling you this is because you are not ashamed of Matthew, nor should you be, he's an amazing boy, and will do very well in life."

"Thanks so much for that, Mother. What a shame about poor Esme, I wonder what happened to her? Laura will always be proud of Matthew as I am too. Strides need to be made in helping children with autism. Maybe in the future it will happen."

Kate cut into the conversation at that point.

"I am so glad that Matthew has you and Laura as his parents, he will do well in life, I just know it."

"Thanks sis."

"By the way, when are you and Laura getting hitched?"

"Well, I don't know how she feels."

Kate jumped out of her chair, strode over to him, grabbed his shoulders and shook him.

"For goodness sake Simon. I know I was guilty of breaking you two up, but now do I need to spell it out, Laura adores you! Get round there and ask her to marry you. And don't come back until you've done it; you've wasted enough time already!"

For once in his life, Simon listened to his sister; they were the wisest words she ever uttered. He knew Laura was his soul-mate, and three months later, he finally married the love of his life, and they both vowed to work together to give their son the best understanding of life they possibly could.

Epilogue

2016

Matthew had fulfilled all the prophecies made about him. He had passed his 11-Plus with ease, then made it to Oxford and left there with honours. The world was his oyster, but he knew exactly what profession he wanted to go into. He loved animals, and understood them more than people, so he became a vet. He set up his own practice and had vets working for him, and just like his mother before him, when his success grew, he opened other branches.

He was not known for being a great conversationalist, but people had huge respect for this man, who was so gentle and caring towards their pets, and there was a waiting list for people wanting to register their pets at his practices.

If it had been left to Matthew, he may never have got married, but it was clear to see, from the moment she first sat next to him at school, Sarah was smitten, and they grew up together and became childhood sweethearts. Sarah liked that he was different from the other boys. To her he was special and wise, and kind. He found hugging Sarah very comforting; she took over from where his mother left off, and with her love and patience, they built themselves a very happy marriage. They were blessed with twins, Kyle and Karen, who were born in 1990. The twins always accepted their dad was a man of few words; it was normal for them. But after the dawn of the new millennium, people were beginning to recognise autism, and much more was done to help children who suffered from it. Special classes were set up for

211

them inside schools, and teachers learned new ways of teaching them.

Matthew had grown up knowing he was different from others, but it had never stopped him from achieving, and he further challenged himself by joining a group of people like himself, and giving talks about how autistic people view the world. His family were extremely proud of him; it had been the hardest thing to do, and by 2016, at the age of fifty-four, he gave up his time to go round schools talking to the students, which raised even more awareness of autism. He attributed his reason for the milestones he had achieved to his parents, Laura and Simon, for their unwavering love and support during all his difficult times growing up, and this made him so grateful for his own loyal wife Sarah, and his children. Matthew was a very contented man, who did not have to pretend to be something he was not; he could be himself and still be loved.

Simon married Laura in early 1972. It seemed everyone knew before they did that these two were destined to grow old together. Whenever they were together, their love for each other shone through, and their total commitment to making Matthew's life as uncomplicated as possible created a bond that would never be broken. In 1973, when Matthew was eleven, his sister Isabel was born. Although there was quite an age gap, from the moment she was capable of attracting his attention, Isabel adored him, and followed him around everywhere. He was her hero, and if he found her tiresome, he never showed it, as he had so much patience.

In 1995 Isabel married Henry Wilson, a city banker, and they had two daughters, Lily born in 1996, and now at University, and Tara born in 1998. Tara was very close to her grandmother Laura, there was a similarity of nature and a feistiness they both shared. Tara was very fond of her glamorous granny, and her handsome granddad Simon, and spent quite a bit of time with them until she grew up. Now she was eighteen, her parents wanted her to go to university, and she was a bit of a rebel. She had found herself an unsuitable boyfriend, who had himself dropped out of sixth form studies. Right now she felt there was only one person who would understand her, so she went to see Laura.

Although Laura was now seventy-two, and Simon one year older, they still kept themselves very fit and enjoyed good health. Simon played golf regularly, and they both took long walks with their dog. They also enjoyed swimming and the occasional game of tennis. As grandparents go, they were both fun to be with. To them age was just a number, and they had always made themselves very approachable for the younger members of the family.

When Tara arrived, Laura had just come back from walking the dog. Simon was doing some work in the study, and as this was such a personal subject, Tara was relieved to speak to Laura alone.

Laura went to make them some coffee, and then they both sat down together. She watched as Tara took a sip of her coffee, and her mind went back momentarily to the day she told Simon he was a father.

"Granny, I am pregnant, and you know how Mummy and Daddy hate Lee. What shall I do?"

This didn't really take Laura by surprise. The world had changed so much. Couples lived together before marriage now, had babies and married later, or sometimes not at all. But in the case of Tara, she was only eighteen, young like she herself had been.

Laura went over and hugged her. She knew that right now she might be in a lonely place, and who was she to judge?

"What do you want to do, Tara?"

"I don't want to go to Uni. I want to move in with Lee and have our baby. I love him, but you know Mummy will freak out."

Laura's memory went back to her dear Aunt Agnes, who had stood by her, and helped her build her life. She still missed her; she had been like a second mother, and she had now been gone since the year 2000, along with her parents, who had passed away in the early part of the twenty-first century.

"All I can say to you, Tara, is it's your life. You only get one, so do what your heart tells you to. Your parents will probably welcome a new grandchild. There is no stigma attached to being an unmarried mother these days, but if you want to be with Lee, then go for it; but remember, you both need to find jobs and support your baby, don't rely on your parents."

"What do you mean about stigma, Granny?"

Laura smiled. "I know because it happened to me; but look at us now, it's all good. Your granddad and I went through hell and high water to be together, but we made it."

She doubted that Tara would understand what she, as a seventeen-year-old girl, had been through to keep Matthew, it was all so long ago. Suddenly in her mind she saw herself, young and uncertain, scared of life and all it threw at her; but looking back she was glad for the life she had lived, because now she appreciated just what she had, a family to be proud of, a husband she adored, and just like her aunt before her, she would be there for Tara no matter what happened.

"Thanks Granny, for being so understanding," said Tara, kissing her as she went out.

Simon came down the stairs, just in time to kiss his grand-daughter goodbye, but not before she had whispered to Laura that it was their secret.

"What did Tara want?" he asked.

"Nothing much, just women's stuff," said Laura. Then putting her arms around him she said, "Simon Richards, have I told you lately that I love you?"

He returned her hug. "Maybe, and have I ever said I am married to the loveliest woman in the world."

"Go on with you!" she laughed. "I know you have only come down 'cos it's lunchtime," and then she went into the kitchen to put the kettle on.

Simon sat down in the chair, remembering the girl of fifteen he had fallen in love with. In his eyes she was still that girl, and she had proved herself to be courageous and independent, a woman of character. What a lucky man he was!